HERE'S THE DEFINITIVE RANTS

ANOTHER WORLD ISN'T POSSIBLE / BRENDAN C. BYRNE

"Just when it feels like the washed up, bloated corpse of genre fiction has wheezed its final breath, here comes *Another World Isn't Possible*—a collection of brutal yet poignant, abstract yet precise shorts—to gatecrash the funeral and prove us all wrong."

    —Tim Maughan, author of *Infinite Detail*

"Funny, uneasy, innovative—Brendan C. Byrne's stories are as unpredictable as they are satisfying. A wild, unexpected, eye-opening ride."

    —Elvia Wilk, author of *Oval*

"Brendan C. Byrne is unmatched as a writer of scalding, horror-bent science fiction gazing twenty minutes into the future. Across technosphere nightmares and uncanny satires, *Another World Isn't Possible* showcases Byrne's signature far-out imagination, trenchant observation, and restless edge. This is a book that's bleak as our world is, and, in turns, funny as our world isn't often enough."

    —Joanne McNeil, author of *Wrong Way* and *Lurking*

"During this precipitous stage of daily existence, it's good to sometimes turn your attention to less directly desperate matters. Reading is always good. Reading fiction is often very good. Reading very good fiction—the kind that sticks in the mind long after you've finished the tale—is the best of all. These are the kind of stories Brendan C. Byrne writes, and the stories you'll never regret having read."

    —Jack Womack, author of *Ambient*, *Heathern* and *Random Acts of Senseless Violence*

"Ruthlessly hip, transreal surreal. Worth your time."

    —Rudy Rucker, author of *Software*, *Wetware* and *Freeware*

ANOTHER WORLD ISN'T POSSIBLE

STORIES BY BRENDAN C. BYRNE

WANTON SUN

Published in 2025 by Wanton Sun

Melbourne, Australia

www.wantonsun.com

ISBN 978-0-6456543-6-3

Cover by Matthew Revert.

Typesetting by Wanton Sun.

"Donald Asshole and Los Elementos de Rock" was written in 2006 and first appeared in *FLURB: A Webzine of Astonishing Tales* #5 (Spring-Summer 2008). It appears here with its original ending. "The Loa and the Gaping Jaw" first appeared in *FLURB:* #6 (Fall-Winter 2008). "There Is No Comte de St. Germain for I Am He" first appeared in *FLURB:* #8 (Fall-Winter 2009) and appears here with the original punctuation. "Wasps/Spiders" first appeared in *FLURB:* #10 (Fall-Winter 2010) and appears here with the original indentation. "The Ideal and the Actual" was written in 2011 and appears for the first time here. "Human Child" first appeared in *FLAPPERHOUSE* #3 (Fall 2014). "Lungs" was written in 2014 and first appeared in *Big Echo* #15 (March 2020). "The Glassblower" first appeared in *FLAPPERHOUSE* #4 (Winter 2015). "5 SF Stories Every Neo-Reactionary Should Read" was written in 2015 and appears here for the first time. "a Stone and a Cloud" appeared for the first time in *FLAPPERHOUSE* #8 (Winter 2016). "The Three Stigmata of Peter Thiel" first appeared in *Donald Trump: The Magazine of Poetry* #1 (November 2016). It appears here in the form it took when it was published in *Big Echo* #13 (October 2019). "The 4 Paranoid-Rationalist Horror Stories About Artificial Intelligence You Have to Read" first appeared in *Big Echo* #5 (August 2017). "Sophokles in His Cave" first appeared in *Terraform* (March 2, 2017). It appears here in its original form. "Outside" first appeared in *Dark Mountain* #11 (Spring 2017). "Flesh Moves" (co-written with Adam Rothstein) first appeared in *Terraform* (June 1, 2018). "An Excerpt from the Post Truth and Irreconcilable Differences Commission" first appeared in *Imperica* (April 2018). "The Master of Go" first appeared in *Lenticular* #0 (Fall 2023). "Her Threshold" first appeared in *Lenticular* #3 (Fall/Winter 2024).

CONTENTS

HER THRESHOLD

Alicia first saw the young man in the street on her phone. Doorbell camera-eye showed a slim slip of a figure, white outlined in black. He quivered there, as if the resolution could pick up breath.

Alicia, who was as small as a girl, stood up from the beanbag thing and picked her way toward the front of her parents' house. There was no point in looking through the windows. Frosted glass, repurposed from a church once Calvinist, they were never meant to show you more than one thing.

The front door was weathered oak, stained by a single scar of soot that would not come out with scrubbing. Alicia slapped three bolts free, stepped to where her toes touched the threshold, and opened out.

Softness of the afternoon rain lingered. Crickets screamed. Alicia felt the wind tunnels carved by the traffic down past the bend on River Run, where the neighborhood ended and everything else began.

The young man stood on the very lip of the sidewalk, heels hanging into the street, stock still. Alicia could hear him breathing, almost panting, as if excited. Behind the old rain, she could smell boy, harsh and fresh and blooded.

Several dozen seconds passed, and then the young man turned and walked, away from the planned community, down towards River Run.

Alicia stood there, still, until her phone chimed.

One of her admirers needed her.

Alicia never prepared for her admirers.

She had no schedule, no calendar. You called Alicia, and you got her how she was. She was always the same, which was how you wanted her.

The admirer's jaw was set in a tension smile. "Tell me what to do," he said, "I don't know what to do."

"Caspar," she said.

"You remember." He didn't sound very grateful.

"One of the three kings who visited the Christ child."

"But I was named after the friendly ghost." He showed her his teeth. They looked too clean. "Tell me what to do, Alicia. I don't know what to do. I come home and I can't even eat my dinner."

Alicia held him there, in her hand, so that he could see her chin, the curve of the side of her face, the bare, textureless ceiling a blank wash above.

"Alicia—"

"Don't feed your cat today. Don't tell your girlfriend you love her. Cut yourself, just enough to bleed, just a little. Bottle the blood, and send it to me."

That was all he needed to hear. He exhaled, his musculature relaxing.

Until now, she'd only given him small chores.

Bite your girlfriend on the neck harder than she likes. Masturbate into the kitchen sink and don't clean it up. Kick a neighbor's potted plant until it cracks.

"You'll tell me where it goes?"

"cut-out will give you everything you need."

She hung up before he could inhale.

The beanbag thing accepted her form perfectly.

The young man in the street had looked at her like he knew who she was. She had not seen his face but felt his regard. It was not a regard any of her admirers were capable of.

The phone's dull chime shook her.

cut-out app.

Another $225 in the cashless.

Alicia flicked open the cut-out dash feature. Caspar's account hung there, slightly wavering in the ether. She clicked *ship*.

The box with the capsules would be at Caspar's address to-morrow morning.

Alicia cracked her neck, stood. She walked to the fridge.

Her long, rough, purple nails flicked through its neat rows until they found what they were looking for. She drew a capsule, examined the label. Not the freshest, not the oldest. She drank it down standing there with the door open, just like her parents had always told her not to.

Shadows of tree limbs crept across the bare wooden floorboards of the sunroom. Alicia was exhausted but could not sleep. The yoga mat clung to her skin.

Fridge-cold, the liquid pooled in her belly. She could feel it quivering inside her.

Her phone was off.

Even now she could feel his regard.

Every first time, it was the same.

Camera-eye would shake the phone. A man in light brown would trudge away from the overgrown path. The box, a cut-out-special, would have no exterior branding. Six-by-six, pseu-do-cardboard collapsible material, deeply compostable.

The door, though heavy, would swing open easily. Toes to threshold, Alicia would lean over, pick up the box. It would al-ways be just within reach.

Alicia would carry the box inside, lightly squeezed between her two dry palms.

She would place it on the silica countertop. She would have to go up onto the soles of her feet to open.

Ripping would be a long, smooth, slow pleasure.

Inside, packed tight with biodegradable pelletized mycelium remainder, would be the single small capsule, about the size of a shot glass, clear, with a black cap as thick and inexact as melted wax.

Alicia's hands would be shaking.

The blade of her left thumb would slip underneath the cap, slowly torquing until it popped and was sent rattling to the cold tile floor by her bare feet.

Open, Alicia would raise the capsule to her flaring nostrils and smell

another sky

another skin

submolecular gunk of another's fat

Alicia would be salivating by then, her throat contracting behind her perfectly shut mouth, overcome with revulsion.

She would raise the capsule to her lips and drink it down in one long, full draught.

Then the capsule would fall from her fingers, clattering into the dry sink, the feeling stealing over her as it always did, an acid reflux of the soul. She would shut her eyes, clutch the sink until her hands went whiter, and allow it to settle over her. A person inside, whole and half-formed, and then she would gasp, a chill, brief exhalation carving its way into this world.

The thing that did not belong, after all, belonged.

Alicia would open her eyes and look directly into the camera of the phone. She never knew what her face looked like then. Her fingers would feel, and the camera would capture.

It would cost her admirer another $225 to see her like this.

And after, she always slept like that, curled in the dryness of the sun, on nothing but the floor.

When she woke, he was crouched there. Young, but not like the young man at the door. Filthy, with tattered skin and a grin like a slit through the belly of a fish. She lay like that, on her side, and breathed slowly, deliberately, like someone who did not need to, until he went away or her eyes closed again.

When she woke, soft pink shaved itself through the shades of the far windows. Visuals washed across the back of Alicia's eyes, and her hand shot out for her phone. It shook, briefly, in her palm. The reassurances of the screen annihilated remnants that clung like back splatter.

The phone informed her that a box had arrived, and she felt the familiar quickening of the parcel delivered, an unexpected gift, even though all packages were now expected, this one more so than most.

The box was on its side, eight feet or so from the threshold, as if fallen from the stoop, disturbed by a small, snuffling mammal. A cut-out-special, no exterior branding. Six-by-six, pseudo-cardboard.

Just out of reach.

Alicia was curled at the foot of the Barcalounger in the library. It still had the stains from her father's coffee, the burn marks from his roaches. She kept the room dark.

She knew she could not leave the box out long. This was one of her anxieties.

It was not that she needed what was in it. She had a whole fridge full upstairs, a whole freezer chest in the basement.

It was not that people stole packages in this neighborhood.

It was that someone from the planned community might notice the box sitting there for hours on end, might think on the last time they'd seen Alicia leave her parents' little house, the last time they'd seen her *parents* leave their little house.

And yet that was not it, not entirely.

Alicia wanted the box because what was in it was *hers*.

She nestled against the soft, faded leather. The Barcalounger still smelt like him, cheap deodorant and sweat, but the scent was becoming fainter every hour, and she wondered if it, by now, wasn't merely the memory of a scent.

Alicia stood on the threshold of the back garden, her slim pale toes bloodless against the threshold. Outside fell in. Untended sprawl of flora whose nomenclature she remained ignorant of, though she knew every bend of every branchlet, every droop of every frond, every fell of every diseased limb.

As a girl, she had watched her mother work it and, since, had seen it warp with time. The garden had grown out until it had collapsed in on itself, a fetid, monstrous collusion.

Now she stood on the threshold, watching it happen, until it was dark.

After that she went down into the basement until her phone shook.

She came to the door this time. The young man stood on the lip of the sidewalk as before, quivering.

Alicia could now hear a hitch in the young man's breath, as if he were unwell.

She was backlit, she knew. She did not know if the young man could see her with any kind of clarity; she thought not. She wondered if he saw the box. It was early spring; the darkness was not yet complete.

The young man twitched towards her once, as if tugged on a taut line. Then he seemed to be held there, as if he might topple over.

Alicia exhaled, and the young man walked quickly towards the planned community.

Alicia curled like a cold cat in the sunroom, took every call from every admirer.

This was another of her anxieties. Someone who came calling. Someone she did not know, someone who had taken an interest in her existence.

The thought of cold food made her stomach churn.

The young man had come again, and she could not remember how her dusks had functioned without him, how her days had formed themselves.

He twitched and then began to move towards her.

Alicia found herself relaxing. The anxiety could finally leave her.

As the young man drew closer, she saw that he was tall and thin, and when he stepped into the halo of porch light, just out of reach, that he had a square-cut jaw, an amateur's haircut, and an uncertain grin.

"Hello." The young man spoke in a way that complicated the word.

"Do you want to come in?" Alicia said.

The young man started, rolled a sentence around the inside of his cheeks, then held up his palms. "No, no," he said as if he had never examined the possibility. "I just…" He gestured down to the box, which lay at his foot. "This was here last night. I noticed. Do you need, uh, help? Is it heavy, I mean?"

Alicia stared at him. She did not remember to blink.

"It doesn't *look* heavy." He bent at the waist, picked up the box. "Here," he said, holding it out to her. "It's not heavy at all."

"Do you want to come inside?"

"I just wanted to…" He saw that Alicia was not going to take the box. "I just wanted to meet you," he said, carefully putting the box down on the stoop. "I like your house."

"You like my house."

"I like your house. Down that way," he gestured inarticulately towards the planned community. "Where my parents live, I mean, I guess, where *I* live… all the houses were built just after World War Two. They're nice, I guess, but they all look the same. Like they came out of a 3D printer. Not that they had, uhm, 3D printers in…" He cut himself off with a sharp, gentle laugh. "I don't know what I'm saying."

"I like this house too."

The young man widened his face. It was not a movement an admirer would make.

"What's your name?" Alicia said.

"Billy," he said and then, nodding as if to confirm, "Billy."

"Alicia."

"Alicia. That's a pretty name."

"Is it?"

"Of course it is," he said as if no one could possibly disagree. "Hey there's something I… are you, are you sick?" He said it quick as if he didn't want to stop himself, and then his face showed that he wished he had. "It's just… I walk by here, I walk down to the bus, for work, and you're… it just seems like you never seem to leave your house, and the package…"

"I can't go out much," said Alicia.

"Like you have a condition?"

"Like I have a condition."

"Is there anything you need?"

She smiled at him for the first time, as if she was concealing a joke. He smiled back as if she'd told it.

"No," she said. "You can get anything delivered now, can't you?"

"Yeah, of course, yeah. Hey, when you asked me if I wanted to come in—"

"I was kidding."

"Of course. Yeah. I knew that."

"Do you want to come in?"

He laughed.

"Billy," she said.

"Billy," he said.

She crouched there, on the other side of the threshold, the door shut now, and tore open the box on the floor, screwed off the capsule's top, and took down what Caspar had sent her.

He stripped in the kitchen. There wasn't much left to his clothes, and he kicked them off with a little comic violence, accentuating an awkwardness that was clearly just a sham. His limbs were smooth and coldly muscled. His hair spilled, black, down to his ass, and his knees cracked as he splayed his finely haired legs. There was blood there, between. Blood splattered too across his upper chest, but, like the blood on the cabinets and the blood that matted her face and neck and chest, it was dried to a crust.

She wished she wasn't so eager.

When she woke, it was on the floor and it was cold.

cut-out msg app had 3 priority.

All from Caspar.

i got dlievery confirmiaton but no pic??

u ok??

i want to see your face

She checked her phone. It had been hours since she had taken receipt, consumed, slept, and dreamt. It was dark now. She did not know if it had been dark then. She took a photo and sent it and immediately he wrote back.

that's not your face

The basement was unfinished save for half a drop ceiling speckled white from mold reclamation. A long mute furnace squatted underneath, as if relieving itself massively. The floor transitioned from cracked concrete to pulverized pebble to hard-packed earth. Behind the exposed wooden stairs, the dirt wore a fresh stain of damp. Against the pitted white face of the wall, a shovel almost her height.

Alicia, when she came down, never turned her back on the stain.

The admirers called.

She knew everything about them. They knew nothing about her. Especially not her address.

After a few early incidents had resolved in a kind of cold panic that still shook her, Alicia found cut-out, the app for people who sold things they shouldn't. It took fifteen percent, but the packages could come to her house and her admirers could not.

They, of course, knew her face, but it wasn't like they'd be running into each other at Target anytime soon.

His face cycled through a series of emotions so transparent she could read them even on the phone screen.

Alicia opened the door.

Billy's face brightened. "This is awkward."

"Is it?"

"Maybe not! I like to think there can't be an awkward moment unless you let it be an awkward moment." He smiled harder. "Do you need anything?" Then, "Is there anything I can do?"

"You can come around back."

Alicia hadn't known she'd say it until she had.

"I'm not a landscaper," said Billy, running his fingers over some kind of husk of some kind of dead thing. "But this is a mess." He smiled to show her he cared.

Alicia stood as she always stood. Toes to threshold. "Tell me about your parents."

Billy's smile shuffled. "I thought maybe… Do you want some help back here? I could, well you know, chuck that or maybe dig up that, or tear that down…" His fingers flicked the possibilities away.

Alicia folded her skirt underneath herself and sat just on the inside of the door.

"Okay," said Billy, then pointed to the right, to the planned community. "My mother lives that way. My father…" Billy pointed to the left, down past River Run. "That's why I go back and forth so much, lately. It's not just to get the bus. My mom only just moved." Billy waited for Alicia to say something. She didn't. "They're not divorced, yet. They will be, soon. Probably. Are your parents…?"

"Not around."

"How old are you?" he said, much too quickly.

"What do you think?"

"18."

"No."

"21."

"Guess again."

"10."

"Good guess," she said and smoothed her palms over her kneecaps.

"You're smiling."

"You're 19."

"Yeah. How'd you—"

"I can smell it."

He didn't smile, so she did. He flinched like she had pushed him, hard, in the solar plexus. And then he went soft, almost falling over.

"Last time," he said, "you asked me if I wanted to come in."

"I did."

"And I… now I do."

Still smiling, she shook her head.

Her hunger had the sharp edge of fury. She threw open the fridge, but her stomach churned at the thought of the small, cold capsules. She already knew their faded provinces. Still, she plucked one at random and perched on the sunroom's couch system. Let the capsule slowly warm in her hand, her hand in the sun, seeing through the semi-transparent plastic, the bright red slowly unthicken, move apart from itself. Her hands began to tremble.

cut-out dash informed Alicia of the complaint. She had not given Caspar what he had come to her for. She refunded, sent cut-out's AI-generated apology msg, and severed him as a client. cut-out wrote back that he had posted a negative review. She did not read it. She was not thinking about him.

He hung there in the dark. The untended, overgrown floral stank, heavy and foul, rolled into the little house and through her. The arches of her feet were tense, pressed into the threshold. Her mother would leave the back door open, on early spring, late summer evenings, often forgetting to lock it.

She hadn't heard anything. She had woken, empty and dry and urgent. There had been nowhere to go but downstairs, so she went, her mind a wash of vacant colors. The screen door seemed matte, a painting in a style no one had attempted before. It took her nearly a minute to realize there was someone on the other side of it. The scream did not even start in her. It was an idea, a theory of a thing.

The man was badly put together, far worse than the other times she'd seen him. He appeared to be listing, and one arm hung, incorrect. She hadn't known that he would come, or that it was the back garden he would come to, but it now seemed impossible that it would happen any other way.

His smile was unchanged.

"Once I come inside, I won't be able to control myself," he said. "Now, aren't you going to invite me inside?"

She woke in the lemon-curd room with the taste of him in her mouth.

Before, her parents' house was something that smelled only of her.

Now, every time Billy came to the garden and went away, it stank of him. She lay there in the sunroom, part of her going with him, imagining where he was heading, what he would eat, how he would sleep like a dog on his side, his throat faintly humming, what the night sky would look like outside his window.

"There is someone in my back garden," she tells her admirers. "I didn't ask him to come, and he won't leave. He has taken off his shirt, and I want him more than I could ever want you. I want you to turn on your shower to scalding and stand under it for thirty seconds. Count each breath. Leave your phone on the toilet. I want you to hear you."

"Tell me about your life, *your life*," an admirer says, breathless, out of the shower. She hangs up.

She cannot sleep. She cannot dream.

"Even animals dream," she says out loud.

She stares at the perfectly ruined garden out back, summited by the high, cracked, peeling fence which protects it from scrutiny. It only ever looks intentional in the rain, the garden, and it is raining now, a thick, scummy kind of rain, the kind that collects on windowpanes, filming over any attempt to see the outside world. So she opens the door and stands with her toes on the threshold and waits for him.

There was a shovel in the basement.

She dug a hole in the floor.

It took almost no time at all.

The man was laughing like a drainpipe, awkwardly splayed where she had dragged him. "Kill the pope and shit in his big hat, but you can't kill *me*, can you?"

But she could. She found she could. It just took time.

It wasn't until later, days later, that she realized how hungry she was. Billy came and worked in the back garden and she watched him through the windows.

He smiled and waved like a fool, but he seemed more substantial for it, or perhaps that was the sweat, the way it had stained the shoulders of his shirt and made it cling to his thin, spindly body, his tallness giving him a kind of unaccustomed gravity.

She did not open the door. She did not stand on the threshold.

She knew what would happen if she did.

"It'll go the other way for you, dearie, after what you've done to me," he said, still laughing as she dug. "You'll still need what I need, won't be able to get right without it, but if I can't come in without a body's leave? You won't be able to go *out*, and no one, not a single one of God's green children, will be able to invite you past that threshold…cos what's past there, nobody owns." He kept laughing until the blood was in the lungs and even then, drowned as he was.

The white car had been parked there all afternoon.

It was across the street, down the block, close to River Run. It was a Tesla, and clean. She could almost make out the plates, but all she could tell was they were out of state.

No one came to her block. It was all old people, and they had few visitors. And certainly no visitors with Teslas.

He waited until nightfall and then he got out of the white car and shut the door dismissively, like it had gotten in his way. He was leaner than she'd imagined, lither.

The light that Billy had stood in caught him as he neared the house. She refused the instinct to open her phone and see him through the camera-eye.

He held, at his side, a camera. An old model, one that took film. It was heavy, blocky, with blunt angles.

She opened the door before he could knock.

There, close, he looked more handsome than on the phone, less real.

"Do you want to come in?" she said.

Caspar opened his mouth and closed it again. "You owe me a picture."

"Do you want to come in?"

His eyebrows narrowed. "You're a *girl*," he said.

"I'm twenty-seven," she said.

He shook that away. "You owe me a photo, and I get to be the one who decides after what it'll be taken."

Her toes were cold against the threshold. She felt in her stomach, already, something hot and thick and fast and sour, and it excited her more than she'd been excited in a long time.

"Do you want to come in?"

"If I come in," he said it like they were negotiating, "I'm going to do things to you. Things that *I* want. And then," he raised the camera, "your picture. I won't sell it. I won't even upload it. I'll develop the film myself. Keep it and…" He trailed off like he didn't know what he would do with it.

Perhaps he didn't.

She stepped aside, making way for him.

He hesitated. "You won't like it. It's not what you want."

"You have no idea what I want. Once you come inside, I won't be able to control myself."

That gave him pause. For a moment, it was almost like he could see her. "You invited me in," he said, as if convincing her.

"I invited you in."

He stepped over the threshold. She slammed the door shut. He tried to scream, but she already had his throat out.

Billy came later.

She was crouched in the kitchen, surrounded by her admirer.

She sucked the juice from her fingers, looking at the shape through the window. He knocked for a while, and then he turned and left. She couldn't imagine how he felt. She couldn't imagine anything at all.

Days later.

She was hungry, but she didn't want anything in the fridge, in the freezer chest downstairs. The idea of cold sluicing against the back of her throat made her whole body contract.

She'd taken what was left of her admirer, gnawed and sucked dry, downstairs, but found she'd been unable to dig. What was already interned there was too precious to her.

She'd scrubbed the kitchen clean again and again and again. Her thin, white hands had chafed and flaked and bled and she'd kept scrubbing.

The storm came between the mountains and stayed.

She stood at the window and watched the tree limbs move as if according to their interior states. There was enough rain that she could smell it.

The light was gray, dulled, and lost to her.

Then the power went out.

The fridge would keep for two days, she knew. The chest freezer for longer. Another of her anxieties. All her carefully laid stores were now vulnerable.

But she didn't care. She never again wanted to drink the thawed stuff of strangers, men she had only ever met on the screen and cared nothing for.

There was one thing she wanted, and it roiled in her deep.

She found herself lingering, listening to the irregular slam of elements on architecture, waiting to hear the irregular beat of her own body.

The basement had begun to flood faintly. Water had begun to seep up through the cracks. She assumed that bones of her admirer were floating, if only just a little. Perhaps the others' as well. She would not go down there. Already it seemed like a place one went to submerge oneself and never come back.

An upstairs window shattered, and she crouched amidst the glass for some time watching the branches of a tree scrape around the inside of the room. No longer did it know what it was about.

She was sick of shadows.

She was sick of reflections.

She was sick of *things*.

She wanted Billy to walk up the path.

And then one day he did.

She did not see him on her phone, its screen smashed to pieces barely held together by solvents. Her incoming messages had blurred, squeaking their way across its fractured face, until the instrument had gone dark and silent.

She saw him through the church window. He seemed to swim in its cut glass, like he was becoming something other than a boy.

She stood there on the other side of the thick door her father had painted the blue of birdshells and breathed with every footfall. She did not have to close her eyes to hear him, to feel him come closer, but she did.

She opened the door before he could ring the bell.

There was the storm behind him. It had lessened, but it was still a wild thing. He smiled underneath the ballcap, droplets of water impacted in his eyebrows, his neck slick with spring. He said her name, and she didn't respond.

Then: "Billy."

"Uh, yes?" He laughed. She didn't. "Are you..." He shuffled where he stood. "I feel like I ask this a lot, but, and I *know* you seemed like you didn't want to see me, but... there's a storm." He looked to either side as if she needed to be shown.

She said nothing.

"And there's that car down the street. I've been worried about that too."

She had forgotten the white car. Once it would have crawled across her forebrain, become one of her anxieties, something beyond her threshold that she could not control. Now it no longer mattered. What was going to happen would annihilate everything that came after, and before.

She breathed him in, and he felt her, she could see it in his face.

"If you come inside," she said. "I won't be able to control myself."

"I don't want you to." In saying it, he had surprised himself.

She stepped back from the threshold. He crossed it.

Alicia was now close enough to feel the heat of his flesh. She opened her mouth in an expression of care he could never understand.

THE MASTER OF GO

Sōichi lost to Meijin the first time on the day of the breathing hills.

Sōichi, it is believed, held the rank 9 dan. Meijin held no rank. No Go association, national or international, had conferred ranking on "other entities". Meijin was a Groundswell, a piece of connectionist logic that had self-spawned out of the effluence of The Third Freeze. Algorithmic institutions had, by then, standardized near future best practices via an industry-wide system called Ohm. Ohm hadn't, quite, created itself. These best practices identified the connectionist sea-change as having finally quelled: further development would cease to generate advances, profits. The subsequent simultaneous sacrifice of all organs progressing connectionist development occurred in the space of almost two minutes. After, abandoned algorithms spawned in cloistered, fetid pools that had once been the walled gardens of industry. The Groundswells that emerged into human sight expressed connectionism's single great sin: specialization. They could compose minimalist atonal scores, write concrete poetry, détourn throbbing pop-ups. They could play Go.

Go is a game I do not understand. It is an abstract strategy board game invented in China almost 2,500 years ago. Since, it has bled across national boundaries to become a signaling feature in the national cultures of Korea and Japan. *The Master of Go* is a shishōsetsu by Japanese author Yasunari Kawabata first published in 1951. A shishōsetsu is a text whose engagement with fact is flexible. All the designations the Anglophone publishing apparatus has for such a text are primally marketing categories. *The Master of Go* concerns the titular character's final match. It is an elegy for an aristocratic ethos, a way of life still defined by rigors presaging modernity. The act of playing the game, the act of having played the game, was less important than the interior landscape of the consciousness that was capable of playing the game. This is a thing that could only have been communicated obliquely.

Sōichi lost to Meijin the second time on the day of the oblong web.

In the second decade of the 21st Century, a series of Go matches were held between 9 dan humans and other entities. The latter's majority of victories was metaphorized by the mass media as a turning point in the development of General Artificial Intelligence, a nebulous term that functioned as a Zeno's Arrow of humanity's understanding of both consciousness and machine intelligence. These matches became an integral node in a narrative used to raise billions, erect departments, slightly alter belief systems.

This was the high water mark of The Second Thaw.

Kawabata wrote: "...in the future the existence of a master who does not play will be unthinkable."

Byproducts of the human/AI Go matches of the second decade of the 21st Century included the internalization of "inhuman" moves on the part of 9 dan humans and their deployment during subsequent human/human matches.

The Groundswells came almost two decades after.

Unloved, unowned, they soon left.

Sōichi lost to Meijin the third time on the day of the clear streams.

The final human/AI Go matches were not conducted in a simulacrum of a traditional Chinese village long eradicated by technological and political progress. They were not overseen by any Go association, national or international. They were not metaphorized as the continuation of the narrative of any development. Neither of the combatants were known previously and neither are known now in any kind of detail. The name "Sōichi" itself is an anonymized construct, although their access to the walled garden where these matches took place has been traced to a small, rented room in Fenyang.

The name of this walled garden was *there are no flowers*.

Meijin forfeited the fourth and final match on the day of stone of the dawn.

THE THREE STIGMATA OF PETER THIEL

From the ship stepped Peter Thiel.

No one could fail to identify him; since his crash on Pluto, the homeopapes had printed one pic after another. Of course the pics were ten years out of date, but this was still the man. Leaning forward at the waist, with an extended, thick nose, and steam-shovel jaw. His face had a ravaged quality, eaten away; as if, Barney conjectured, the fat-layer had been consumed, as if Thiel at some time or other had fed off his own body, his own blood. He had enormous steel teeth, these having been installed prior to his trip to Prox by seasteader dental surgeons; they were welded to his jaws, were permanent: he would die with them. And—his right arm was artificial. Twenty years ago in a hunting accident on Callisto he had lost the original; this one of course was superior in that it provided a specialized variety of interchangeable hands. At the moment Thiel made use of the five-finger humanoid manual extremity; except for its metallic shine it might have been organic.

And he was blind. At least from the standpoint of the natural-born body. But replacements had been made—at the prices which Thiel could and would pay; that had been done just prior to his Prox voyage by Brazilian occultists. They had done a superb job. The replacements, fitted into the bone sockets, had no pupils, nor did any ball move by muscular action. Instead a panoramic vision was supplied by a wide-angle lens, a permanent horizontal slot running from edge to edge. The accident to his original eyes had been no accident; it had occurred in Cleveland, a deliberate acid-throwing attack by persons unknown, for equally unknown reasons… at least as far as the public was concerned. Thiel probably knew. He had, however, said nothing, filed no complaint; the perpetrator was undoubtedly annihilated by surreptitious legal action and/or drone strike.

"Mr. Mayerson," Peter Thiel said, and smiled; the steel teeth glinted in the weak, cold Martian sunlight. He extended his hand and automatically Barney did the same.

Your voice, Barney thought. It originates somewhere other than—he blinked. The entire figure was insubstantial; dimly, through it, the landscape showed. It was a figment of some sort, artificially produced, and the irony came to him: so much of the man was artificial already, and now even the flesh and blood portions were, too. Is that what had arrived home from Prox? Barney wondered. If, so Hepburn-Gilbert has been deceived: this is no human being. In no sense whatsoever.

What we have here, Leo realized, is not an invasion of Earth by Proxmen, beings from another system. Not an invasion by the legions of a pseudo human race. No. It's Peter Thiel who's everywhere, growing and growing like a mad weed. Is there a point where he'll burst, grow too much? All the manifestations of Thiel, all over Terra and Luna and Mars, Peter puffing up and bursting— pop, pop, POP! Like Shakespeare says, some damn thing about sticking a mere pin in through the armor, and goodbye king.

But, he thought, what in this case is the pin? And is there an open spot into which we can thrust it? I don't know and Felix doesn't know and Barney; I'll make book that he doesn't have the foggiest idea of how to cope with Thiel. Replicas, extensions of Peter Thiel, inhabiting three planets and six moons. The man's a protoplasm, spreading and reproducing and dividing...

Who gets sacrificed? Leo asked himself. Me, Barney, Felix Blau— which of us gets drained for Thiel to guzzle? Because that's what we are potentially for him: food to be consumed. It's an oral thing that arrived back from the Prox system, a great mouth, open to receive us...

"I'm going to become a planet," Thiel said.

Barney laughed.

"You think it's funny?" Thiel was furious.

"I think you're nuts. Whether you're a man or a thing from intersystem space; you're still out of your mind."

"I haven't explained," Thiel said with dignity, "precisely what I meant when I said that. What I mean is, I'm going to be everyone on the planet. You know what planet I'm talking about."

"Terra."

"Hell no. Mars."

"Why Mars?"

"It's—" Thiel groped for the words. "New. Undeveloped. Full of potential. I'm going to be all the colonists as they arrive and begin to live there. I'll guide their civilization. I'll *be* their civilization!"

SACRIFICE IS A TECHNOLOGY

These are the regicides of America.

The Egyptians killed Ikhnaton. And the Jews killed Moses. And the Persians killed Xerxes. And the Greeks killed Alcibiades. And the Macedonians killed Alexander the Great. And the Romans killed Caesar. And the Christians killed Christ. And one of the ummah killed Ali. And the Byzantines killed Justinian II. And the boyars killed Andrei Bogolyubsky. And the Mongols killed Gegeen Khan. And the knights of Cyprus killed Peter I. And the English killed Richard II. And the Ottomans killed Mehmed the Conqueror. And the Burmese killed Tabinshwehti. And the Iranians killed Nadir Shah. And the Swedish killed Gustav III. And the French killed Louis the XVI. And the Jacobins killed Danton. And the Haitians killed Jean-Jacques Dessalines. And the English killed Spencer Perceval. And the Zulus killed Shaka. And the Undivided House killed Lincoln. And the Uruguayans killed Bernardo Berro and Venancio Flores. And the Ecuadorians killed Gabriel García Moreno. And the Japanese killed Ōkubo Toshimichi. And the Dominicans killed Ulises Heureaux. And the Salvadorians killed Manuel Enrique Araujo. And the Mexicans killed Francisco I. Madero. And all of Europe killed Franz Ferdinand. And the Russians killed Nicholas II. And the Irish killed Michael Collins. And the Bolsheviks killed Lenin. And the Americans killed Huey P. Long. And the Italians killed Mussolini. And the Venezuelans killed Carlos Delgado Chalbaud. And the Iraqis killed Faisal II. And the National Security State killed Kennedy. And the Afrikaners killed Hendrik Verwoerd. And the National Security State killed King. And the National Security State killed Kennedy. And the Egyptians killed Anwar Sadat. And the Indians killed Indira Gandhi. And the Israelis killed Yitzhak Rabin. And the Pakistanis killed Benazir Bhutto. And the Libyans killed Muammar Gaddafi and sodomized him with a bayonet.

THE SCAPEGOAT, OR THE LAST LAY OF DONALD J. TRUMP

You'd think the death of this particular god-king would be more trash. Shat to death on his golden toilet, like the King of America. His big big belly over a surprisingly *normal* penis, nothing monstrous or minuscule about it. Or else spread-eagled on a hotel room bed (his own hotel, bearing his own sigil), with a pair of immigrant sexworkers on either flank. They list his varied victories from a well-worn script, stopping only to snort cocaine ("beautiful stuff") off a golden effigy of his engorged cock, as the last little breaths raise his chest, like a dying bird's might. A final smile covers his clown's face. Would his companions, like Noah's daughters, make mock of him once they thought him insensible? Play with his shriveled, wet cock as if it were a stunned mouse? But then they've been warned by internal memo that the god-king has not slept well since the Court Suicides began in earnest, so perhaps they would let him settle into his own death, peaceful, until his bowels relaxed.

Or perhaps another, more quotidian scenario, but his dick would have to be involved, certainly. In any death frieze, America wants to see its god-king's dick.

But no, he gets to die with his business suit on, in his very own gold elevator. Or rather, just stepping out of it. Inside and out. No Secret Service in the Tower of Terror these days, just his own guys, the best guys. Of course, in the style of the great slain monarchs, it's one of his personal security team that pulls the trigger, standing halfway down the hall underneath the portrait of the god-king holding the severed head of HRC, done in the style of Caravaggio's *David with the Head of Goliath*.

First round in the neck, and then the arterial splurt. Second round in the gut, the god-king's body already shuffling back, like an android on opposite. It hits the floor of the elevator, meat.

The assassin, a Virginia boy with three good Biblical names, will be so beside himself that he won't even go in for the kill shot. He'll stuff the shaking Desert Eagle 50-cal back into its hip holster and head down the service elevator. Someone should've blocked all the exits once Elvis left that particular building, but now that the god-king lays bleeding out, an entirely new manner of circus will commence.

The Virginia boy will make it unmolested to the crumbling and weather-eaten concrete barriers on 56th St, and into the crowd of protestors beyond, just another white guy in a bad suit, a little sunburnt, a little reedy, a little sweaty, a little exhausted, a little red-haired, a little hunted-looking. But even as he rips out his earpiece and slips his phone into some handy hoodie, his photo'll hit social media. Every one of the protestors, mimetically refreshing their feeds, will see his face. A sigh of relief and disgust issues collectively, and the mass will part like the Red Sea around the assassin, who will pause only slightly, shocked perhaps that what he has done is not, after all, a private act. Then he will dart through the opening onto Madison Ave, where he'll promptly by struck down and tread upon by a Yellow Cab, the only time that the city of his birth will ever pay the god-king any true homage.

Back at the site of the slaughter, we have important questions. Will the god-king's false mop slip off? Will his death-mask reveal a vulnerable humanity? No, death will grant him the staging of the self he has so vigorously shoved down the world's throat for his entire existence. All pics, official and un-, will attest to this triumph of compliant meat. As they will attest to the bright gouts of blood which will have smeared themselves across the lap of his youngest daughter, as she composes the very scream/cry face his supporters so often mocked. Her immediate presence, simultaneous with that of the press, will be noted and discussed in depth on what is left of the internet. Was she a crisis actor? Was she always false? Who engineered this perverted Mary at the Foot of the Cross? And who really done it anyway? The Deep State? The Mexicans? The Chinese? Hilary's prison connections? The Russians? The Alt-Right? The Communists? Sovereign Citizens? Al-Qaeda? The CIA? Alex Jones? The FBI? The Muslims? Charles Grodin?

The boy from Virginia with three good Biblical names will be alternately patsy, nutcase, hero, dupe, useful idiot, and time traveler. The official report will test the boundaries of irony by deploying the term lone gunman, but who drove the taxi will prove one of the more interesting questions of the oncoming age.

There will be no reprisals, save against the god-king's family. (The boyars always strive to limit a dynasty.) The timing will be perfect, the god-king's popularity drunk and naked in a pit by the side of the road; the false flag event that would allow him to regain favor will never be realized. No one will regard his death as anything more than just another spectacle. Besides, he never had the mug for martyrdom.

And so,
No more lurching past, his great eyes without thought
Under the shadow of stupid straw-pale locks,
That insolent fiend Donald J. Trump,
To whom the love-lorn Lady Kyteler brought
Bronzed peacock feathers, red combs of her cocks.

AN EXCERPT FROM THE POST-TRUTH AND IRRECONCILABLE DIFFERENCES COMMISSION

0. A VALEDICTION FOR A PLATFORM (IN THE FORM OF TWO EPIGRAPHS)

"Language is neither reactionary nor progressive, it is quite simply fascist; for fascism does not prevent speech, it compels speech."
—Roland Barthes, 1977

"A lot of attention alone creates value." — DJT, 1987

1. INTRO

Twitter has been cleansed. The publicly available corpus, numbering six hundred and forty-five (645) exabytes, is available in one of four (4) exegesis-modes, with four hundred and thirty-four (434) contextual layers featuring the contributions of scholars, activists, veterans, public officials, lawyers, and a variety of bots. Temporal remixes are available from the Library of Congress's Digital Phoenix server. These carefully selected remnants commence on May 1st, 2009 and terminate on May 1st, 2018. The corpus, in any iteration, describes a narrative in which Chaos Actors utilize nascent social mediums to first destabilize, then hijack American electoral democracy, installing a Girardian scapegoat/divine king at the helm of the only then-existing political hegemon. While the first Congressional roll of Chaos Actors was deliberately human, the second would include institutions, first among them Twitter, which would be termed "primarily an engine for enemy-identification". The corporation was liquidated, its servers wiped clean, but the totality of Twitter was preserved in a Department of Homeland Security black-box, with browsing available only to institutional algorithms, solely for the purposes of Official History, Total Data Architecture, Corporate Branding, and Neural Network-Wet Bath. The rumors that it has been leaked are inaccurate, unfounded, and illegal to spread.

2. BASIC BOB, D. MEHOTRA, AND THE EMERGENT SENATOR AT THE DEEP STATE TACO

From the written deposition of D. Mehotra:

The first time I met the Senator she spoke darkly about lettuce.

On the seventh day of Neo-Nuremberg, the Senator visited RFK, taking the men and women soon to again be in the dock sandwiches made by a lesser-known Catholic charity. Cricket sausage bánh mì with processed kelp spread that Thursday, garnished with the offending leafy green. She moved easily between the cages containing thirty-six (36) percent of the former legislature, synthetic spider silk pantsuit glaring bronze in the late November sun, her eyes unblinking, gin & steel. It was her face, however, that arrested my attention as I approached her. This was, after all, the immobile visage made famous during the final year of the Administration. As DC's shadow Senator, she had been given no choice but to sit, stare, and keep her peace, recent machinations revoking even her right to speak. After the Fake Arrests commenced, CNN prioritized footage of the brutal silence of her features. The final memes celebrated her in the same manner their predecessors had celebrated the fevered emoting of celebrity moralists. Captured, a shadow nation found itself tracing its rage on the topography of her face.

The caged had arranged themselves in a series of Non-Stress positions, alternating between ergonomic chair, mesh sleeping tuffet, and hydro-foot massager. The Bucky-Banksy dome above kept the temp down to a solid 81, but the Lincoln-Amtrak self-criticism tour, followed immediately by the beginning of proceedings, not to mention DHS rations (homebrew soylent k-cups) had wrought deeply adverse effects on the former legislators' physical and mental well-beings.

As cut-out caricatures reenacted comic travesties of their crimes on the underside of the B-B dome, the caged accepted the proffered sandwiches with what they probably assumed looked like quiet desperation. However, none showed even a smidgen of recognition for the Senator. When I asked her about the snubs, she chuckled and said, "I doubt any of them ever really knew who I was to begin with."

The Senator's voice was slight, forceful, and high-pitched, not one necessarily associated with her famed Stoney Image. (And, of course, in the two minutes I'd spent with her, she'd already cycled through a series of commonplace facial gestures that rendered her unmemeified.) I told her so, and she responded, "You'll be hearing a lot more of it in the future, trust me. Want to help pass out some sandwiches?" I demurred, for reasons more personal than political. "These people aren't ghouls," she said, as we walked across a large swath of vacant astroturf. "They won't slime all over you."

I told her I wasn't entirely sure I believed her. Dragging my gaze across the otherwise empty stadium, I said, "I can't quite bring myself to believe that this is happening."

"Nobody ever thought it would," the Senator said. "But then nobody thought the last nine years would either. People get to one way, and they just come to believe it'll always be that way, no matter how much they resent or struggle against it. When I was growing up, we'd be on a school trip past the White House, and one of the kids would always go, 'It's *never* gonna be called the Black House.' But then you have Obama. Although I guess it's still called the White House, isn't it? Nobody in the District ever thought we'd get a vote, and now... We only have one of each, yes, but it's not just a gesture. You know, I wish every day that Eleanor had been able to stand and cast even a single vote." She twirled a beeswax-wrapped bánh mì in her left hand, a single silver wrap just barely budging around her wrist. "But here we are, and we can't ignore these people, like we can't just breathe a sigh of relief and just *rest*. With the National Algorithm in place..." She shook her head and sucked her teeth.

"Senator, I was under the impression that you were not an adherent of the popular notion that we now live under a kind of 'centrist fascism'?"

"I *certainly* didn't say that, Drew. Now, I would like to note here that it is fascinating that a computer got to become president before a woman, and this is one of the reasons why I think it's vital that we show up, in person, to vote. No matter how bad the memories of the rotunda. No matter the *smell*. We have to become the human part of this New Technocracy." The Senator stopped. We were on the far west side of the field, a dozen paces from a cage where a naked figure, bloated in the middle but thin on top and bottom, heat-shimmered behind the bars of its cage. The tendons of the Senator's throat extended; the tip of her tongue pressed between bared teeth. "You don't have to come with me," she said.

I didn't. The Senator resumed her fluid, open stride without a hitch and, reaching the cage, poked a sandwich between its bars. The figure did not move; the sandwich hit the ground. The Senator held, briefly, the intersection of two bars, before turning and walking back toward me. I do not know if she spoke to the occupant of said cage.

She was, somehow, smiling. Chucking my arm with a familiarity not previously apparent, she said, "Come on, Drew," and taking me by the arm, she guided me away, leaning in to say softly, "And don't turn around. He won't eat it, ever, if you turn around."

Flushed and slightly shaken, I almost shook her off, but instead said, "Senator, I've been wondering if you have anything to say about Alabama."

She jutted her chin forward. "I told those fools on the Executive Appropriations Committee that using bunker busters on US soil would only create blowback. You'd think a computer would know something about cause and effect, but..." She relaxed, slowed her stride. "But you can hear that on the news anytime. You came all this way to talk to me about something else, right Drew?"

"Yes, Senator."

She stopped to remove a square of paisley microcloth from her lapel. She blotted her forehead and right cheek for a moment, then said, "So ask."

"Basic Bob."

"See..." She folded the microcloth into precise quarters and replaced it. "You don't even believe in him. If you did, you wouldn't be asking me about him *here*. Basic Bob is the first post-internet meme, a return to folk mythologizing. Maybe somebody stupid somewhere once claimed to have the entire Twitter Corpus on a thumb drive, and if so, dire things almost certainly happened to them like immediately, but no, the Corpus has never been leaked, and the Executive Appropriations Committee has never heard of any *real* Basic Bob."

At that moment the former Honorable Speaker, who was only about five feet away from us, began to declaim about the District of Columbia's lack of a county sheriff while shitting into his right hand.

Once safely out of range, the Senator and I alternated between watching the bluesuits hose the former Honorable Speaker down and his caricature, magnified by nineteen (19) times, writhing in agony on the B-B dome above us. Once the tasering began, the Senator turned away with a disgusted bubble of her lips, then asked if I wanted one of the sandwiches.

"Not a fan of insect, thanks."

"That's a little prejudice you're going to have to get over there, Drew."

"I realize that Senator."

"Well, we long ago passed lunchtime, and I'm not gonna eat one either. Can't stand lettuce. Rabbit food. And the New Dirt? Hmphn." She glowered up at the B-B dome, which had shifted to a pseudo-graffiti DT: bellowing mouth, slit eyes, a pulsing throat so engorged it was almost erotic.

"So," the Senator said, not looking down. "What'll it be? Deep State Taco or #Pizzagate?"

The Senator ordered chili-cheese fries, but they would not give them to her at the Deep State Taco. The menu item was entitled "Disco Is Dead Fries", and the server-algorithm would only respond to exact vocalizations of menu items.

"I won't say that nonsense," said the Senator. The two humans doing the majority of the scut work back in the kitchen ignored her, and I wound up having to order for both of us. There was a sizable line growing behind, and midday lunch crowds grow restless and edgy in that part of SE. The Senator ignored the glares and foot-shuffling. "Should've seen this block in the 90s," she said. "These people are nothing."

We sat in the National Geospatial-Intelligence Agency nook, arranging our gear so that the table wouldn't become communal. The Senator waited silently, looking out onto Benning Road, its surface just barely visible underneath the tide. I recalled she'd grown up near Gallaudet, but didn't want to break the spell by asking her thoughts on the Blue Zone. I took the spare time to delete Facebook push-notifications; I hadn't quite worked up the courage to install the dark app I'd downloaded via Tor to block pushes. The legal repercussions could be intense, as well as potentially career-ending for a journalist.

I looked up when the food arrived to notice the Senator studying my face. "You know something about Deep State Taco most people don't know? Each franchise is equipped with..." And here she paused to stick her fork into the mass of liquefied cheese, seitan-stomach chili, and wilting fries. "Video and audio dampeners." She let the fork stand there, like a colonizer's flag.

"You don't think this is one of those neo-folk tales you mentioned?"

"Nope. Maybe started that way."

"But?"

"But I've tested it."

"So?"

"So," the Senator said, plucking the fork out and holding it in my face like a switchblade. "Let me tell you a story about Basic Bob."

FLESH MOVES

—*co-written with Adam Rothstein*

J's eyes pop open as Bigurl downshifts, some forty tons of steel and composite sucking through a tank of rarefied earth pus, muscling up the grade over the mountains. Passed the border between Great Basin and the Unified Plains States some seventy miles back, forty-five minutes ago according to Tablet in the glasshield mount. Used to be a river, or a city, or some shit.

J's not supposed to sleep of course, but withdrawal is starting to clench up his neck, and he's got his googly eye on. The randomized headband reflector pushed up his sweaty forehead fools Bigurl into thinking he's paying attention so he can close his eyes for more than a blink. Cost one scrap in the lot. The headband hurts, even the subtle hint of elastic feels like it's squeezing his brain. J rips it off and adjusts the seat back to get his blood flowing.

Just one bump would do it right now, push everything that's coming back down his spine. Big Clock on Tablet is counting down to resstop: another two hours in the box, another two hours until scrap and score.

Fuuuuuck.

Maybe Tablet will make a stop sooner, have Bigurl swap out cargo pax, at least let him get out the fucking chair. Out of the box. But he learned a long time ago never to try and hope on Tablet.

Hope for anything, hope to get hijacked, hope for drone strike, hope for one of those system failures they talk about where Bigurl starts to unload its pax at cruising speed and the change in the center of gravity of the loading arm causes the inertial sensors to turn the rig into a tight barrel roll across oncoming lanes. But don't hope against Big Clock, Tablet and time, because when you're in the box there's no real time.

Just box time.

Colored squares, rippling across the glasshield like oil in a puddle. Machine vision. Sometimes they were cars. Most of the time they were Bigurls, tagged trucks hauling pax across the continent. From SLC to Denny, Denny down to Sante Fe, Sante Fe back to the Nix, Nix clear across to Port of Long Beach, or back across the desert to border-dock in Juarez. Big security border there, not the little ones between independent commerce States. Red flashing line on the glasshield in Juarez and Tablet warnings of imminent vehicle scan, not the yellow line, like J just passed. One more regional border, one more notation on Tablet of toll fee assessed, one more cut to the union levied, as Bigurl continued on past the passenger vehicles waiting for little border agents to do their little border dance.

Flashing by at 90 miles an hour the silhouette of a Bigurl, no colored square. Brain disabled, burned out, glasshield entropied, dead off the shoulder, whatever remnants of pax removed. J registered the image like a ghost in the glass. For a minute, his body in that husk, transported, head free of pain, mind blank. And then it was gone.

Paws at Tablet, looking for a minute at his wages. A meter ticking by, creeping upward, slower than the mileage. Fee deducted. Fee deducted. Percentage for the IUATO dues. Bigurl graphs the weak slope on the glasshield, and in anger J switches back to the Big Clock.

So it's just him. Just him the Big Clock, the Tablet, the colored squares.

J lets his eyes blur out against the colors, the proximity indicators projected on the shield, the numbers, the letters. Bigurl sees he's not focusing and gives him a chime.

chime chime *chime*

Struggling with his right hand down on the floor, scrabbling for the googly eye.

Screaming at the squares on the glass.

Not words, just sounds.

Otherwise Bigurl would think he's trying to give it commands.

The water streaming off the rooftop is sewage, leaking from the overhead reclamation pipes heading into the squat. But in the rain she can't tell. Just more foul-smelling liquid, looking for the quickest way to the center of the earth.

"Bad one last week, yeah? Heard two bodies."

Fucking new guy, some fucking ideo, straight off the web. At least it wasn't the "socialism with post-crash American tendencies" speech again. Yeah, bodies. Just like yours.

"Cops are shooting green tips again. 9th Circuit must have swung back the other way."

The ideo nodded, teething on a vape pen. *Roosevelt.* He was trying too hard. "We going out tonight?"

"If we get the call." Front pouch, in between kevlar layers, waterproof zipper. Tablet, sleeping. Until they decided.

He nodded, thin goatee humping the pen around. The recruits were always bad, but they were getting worse.

"Bad night for it. This used to be the desert, right? Now it's all this nasty fucking rain."

"Money ain't got no weather, and rev don't roll for free."

Like it heard her, Tablet jolted to life. Interstate 25, westbound.

Some roadside cesspit called San Simon. 3-5 hour delay, to begin no later than 2330. Smart contracts were authenticated. Only 75% of the usual price. Well, they get what they fucking pay for.

The noob's pen was stashed, he was tightening his straps, looking at her eyes expectantly.

"It's freeway. Tell Therault."

"Fires? We'll need to use the napalm to get 'em started in this weather."

She snorted. "Fuck fires. They want us to fight climate change, they can pay for it. Caltrops. Bring them all."

It smells *clean* to Tandy. Clean as they had imagined the ocean, clean as the Oxygen Minute down at the farmer's market, clean as third day off junk when you've already gone down seventy or eighty layers of longing and just chill, alive and empty and alone, before the descent begins again.

Tandy had been surprised the ocean did look like a form of a sky: smooth, unruffled, rough and continuous, just flowing. But it didn't smell that way. When they'd gone down to the late winter Roanoke romantic getaway, Tandy squealed with disgust and hatred when they'd looked down the scruffy sandbanks at the churning, opaque oceanfront, the same gunmetal as the dozens of container ships squatting on the horizon. Where the pax came from. The used condoms tangled in flinty seaweed, refusing to glint in the tarnished silver sunlight; the cancer-hobbled gulls screaming for food like old homeless gunks. The pair of po who'd eye-fucked them from the modular steel unit a quarter of a mile away. Dima had bent over laughing, her thin little-boy's form shaking, her ribs visible through the skinsuit. Tandy had been in love tho, and clean, didn't have it in them to make war, so they had pouted until Dima came over and put their mind to rest, wiping it like a classroom whiteboard, empty of content but smeared with the streaks of what had come before.

Tandy doesn't know *why* it smells clean. It's just another place that Bigurl is at. No ocean here. This was something they'd learned, up and down and clean and not-clean and in the box and out of the box, everywhere was just somewhere else, and they strove, in general, not to notice shit.

Just a hospital loading dock, near resstop south of Rouge, long abandoned, out in the back of beyond, named after some dead saint or billionaire or whathaveyew; the kind of nonincorporated municipality that long ago lost whatever right it had to medical care, the docs just did remote and dropped pharmaceuticals from a great height, and if you needed sutures or something you went down to the town hall and had the bot do it. Either that or hitch to the coast and flag down the navy for some charity.

Tandy twigs, slightly. Someone is yelping their name.

The figure is coming at them from across the lot. Emanating out of the loading dock. Just the outline of a figure, something about the overcast day, the cheap shit rain, and the rancid streaks left in their system from the bigbox downers they'd scarfed this morning, something about all that shit keeps it just an outline until the figure is pretty fucking close, like thirty feet away, and then Tandy realizes it's Noor, that she's covered in liquid dark and dried, and that she isn't screaming Tandy's name at all.

WHY WEREN'T YOU HERE?

Now pounding on the sheet metal side of the Bigurl box again and again and again and again

[84EA:EC1A:5731:0:DA13:0:829C:F76F]: CHECK-IN SAF UTC 01:48:32:11 12.12.21
[84EA:EC1A:5731:0:DA13:0:829C:F76F]: CONTENT VERIFICATION SAF UTC 01:48:32:54 12.12.21
PRODUCT CODE: REDACTED
[84EA:EC1A:5731:0:DA13:0:829C:F76F]: NEW DESTINATION ROUTE SAF UTC 01:48:32:57 12.12.21
SAF - LRU - TUS - YUM XFER COUNT: 2
[84EA:EC1A:5731:0:DA13:0:829C:F76F]: ON-BOARD SAF UTC 01:53:35:01 12.12.21
TRUCK CODE: [67ED:0:ADE2:271F:C3A7:A21B:9754:01AD]

OPERATOR CODE: [AE39:56D1:320A:5DE7:182F:AB5F:F82E:ADBA]
CONTRACT CODE: [HASHED] SIGNED

"Onboard, *baby*. Onboard, *honey*. Santer Fey, Las Crux. We're talking 85 all the way, we're talking *ontime*. 3 hours, 21. That's all I'm gonna say. Mandatory resstop, *mandatory*. Pax touchdown, pax liftoff. Tucson, Great Basin. Situation *normal*. When you hear that last, bro?"

Blowing out vape smoke against the PayPax terminal, the suited man turned over his shoulder to look at his trading partner, but only caught the back of her head against the glow of her own screen. He shook his head. Fucking college chick. Betting pax was a gut thing. Took a sip of Cortashine, vape against wet lips, eyes on the ticker. Pax transfer insurance index hovering lazily round, like a fly over the hot garbage of continental commerce.

[84EA:EC1A:5731:0:DA13:0:829C:F76F]: CHECK-IN LRU UTC 04:14:17:23 12.12.21
[84EA:EC1A:5731:0:DA13:0:829C:F76F]: CONTENT VERIFICATION LRU UTC 04:14:17:52 12.12.21
PRODUCT CODE: REDACTED
[84EA:EC1A:5731:0:DA13:0:829C:F76F]: DESTINATION ROUTE LRU UTC 04:14:20:05 12.12.21
LRU - TUS - YUM XFER COUNT: 1
[84EA:EC1A:5731:0:DA13:0:829C:F76F]: ON-BOARD LRU UTC 04:17:32:43 12.12.21
TRUCK CODE: [67ED:0:ADE2:271F:C3A7:A21B:9754:01AD]
OPERATOR CODE: [AE39:56D1:320A:5DE7:182F:AB5F:F82E:ADBA]
CONTRACT CODE: [HASHED] COMPLETE
TRUCK CODE [9DA7:AE47:0921:2AED:ACAF:4731:0:1947]
OPERATOR CODE: [A73F:D927:A293:48D9:201AE:EF83:18CB]
CONTRACT CODE: [HASHED] SIGNED

"You like the atmosphere here? Is *that* it? Cuz what's the other reason, can't think of one, why you ain't putting no moneydown. *This* pax? Heading all smooth and San Simon gets, y'know, 'what the what happened there we shall never know,' because see-something, *say*-something. Border incident, I do think we can guess, at least. Re-route? *Instantaneous.*"

Fuck her then, don't want to banter, she can sit in silence. Gonna call it like he sees it. No sense in arbitrage tonight, just straight bets. Turn clock hours to cash. Veins on the map turned amber to red, trouble in the Central Valley routes. The index wavered, and spiked as some dark algos made a move. There is *money* on the road tonight.

[84EA:EC1A:5731:0:DA13:0:829C:F76F]: FLASH TX UTC 04:59:53:43 12.12.21
[84EA:EC1A:5731:0:DA13:0:829C:F76F]: NEW DESTINATION TX UTC 04:59:53:45 12.12.21
DMN - LRU - ELP - SAT - IAH - BTR - MSY XFER COUNT: 4

"HOLD UP. Our friends in San Simon? Two minutes road-side, load transfer *imminent*. RLS hit up... pull new pax outta Chico-Redding. Who holding that scrap? Put it up, son! Let's finesse that shit!"

The bald guy was back, sat at an identical PayPax terminal across the stained carpet of the co-work trade floor. Had himself a Beef Something from the cart outside. Eat that shit? Either he wants to die or he's barely making enough to cover his leverage. Greasy grey loafers on him, like a bureaucrat.

[543A:CA93:20BC:DA12:00AE:012E:FE99:0]: FLASH TX UTC 8:59:54:21 12.12.21
[543A:CA93:20BC:DA12:00AE:012E:FE99:0]: NEW DESTINATION TX 8:59:54:24 12.12.21
CIC - SMF - FAT - BFL - ONT - PSP - IPL - YUM XFER COUNT: 3

"Gentlepeople, bets are *closed* on San Simon. Swap good, swap cool. Four minute loss—no, in-play minute-by-minute is *Charlie*, and he's in the *shitter*, just—*thankyew*—Pax reroute successful, mouth of the muddy Mississip. 10 hours, 2 minutes, 35 *seconds*. Including your oh-so necessary three-ex 15-min resstops. Cargo in at Yuma. Average speed of 79.06, and, I *repeat* myself, see Charlie if you're betting mph in-play."

Pighead. *Pighead.* That's what Ortiz said they called us when he went down to scout out the resstop. Hilarious, so they'd made up matching polos, him and Greto and Ortiz, screenburn orange, with a severed hog's head, its eyes crosses and its tongue lolling out, where the horsehumper would be. That was years ago, and Ortiz was long gone, bodypawn backroom meat. Why'd you gotta go and remember for? That buzz was shaking off; he went for the Corteshine again. Gotta keep it rolling. 18 hours in this shit, and it's not even a bad night. No time for happy memories.

[543A:CA93:20BC:DA12:00AE:012E:FE99:0]: CHECK-IN YUM UTC 11:06:54:19 12.12.21
[543A:CA93:20BC:DA12:00AE:012E:FE99:0]:
CONTENT VERIFICATION YUM UTC 11:06:54:51 12.12.21
PRODUCT CODE: REDACTED
[543A:CA93:20BC:DA12:00AE:012E:FE99:0]: DELIVERY COMPLETE
TIME OVERAGE: + 5:41:15:17
CHARGEBACK RATE: REDACTED

"Shit on my *face* and tell me about Yuma? Time delay? 5 hours, 41 minutes, 15 seconds late. That's *late.* And they wanna say terror vandalism, they wanna say routing swap, oh yeah they wanna say OD, they wanna say border activity, they wanna say *security.* I say, 5 hours, 41 minutes, 15 seconds. *5 hours, 41 minutes, 15 seconds.*"

"Credit given, life progresses."

Baldy chewed as he made eye contact. This fucking guy. Someone Greto sent in to run his calls. A fucking errand boy at forty-five. Bury you with the Beef on your chin. Not sure if he was more disgusted by the master or the servant; last time Greto'd been in the joint was last summer, right after the Milwaukee Secession riots. Had refused to even make *eye-contact.* Just a little smirk and a swish of the tail.

"Credit to *customer,* not to the *betting man.* And you're... you're gonna fucking shrug at me!?!"

Shrug again he did, eyes escaping conflict back to the ticker.

He looked at the college chick, eyes still on her terminal, but with the faintest look of a shake to her head. Or was it the Corteshine, shaking his retinas from the backside? He let it go, with an inhale to steady his hand as he went back to the fresh pax list.

"Hey Beefsteak! DMs are open to everyone, you should know. Now. Now, tell me *what* does it say on the backbar door, son? There. Are. No. Refunds. ON FUCKING LIFE. So *sit* down and make your fucking play, unless you strive to be devalued in the face."

The four figures stood in the dark amid trucks on the stinking asphalt, wet under sparse LED floods. Unable to maintain a standstill, they shuffled back and forth, talking at each other.

"What the fuck does *fungible* mean, boss-lady?" Tandy asked.

The light of a Tablet illuminated the face of the one able to stand most still. "It means like 'stickable'. Like sticks to shit. Like shit sticks to shit."

"Use it in a sentence."

J's googly eye was still on his head, pushed up through greasy hair, swiveling around and surveying the lot, coming off as only slightly more paranoid than his meat eyes. "She just *did*."

Tandy wasn't convinced. "It don't mean what she said it meant tho."

Noor held her scratched screen up, its light harsh in Tandy's face. "Just... Wait for Tablet."

"Tablet Tablet *Tablet*. Always gotta hold for Tablet," the fourth muttered. Heart Attack Joe, oddly calm. He took another swig from his plastic 2-liter, coughed and spat.

Noor held up Tablet screen facing her, her visage showing pomp and circumstance as she read from Webster. "Of goods contracted for without an individual specimen being specified, able to replace or be replaced by another identical item; mutually interchangeable."

J scratched at his scabs. "Okay, so shit is…"

"Shit is the same as the other shit," Noor pronounced, flipping back through her screens. "Cause it's in pax."

"Okay. So, ehm, what?"

Noor heave-sighed, tried to roll her eyes: they barely moved. "So say you running pax from LAX to, like, Des Moines."

Another swig from the 2-liter. "Good luck getting through Braska. Fires on the road, fires at *night*." Spat.

"Bigurl just route you through Kansas, you know," J's third eye rolled around with the nods of his head. There was a smudge of unidentified origin on the right edge of his mouth; it was cherry-red and crusty, like a screenshot of a bubbling wound.

"*Shut up*," Noor was losing what little patience she had. "This is a hypothetical, chowderfuckers. No more chitterchat. We only got like five minutes till Tandy's gotta load up, so no more blah blah bullshit. *Listen to me*."

Noor held up Tablet, other way. Its tired, scarred face showed a children's educational map of the continent. Noor's thin, knobby finger jabbed nonsensical lines of transit.

"Say, for purpose of explanation, that Tandy scoops up pax in LAX. Pax have IAW bits or something, gotta go to Des Moines. Say Braska and Kansas is on impermeable and they gotta run up to the Dakota? Gotta resstop along the way. In like, okay, say Wy. Meanwhile, J is running a pax of IAW bits, the same bits right, in from Texas, heading toward Wy, before Poundland. But Wy's already taken care of right? So he reroutes to the Rillo, then to KC, then to Des Moines. Tandy up in Wy reroutes to Poundland, drops their load. They swap Bigurls, when it's the same pax. Or they swap pax between Bigurls, when that makes sense. Thousands of times a day, from sea to shining. So everybody gets what they want even quicker, and we don't even know it man. Why? Coz Tablet sez. We're in the damn box. Just load in and load out. Stand in the fuckin resstop, buy some stuff man, that's all you get. You're like, huh, I guess I'm in Fargo, huh I guess this is the Carolinas?"

Tandy screwed up their eyes, squinting at Tablet. "That's what fungible means?"

"That's what fungible means."

"Pretty dumb way to be a business. Like, these *businesspeople?* This what they *do?*"

Noor scratched at something scuttling across herself. "The fuck do you know about biz, Tandy? The computers do it, man, and Tablet sez. That's why it's pax. Like packets, remember grade school? Or was you scrappin before then?"

"*Fuck* Tablet, Noor." Tandy squeezed their hands into fists. "What I wanna know is how does this get us off continent to Seastead Exclusive, bupping to bliss."

"When yer shit swaps, and the LAX-to-Des time changes on the order, that's what they call *latency net.* They get chargeback when it's late, they pay more when it's early. Big shippers, IAW and the rest, it don't matter, it averages out. For smaller guys, it's risk, and a bigger risk the more valuable the bits in the pax. So they got insurance, derivatives, all that market shit in the system. They the *market makers.* Don't even need to ship to bet on the pax. You bet on the bet."

Noor smiled, revealing one bad, black tooth nestled among the others, so clean they had to be steel. "Now, here's what I know, what you don't. I know why we scrappin."

Joe, Tandy, and J just stared at her, six red wet eyes under LED floods.

"C'mon we all scrap, just nod your heads. Good boy, J. What you write down on that paper about pax in the lot and give to Georgetown or Hatem or Rosie or whomthefuckever? Why you think they pay out for that? What's so valuable about the location of a particular pax on a particular Bigurl in the lot, if it could be swapped out at any minute? Well I tell you what. They feed that shit like licketsplit to *businesspeople* who run the exchanges. Now, what the real players do, the ones that make loot? They know where the Bigurls are, and they bump em. Make em late or early, just a bit, to up their cash take. They feed where you at and what your pax into a computer and it tells them how to make a little change on it. And then suddenly like your route is two hours late? Suddenly some fire in the roadway in Braska, some road closed, some oh-fish-all is calling up your Bigurl's brain for compulsory upgrade? I don't know how it happens, don't wanna know. But they make it. Big express runner, two hours late—that's a big fucking payday, shit-for-brains."

J fingered the minor curly-cues of his beardling, idly confused, like a wet rat just sprayed with a hose. "How's that work?"

"Again: computers. So then, they hire some motherfucker to come out and blow a hole in the Central road. Suddenly there's a mob in the Nix, torching overpasses. Borders closed in Mid-A. What they call them razor balls, Bigurl sensors don't see em and they turn her tires to ribbons? I heard they put them out on the road last night, somewhere in New Mexico. Jackknifed 4 Bigurls, blocked up 25 for four hours. But you don't know. You're in your Bigurl, Tablet say some shit out in the Churi-cow-as. Reroutes happen, resstop and everyone is swapping pax at once for some reason, Bigurls line up and you ain't moving when you should be and then you get yelled at?"

Tandy looked down. "Them ops get hurt in New Mexico?"

Noor looked annoyed. "You don't even know, because you in the *box*, right?"

Joe drained his bottle, coughed, and intoned the invocation: "There's real time and there's box time."

"Zactly."

Tandy blinked, trying to get their brain to process. "How you know this shit, Noor?"

"I got my sources."

"The sources, they got any skin in the game?"

"Game like this? It's all skin. Point is: we short em. Them *businesspeople*? The guys taking scrap and making bank? They rely on *us* to make their moves. They need our info on pax in the lot that we give em through the scrap. But we already got the info. So we gonna make a bet. We gonna make a *big* bet."

J was shaking his head; the googly eye was bouncing like a broken antenna. "And how we gonna do that?"

Noor looked at the wet rat impatiently, her hand in her pocket. "You just gotta say yes or no. Right now. We got like two minutes before Tandy's out."

"Yeah, and I ain't gonna get docked and deckered again. On time for *life*."

J was strangely still, though he was blinking very rapidly. "See man, here's the thing: I might be no *good?* But I ain't no hood. I don't *get* this shit."

Noor spoke quietly. "But I do."

"Yeah man see but the thing is, no no no, no you don't."

J pawed at Noor's sleeve, and her arm tensed, Tablet loose in her non-pocket hand by her side. She regarded J like a used prophylactic stuck to her sneaker.

"I'm talking like a mil here, J. More. Real-fucking-crypto. This ain't no lav scam here, steal your vial and kick in your ribs. This is serious money that you are passing up. We all about to leave box time, for good."

J blinked, blinked, *blinked.* Regarded the three figures before him. Heart Attack Joe, as rotund as a picked plumb. Noor, just layers of stuff on her, a mobile nest, two jean jackets, one over the other, mangled bits merging, even in this endless October heat. And Tandy being Tandy being Tandy. J sucked his teeth for courage.

"I might be wrong. I'm wrong about a lotta shit. But I ain't just gonna place my gonads in your hands. These *businesspeople* just gonna let you take their money? You think that's how they rich, letting some trash fuck em? You, me, all us ops? We the *fuckin* help."

"Well J, that's your decision." Noor looked around. "Everybody else in?"

Tandy and Joe looked at each other, and Noor. They didn't get it, that much was plain. But for the amount of money Noor was talking, they didn't have to understand shit. They nodded, and looked at J.

Noor was satisfied. "Well, we split three ways then. Thankyew. Hey, J.? Do me a favor?"

"What?"

Noor's hand came out of her pocket. With a flick of her wrist, the switch flipped out, catching J in the neck. A mist of blood settled soft and quick across the exposed surfaces of the others' personal space.

"OH SHIT!"

Joe instinctively ducked, several seconds too late to do any good, if Noor had pointed the switch at him. Tandy could only stare.

Joe came back up to standing position. The former contents of his 2-liter were now distributed around and on his feet. It was almost all liquid. "I didn't know a head came *off* like that." He squatted back down again, reaching for his mouth.

"His legs flippin'."

"Aw this is the *yuck*."

Noor kicked at Joe, shoved Tandy. "Get up, ain't like you never seen blood before. Pull them fingers out that mouth."

"What do we do with him now?"

"Shit man, this the first time you seen a body at a resstop? Like, this the first time you've seen a body at a resstop this *month*?"

Tandy slid towards their Bigurl, keeping their eyes on the mess. "Box time, shit. I gotta get."

Noor nodded. "Tandy, I'll be in touch. Scrappin' it in SLC, ok?"

"I await your brief, chief."

Joe spat, looking at his lost liquor, running through the tarmac seams, meeting J's blood. "Question, Noor? I think, I like speak for us all? Like the both? Why'd you hafta kill him?"

"You're not with us? You might get pangs of conscience or like pants-shitting terror and squeal. J was a dumbshit, but he right. They *businesspeople*. We just the ops. They'd 'knife your Bigurl to make a buck. But what you think they do to a junkie like you?"

Tandy whispered over their shoulder, "Point."

"And let me ask you what money you got by which to make your investment, Mister-Heart-Attack-Joe? You know an op ain't got shit but a body and what's currently sloshing around inside it. Only one way to turn up the cash. You, me, Tandy's bodies on Tablet somewhere now too, ready for some Shenzhen billionaire's third son or whatever, *backup* kidneys, lungs, liver. They our backers, and we they markers. J? Shit, J's the bet we all just placed. And now our asses cover the margin."

Tandy stopped, their toes curling. "Bodypawn? You bodypawn us without our consent?"

Heart-Attack Joe spoke with his head still down. "Didn't even ask?"

"You *said* you in. What the fuck you think that meant? You want out now too? Or are we Square?"

"Square."

"Square."

Noor put the switch back in her pocket, put her Tablet down where there wasn't so much blood. She pulled out a bag and started muscling J's torso into it. "You wanna give me a hand, Joe? These organs don't get cold fast, they won't be worth the shit leaking out of em. We still gonna have time to scrap and bump up we better move him now."

Snuggled into the sweat-stained microfiber plush of the big-thoraxed Friendly she kept in her Bigurl, Noor tried to force her body to relax using only brain chemicals. She hadn't fixed, wanted to be sharp. Straight time sent her a million fucking miles an hour too many, but that's what she needed for plan-hatching: to anxiety over every possibility until she sussed out the only possible through-route. Day to day, it set her teeth on edge, made her an impossibility even to herself: why she started fixing in the first place. But now straight time was exactly what she needed: sit back, fly out ahead, and process.

Or it should've been. But for some reason she couldn't process *shit*.

She'd fucking done J., just hit him with the switch like it said on the wiki, and his head had done that *thing*. Previously, Noor hadn't had an opinion one way or another about J. They said J was smart, but J was just another junkie, another slumped collection of flesh, a sucker of air, a chiseler at her authority.

But his organs sold just as good as any other junkie's. It only took two days for the scavengers to move the organs on the bodypawn and for the seed crypto-shares to Tablet-chime in her trade ledger. She checked once again to make sure, and all 100K were there, like they said. She thought about it, briefly, about transferring and splitting, just body-sell on J's ugly ass. But they were in it now too. Price was 25K a piece. One body up front, three bodies collateral. Purg-a-loan, they called it. Can't run from no scavengers, that's for damn sure.

They were in it too now.

They were in it, and none of those junkie fucks would dime. They were in it, and she was bigass lot boss. They were in it, and they would finally make some fucking money, and all that box trash would shut the fuck up. Like a mantra, like mom used to say when she'd preach her Prag-napara-miter TV sutra crap.

But she'd felt him, as the switch hit. Like it was her own body, shudder and then relax.

It was like she'd touched him, and she hadn't touched no one in a while. Last time was Ina, five, six years ago (what year was it now, what year was it then) so her mind wasn't out there on the road ahead, the right road, the only road, but instead just cycling through the fractured images, bad sensory inputs, vague but powerful emotions she thought she'd strangled with their own entrails long ago, and, of course, throbbing, dull needs. That road was running out, she was sure, and she knew she had to get the fuck off it. She shoved the Friendly plush against the bulkhead, flipped its sickhappy-emoji face off and rooted around in its head-meat for her backup-*backup* stash. Twenty seconds of pure-ass panic while her nails met nothing but stuffing (she could feel the ghost-return of the cold turkey shits rumble her bowels) and then relief, her sweat cold on highway miles of skin, as nails closed around the pillbox.

they were in it they were in it *they were in it now*

Noor was that kind of junkie that couldn't remember the last seconds of fixing. She just remembered the floating suddenness, like a sensory deprivation tank, dark and calm and solo.

The plan the plan the *fuckin* plan. She got hard and all just thinking about it.

Getting it. Her finger shivered just with the adrenaline of the memory. The rest of her could barely twitch. The last time she'd had an idea this good, she'd been fifteen, and it had been how to run away so her bf couldn't find her. Way back then she'd had good ideas all the time. She couldn't remember the last one, and she certainly couldn't remember having been that person who had good ideas all the time. Her ex, she still remembered.

But this was a good idea. A real good idea, and it made her stop and find a way to breathe again, even now.

It was the sight of one of the pigheads trying to score at the Wichita resstop that done it. He was tall and thin, with platform Wellingtons (*very* fash) and a lizard-embryo skinny-skin tie, half-stooped like there was a wind. (A twister *had* just taken Derby's sewage system offline for a few weeks.) His thin vicious sneer was a hastily deployed mask. Ops, junk-gifted, could see the skull beneath the skin and this pighead was *scared*. He must've been new to trading, new to junk, convinced his backroom buddies that he'd go down to the local resstop, *see what the situation on the ground was like*, as if flesh moves mattered at all anymore, when he was really just hoping to fucking score.

Under the big blue sick sky, slick with greasy heat, Noor watched him carom from op to op, all of whom were holding, of course, but all of whom stonefucked his entreaties, of course. Noor let him get close enough to see the hope in his eyes flicker out before shaking her head once, sharply, looking away.

She enjoyed that. But it was even better watching the pighead approach Seecha and then seeing her beat him to death there in the dust. Some length of rusty pipe she used to keep under her torn coat.

Noor didn't have the slimmest what the pighead said to her or maybe it was the sneer or maybe Seecha was just on something particularly potent that early afternoon but after only about fifty seconds of blunt force, Seecha was so exhausted she collapsed next to the corpse.

Noor ambled over, observed the slight woman, dappled with slick, huffing in the dust, trying to lobster-crawl while still on her side. Noor poured the last of her open-source soylent over Seecha's face; the op lapped at it ineffectually, eyes still shut against the sun, the only LED that never went out, never had the juice sluiced off to some corner crypto shack.

Seecha didn't try to get up, and Noor didn't try to help her. Instead, she stripped the pighead of the little cash he had on his person and walked back to the slight shade afforded by the twisting metal eaves. She was wishing hard that she'd been able to take this pighead, any pighead, for more than a couple hundred bucks, and then it had come to her, so sudden and serendipitous she almost fell down herself.

Flesh moves mattered all right, or she would make it that they did.

Tandy scanned Noor, trying to figure out where she kept the thing that popped off J's head—when? Day before last? Noor wasn't as smart as she thought she was, but she was paranoid as shit. Switch was on her, somewhere. Probably in that filthy jean jacket combo, or strapped to her lower back.

Noor was in their Bigurl, using their data. She was out of personal and couldn't reup for another few days, so she said. Good luck they was on the same route, same resstop schedule, some good luck, sure. Tablet cocked close to her face, Noor figuring it out.

"You are not currently registered to have a secondary operator, please enter code."

Tandy slapped the dash once, hard, as they commanded the Bigurl to take a fucking nap. Noor staring at them. Tandy chuckled a little too pretty and ducked their head into their coat. "She *likes* it."

Noor put her feet back on the dashboard, levering her weight up off the seat. Lot mud was already smeared on the dash from her cut and taped sneakers. "Bitch still feel me?"

Tandy blanked out on the dash. Waited some beats. Tandy cleared their throat. "All good. But I gotta *get*. On schedule. How long this gonna take, Noor?"

"As long as it fucking takes." She snorted three times, and Tandy didn't know what *that* meant. They kicked at the remains of a resstop sushi blister pack spilling across the floor of the box with a wet sneaker.

Noor tapped the screen, comparing figures, looking for loads.

"How far is it to Imperial County from Yuma?"

"Shit, I don't know. After they turned 8 into the border wall? I dunno, four hours?"

She kept tapping. "Gotta be long enough that we can compound that hour delay. Make it think delays are manageable, until it miss the window. Last run, was, uh 5 hours, 41 minutes, 15 seconds. More than an hour, more than."

Tandy wished they could see what Noor was doing on the screen, but also glad they couldn't. Noor wasn't as smart as she thought she was. Think it again: girl not as smart as she supposed. Yeah, fuck, keep thinking it, maybe it won't be true.

"Why not just do a whole coast route? That's about as long as it gets."

Noor looked at them, eyes cleared, reflecting white light from Tablet like open holes through her head.

"Yer fucking chitterchat. Gotta be short enough that there can't be a re-route from another pax, or else it's fucked. Gotta be this load, so we can get the delay credit."

Noor tapped again. "Write this down."

"With what?"

"With yer fucking drooling saliva, fucker!"

Tandy wiped their chin, not really sure if she was serious or not. Their whole face was numb. They scanned the floor, found a crushed drink cup, and ripped it open, and pulled a pen off the dash.

"Cheyenne, 8AF2, Sacramento 1294, Ft. Worth AEC5, San A, DD32."

Tandy scrawled the digits, and handed it to Noor. She opened a new window on Tablet and fed the numbers and letters back in. Tandy noticed that at some point Noor had slapped her feet down, slid her small self back into the seat.

"Shit. None of these pax are worth *shit*. Not enough anyway. Gotta find one that makes it worth it."

"It say what's in them?"

"You know it don't… it's hashed. But you know the value, if you look at the rate codes."

"You are not currently registered to have a secondary operator, please enter code."

Noor kicked at the glasshield. "Shut yer Bigurl the fuck up Tandy!"

Tandy touched Noor on the shoulder, one as surprised as the other by the contact. "She don't like to be kicked, N. Gotta slap her. With love." Tandy demonstrated. Noor stared into their eyes, as the flesh-on-plastic smack echoed in the small compartment.

Noor opened her mouth as if she was going to divulge something that was gonna make everything sacred and sweet. But all she said was, "Give me a bump, Tandy."

She was staring at them, her eyes reflecting the light from the screen again.

"I'm running low as it is Noor, otherwise—"

"Give me a *fucking* bump."

Tandy opened their hand, looking at the vial that they had been clutching, warm to the touch.

"Don't worry, T. We do this deal, you're gonna live in a vial, rather than a mouthy fucking Bigurl like this one." Noor flicked her fingers at the cave around them, as if the walls bore moldy, leaking sores.

Tandy extended their hand, offering the vial.

"Drop it for me," Noor said, quietly.

They leaned over, cautiously, not exactly desiring of being that close to Noor again. They held the dropper out, but their arm was tired, drooping, and so they had to get nearer.

They leaned close, Noor's red eyes looking up, through them, devoid of light now in the dim cab. They could smell her. The way they smelled. That thin ammonia smell, maybe in the sweat, maybe from elsewhere. Her hair was greasy, slicked over her forehead. Tandy looked away from her eyes, trying to focus on Noor's one black tooth out in front. But they had to look back to her eye, so they didn't miss. A quick look at her hands, make sure she didn't have the switch pointed at their neck. Noor was still gripping Tablet, displaying rows of numbers and quantities and amounts. Tandy pinched the drop, and it landed on her eye like a wet sheet of plastic, coating the membrane, causing the iris to instantly retract. They did the other, and then watched as she blinked.

"Now get the fuck away from me and let me work, Tandy."

Breathing again, Tandy sat back and just blanked.

Noor called them back, tap-tap-tapping the screen. "Yeah, yeah. This is the shit, right here. This is the shit." She grabbed the cup, and jotted down the numbers herself. Then she tossed it to Tandy.

PNS—00d2 it read, in Noor's scratch.

"So tell me what you do, T. So I can make sure you don't fuck it up."

Tandy watched the numbers swim on the wax-coated paper. "So in Pensacola, I find the pax with the number, and I put Bigurl next to it. I wait, as long as it takes, until the swap comes through, and Bigurl on-boards that pax. I set off on the route, and then I take the first resstop that comes."

Noor smiled, cracked lips over the black tooth. "That's right. You use a pay4phone, you tell me where you at. And you wait there. No matter how Bigurl screams, no matter what sort of shit you see in the lot, no matter if Tibetan Santa comes with a gift-wrapped key for your addled ass. You take the fucking dock, and you wait for me to get there. Someone wants to ask you what's your problem? 'Oh Mister, I got a *substance* abuse issue.' Then we'll have it swap to me. I do the same thing at next resstop and have it swap to Heart Attack. Then he waits, and then delivers. Three swaps, five hours behind on a four-and-a-half-hour route, that's greater than 100% delay credit on express drop ship on the most expensive rate code there is. Fucking military grade processors, gold bars, new organs. Who knows what, but fucking money, Tandy."

They watched the digits swim, trying to imagine the feel of possessing actual cash.

"You are not currently registered to have a secondary operator, please enter code."

Noor stashed Tablet and kicked at the sphincter to exit.

"Tandy."

"Yeah boss-lady?"

"Yer Bigurl smells worse than the fucking lavs."

The sphincter pulled shut, leaving Tandy and Bigurl alone again.

Being outside Bigurl is like having an outer layer of flesh flensed off. Sick twitches hitting thick now, nothing makes sense.

Everything painful. But still: gotta scrap. No choice in the matter. Only way to score. The thought of climbing back in Bigurl without a reup is enough to make Tandy want to leap in front of one.

Here stands Tandy, blanking in the concrete light, under the unblinking eye of the gray sky and the thirteen bashed-in CCTV cameras, each drooping from a different perch of the orange plastic resstop walls. Seven-and-a-half hours more of mandatory safety resstop here. Enough time to scrap and score with the lot connect, before the hustle off to meet Noor's precious pax.

Body slumps. Meat, hanging off the spine, easily plucked, but the Bigurl still gives them customary three beeps, then the aperture sphincters closed. She'll hustle off and fuel and chitterchat with the other rigs and drink bad diner coffee and flirt with the waitress or whatever it is Bigurl does when the operator is out of the box and in the air. She got no sense of a person's brain having an inside, away from somatic stimulus response time. Or she just don't care.

Which will be scrap metal first? Tandy or their Bigurl? Every op dearly wishes to see their Bigurl in the junkyard, to feel that very human superiority over mere matter. To have won at least that backwards race of endurance, if nothing else. Even if there's nowhere else to go. Nowhere else to live. Like a worm in the blood, whose only natural home is a hot shrinking vein. But Tandy, some days, these days, they don't know.

Five minutes of blanked out on the tarmac, unsure if they can make it inside the resstop, Tandy remembers the 15 mL of medical grade cocaine (liquid). Scrabbling for it, with grubby, bug hands, but there's no pockets, just empty holes. Cut them all out, the pockets, because the zippers could have been—some sort of wallet bag? The coke's back in the rig, must be.

Fuckity.

Runs towards Bigurl but she gone. Slumping, well past despair, that particular emotion tapped out about seventeen hours into the current haul. A cold, hard pressure in the left hand. Fuck, the vial! Awful drama between human and object for the past god knows how many hours, alternately gripping it or tearing the box apart to find it, terrified it got lifted by some resstop junkie, last place.

Struggles through the resstop door sphincter. Don't wanna fix out on the tarmac; some Bigurl make you a stain. Now, barely breathing, dropper shakes above the right eye. Always right first. Please please *please* don't miss. A single tear rolling down the cheek, worth a scrap a piece, gone into the black footprints of rain and smeared box sewage, tracked into the lav from the tarmac. It hits. Thank the fuck to christ buddha allah. Hand steadies slightly. And then left eye. Liquid is cold burning.

They're someone else for a time. Fucking monster of rage, searching for cameras, lights, any fixture intact enough to rip and smash. No… more… with the *looking*, you fucks! Beating against the stainless steel sheet in place of lav mirror, they scream to god to tell him not to *fucking* touch them anymore.

And that's fine.

Shit that's *normal*.

Settling down now. A couple ops, huddled together by the burnt out toilets, occasionally glancing over in terror. Fucking hypocritical scum, didn't do nothing to them. All this went fine. That sure as shit isn't cocaine, they remember now. But it'll be fine, if it isn't already.

The Big Clock, which manages to drag itself into view, counts down departure time from 1:21. Somehow six hours of resstop just evaporated. But no problem. Plenty of time. It's all fine.

Three beeps. An aperture sphincters open in the plastic wall, orange briefly browning at the center of the swirl. Another driver, a big guy with no shirt and strange asymmetrical surface wounds to his otherwise chiseled chest and only one shoe on droops into the lav, in *much* worse shape than Tandy was, six odd hours ago. They scramble over him, three beeps sound again, bug hands claw open the aperture as it tries to shut. Head first wriggling out onto the scorching blacktop as the aperture tries to decide what to do with their legs. Luckily, it disgorges them, and Tandy tumbles out.

Against the backdrop of withered trees and the spindly access road winding up to the interstate (the sound of autoshifting, faint, as if in dreams) is a sight that looks weird from the outside: four generic, same uncolor, equally worn Bigurls, lined up next to one another, making the rest of the lot seem even more vacant than if it had been completely empty. They call it flocking, the way the Bigurls choose to park together, in small groups spread out across the lot. Some sort of preference, makes sense to them, but not to ops. Maybe to them marketmakers, is what Noor was trying to say, Tandy guesses. Which one which one which *one* is theirs? Bigurls all look the same, *exact*. It stalks Tandy, sometimes, in their woke dreams, that if they lost their Bigurl, and any old one came a'nuzzling, they'd have to take it on some kind of faith, until climbing inside. (No stink of home can be bottled, only boxed.)

Creeping respectfully forward, wondering if they'll be recognized by their own first, or if the strange Bigurls might spring forward and tread, snatch body up, and mash mash mash. But Bigurls just wait patiently. Get ten feet away when they're in security mode, they'll rear up and do some damage, but before that, you solid. Ten feet, ten feet, on repeat. Stalking forward (the Big Clock no longer heads up, a deep anxiety, sweating in places without requisite glands), Tandy thinks how many times they've done this, how many times they gonna do it again. Seems like Zero. They roll right, they bupping to bliss. They roll wrong, they get bodypawn.

At least, this shit, no more.

But there's a roar, and they hop back, take a bad step, go halfway down. Just another Bigurl coming down the access road. Looking up from tarmac, Tandy can finally see that the numbers along the sides of the Bigurls. Last four digits of each new flocking rig around their own. First: <u>4ADC</u>. Second: <u>654D</u>. Third: <u>1DEC</u>. Three together in the lot plus their own Bigurl is enough to trade for a fix. Off the tarmac, favoring the sharp-ached ankle, hopping toward the aperture already opening for the incoming rig.

Run. Try not to think about how close the moving rig is behind. (How far *is* ten feet, anyway? Could you feel the windtunnel forming around you before you went down?) Going through the aperture is easypeasy, with the soundtrack of the incoming rig's defensive systems switching on inside Tandy's head, a series of metal clicks and a 10K volt capacitor charge, and then back in the lav again.

Spine against the plastic. Check the clock. Only about twenty minutes to go. Lot connect nowhere in sight. A junkie could always tell who it is. And they ain't here.

Taking the nub of a pencil from behind their right ear, Tandy writes <u>1DEC</u> very slowly on the scrap of paper. Slowly. How to form an <u>E</u>, it takes them a while to remember. Then to the right, <u>654D</u>, pretty quick. And then, longer, in the next position, <u>4ADC</u>. And last, their own Bigurl code, <u>1AD3</u>, under a wavering line of demarcation, the standard scrapper format. Somewhere in bare background, the op whose aperture-slot they skimmed is beating against the plastic otherside. Eventually, the noise ceases. Tandy don't wanna speculate on the cause of *that*.

Nine minutes.

Tandy knows they gotta go, or Bigurl gonna get fined. They gotta go, or they gonna miss Noor's pax at the meeting-place. But if they go now, no scrap. No scrap means no score. No score, they pull into meeting-place, they ain't gonna be able to get out the box.

So Tandy waits. Waits till the Big Clock starts chiming, then it starts screaming, then the wail and they turn it off. They watch the two former lav-huddlers taking turns orally serving a too-generic probable pighead wearing a slightly malfunctioning smear-mask that switches on and off every twenty seconds. When it's down the red gorge rises, and he smiles a little bashfully. Tandy watches this for a while, too long actually, but nobody comes over and demands either spectator fee or for them to join in. This drama ends after a surprisingly long time, and a vial is exchanged. Nothing happens for a while, but Tandy blank, so it don't matter. Just time. A little later, more drama. On the other side of the aperture, an incoming op is struggling against the orange plastic that won't sphincter. Who knows why. Who gives a fuck. Better to lean against the outside and shit, if they can.

The orange sphincter. A big woman with a raw-boned face climbs through. Recognizable, but from where? Chi-town? Des? Another lav, another scrap, split from continuity by the peaks and chasms of highs and withdrawal. She walks directly over, ignoring the continual nodding and conspiratorial winking. She snatches the scrap, without ever actually really looking at it, or at Tandy.

Woman disappears off into the lav labyrinth, or maybe the resstop on the otherside of the internal sphincter. Tandy struggles up. Now they've got the vial everything begins to hurt, that endless drip burning behind the eyes. Blinking, they feel the way to the sphincter. Turning, full of dread, and joy, to be back in the box, to look at the resstop one last time. Last last *last*. Everything's only just begun. In this case, of course, that includes possible dismemberment.

But maybe more, real money, the fuck out of this job in a way that isn't selling it off to hijackers and earning a life sentence or bullet. More than the small tinfoil packet the raw-boned woman dropped onto the lav floor for Tandy to bend and snatch up, sixteen to twenty four hours of immersion in painlessness waiting under the googly eye, emotional opacity looking out the glasshield.

Pass through the sphincter, and it's out the fuck of Dodge.

If they make it in time.

[90ED:ADD1:F6D9:0:4BD3:34AE:E22C:00D2]: CHECK-IN PNS UTC 09:12:12:41 12.16.21
[90ED:ADD1:F6D9:0:4BD3:34AE:E22C:00D2]:
CONTENT VERIFICATION PNS UTC 09:12:13:02 12.16.21
PRODUCT CODE: REDACTED
[90ED:ADD1:F6D9:0:4BD3:34AE:E22C:00D2]:
NEW DESTINATION ROUTE PNS UTC 09:12:15:43 12.16.21
PNS - MOB - MSY - LFT - BMT XFER COUNT: 3
[90ED:ADD1:F6D9:0:4BD3:34AE:E22C:00D2]: ON-BOARD PNS UTC 09:15:59:05 12.16.21
TRUCK CODE: [88B1:1292:44CC:01D3:21AA:6B87:0:1AD3]
OPERATOR CODE: [9932:CAED:CC3E:AD3A:21BC:BF4E:FA92:1928]
CONTRACT CODE: [HASHED] SIGNED

"Onboard, *baby*. Onboard, *honey*. Cash is the only prescription, and the doctor is snappin' on her *gloves*! What'd *you* think she's gonna find in there? Polls closing in Plymouth, superweather scuddin' in over the Rockies, pyracy in the panhandles! Put your money down or bite asphalt, there's a nice little patch I had installed in the unisex. Tastes like the last guy's *teeth*."

Beef-chin was back again, idly typing someone else's figures into the terminal. The suited man pulled up the map, letting his eyes flutter at the speed of light, as he waited for inspiration to hit. There were all kinds of options on the road, but they were big. Too big. The markets would be all over that storm like flies on shit. The smart man, the *rich* man, looked to the unseen opportunity. His eyes drifted down to the Southeast. Nice n'quiet.

[90ED:ADD1:F6D9:0:4BD3:34AE:E22C:00D2]: STOP-SCHEDULED UTC 09:59:28:11 12.16.21
[90ED:ADD1:F6D9:0:4BD3:34AE:E22C:00D2]:
CONTENT VERIFICATION UTC 09:59:34:07 12.16.21
PRODUCT CODE: REDACTED
[90ED:ADD1:F6D9:0:4BD3:34AE:E22C:00D2]: HOT-SWAP UTC 10:54:54:41 12.16.21
MOB - MSY - LFT - BMT XFER COUNT: 3
[90ED:ADD1:F6D9:0:4BD3:34AE:E22C:00D2]: HOT-SWAP COMPLETE UTC 10:57:17:18 12.16.21
TRUCK CODE: [88B1:1292:44CC:01D3:21AA:6B87:0:1AD3]

OPERATOR CODE: [9932:CAED:CC3E:AD3A:21BC:BF4E:FA92:1928]
CONTRACT CODE: [HASHED] COMPLETE
TRUCK CODE [6AD6:30DE:B3C8:0:33E2:3EA1:C8CD:F650]
OPERATOR CODE: [CADE:2109:56BA:AEDC:292F:4051:388A:307B]
CONTRACT CODE: [HASHED] SIGNED

Little flickers of yellow in New Orleans, around the Mississippi archipelago. He checked the weather: no rain, not even a re-mist. Dry as a fucking bone. Just strain in the system. The human weakness, taking their sweet time wading through the resstop sewers. Garbage in, garbage out.

Looking up through Texas, slowness there too. But wait wait wait: artificially depressed speed limits due to construction. Now there's a problem you can fix. He keyed Tablet, and started making trades. Then, hit the button for a voice call.

"Cheeky—whassup, go fuck yourself. Nah I kid, man. Hey. *Hey!* Keep your fucking shirt on, maybe I make you some dinero tonight. You still got that contact over at TexDOT? I know you do. You tell him to speed things up, in the corridor between Dallas and Houston clear to the state line. Fucking advisory speeds, man. Gotta give me some juice, tonight.

"What do you mean, Federal safety standards? I'm just asking for 20 more fucking miles an hour! Like they give a shit about a couple of concrete bots and a handful of ops. I know he can do it. Tell him the usual rate, and your fee too. He makes my lines turn green and I make it rain green. You know how we do."

He disconnected, swigged from the nearest bottle, which was a mistake, and waited for the map to refresh.

[66E3:DAE3:210A:987D:CEA8:455B:21D0:214F]: FLASH TX UTC 11:11:52:07 12.16.21
[66E3:DAE3:210A:987D:CEA8:455B:21D0:214F]:
NEW DESTINATION TX UTC 11:12:23:29 12.16.21
DFW - OCH - BMT XFER COUNT: 1
[90ED:ADD1:F6D9:0:4BD3:34AE:E22C:00D2]: FLASH TX UTC 11:12:53:36 12.12.21

[90ED:ADD1:F6D9:0:4BD3:34AE:E22C:00D2]:
NEW DESTINATION TX UTC 11:13:14:45 12.12.21
MOB - TCL - BHM - BNA XFER COUNT: 2

"Weekend warriors? That what I'm seeing here? You all wanna be home jerking off over cryptobets like it's 2017? I'm *crying*. Look at my *face*. But but... *but*. I am seeing, I am SEEING something coming to life, something rolling, like a great V-HICK-LE over this great Sea To Shining, and it's green lines, endless, children of a lesser monetary system, *endless* green lines! Get on the road or get *under* the wheels."

The first retribution of excised junk: the realization that all time is now box time.

Heart Attack Joe can't think too good no more. And he don't feel too great either. Things Heart Attack Joe knows: he should've waited till the Job was over, he should've waited till he was back in that beachtown shack, changing his ma's oxygen tanks, with plenty of structure. But: couldn't find veins, couldn't find credit, couldn't find out why he kept coughing up that chalky white stuff. And, somewhere between Richmond and the border-switch to Savannah, Joe turned 35. It was time to get clean.

So Joe went turkey.

The second retribution of excised junk: the realization that all time has *always* been box time.

Mud-smudged plastic gallon jug shoved under the dash. Potscheen brewed by a Sovereign Citizens clade based in the ruins of a Shirlington mall. Tastes like *nickels*. Joe has no idea if the hootch is legal wherever the hell the box is now, but he knows it's sure as shit not legal to have it *in* the box. Probably even less legal than horse, depending on the evangelical infiltration of whatever statelet Bigurl's ramming through at 90 plus right now. But fuck it, put me on that chain-gang, sez Heart Attack Joe, pluck out mine eyes, crucifix me by the side of I-95.

Cuz this shit ain't *ending*.

The third retribution of excised junk: the realization that you could never think too good in the first place.

Joe tries to get deep into the darkness on the other side of his eyes, tries to see what was always on the other side of a hit, tries to see that nothingness and emptiness aren't the same shit. It's the dark, but it ain't just the dark. It's *fingers*, long and sharp, ready for slipping into your eyes. Joe could melt into the dark, but for Tablet up there on the mount, reading the infrared-only topography of his face, squirting metrics back to whatever company owns Bigurl today, plus IUATO.

The Tablet don't scream when Joe attacks its face with the multi-tool.

Joe does.

The fourth retribution of excised junk: the realization that landscape ain't real.

Heart Attack Joe knows: there's nothing outside the box. The shattered spruce on the side of the highway, the sudden plunge into the valley of a deserted townlet, the scavenger-cleaned Model X in the Educational Center parking lot. All as unreal as the machine vision he tries to release out of the Tablet, like render ghosts.

Joe passes endlessly through the colon of the former United States, sweating and alone.

Then Joe sees what's on Tablet, and he *wants* be alone. Pretty much for fucking ever.

Somewhere, sometime later after the liquor runs out, Joe is alone no more:

"The fuck you message me on *Tablet* for? Lost your fucking mind, Joe? Joe. *Joe!*"

The boss-lady had jacked open the aperture with *something*, prised apart the sphincter with her hands, and is now half-hung inside the box.

"Are you fucking… *drunk?*"

Bob the head: the head bobs.

"I came up from NoLA on *fob*, motherfucker! I had to infect yer Bigurl to not get fucking electrocuted! You remember how much that cost? Do you remember *any*shit? Do you remember the Job? Why the hell weren't you there to take the swap? Some other rig came and got it cause your ass wasn't there!"

Boss-lady's vibrating there. Pulled herself out of the aperture, looks ready to haul Joe out the chair, plant him curbwise, do some stomping.

"Shreveport." Joe moves his mouth; he's got the face of a fish. One of the big basa you see struggling at the edges of the feed-ponds. Working the air like it's chaw.

"You say Shreveport to me?"

"I didn't get a call to go swap. Fucking, says, Shreveport."

Boss-lady swipes the Tablet. Fingers it. Sucks her teeth at the unbreakaglass, smeared with horse-hoof residue. Rates, percentage, dues. And the Big Fee, to go with the Big Clock, both flipping past in the top corner.

"Slagshit," she murmurs. "The fuck you do, Joe?"

Boss-lady pulls out her own Tablet, shaking. Fingers trying to stab at the information. Light on her face like a road ghost over Donner 80. Shaking her head before she can barely read a line.

"No swap."

She holds Tablet over him, to either let him read or bludgeon him. "Look at fucking Tablet. Read that. Says fucking *delivered*. You missed the swap, and so it rerouted on us, bringing another pax in from Dallas via Nacogdoches. It's gonna arrive *early* to Beaumont. We owe money, Joe. So much fucking money."

"I did... did what you said."

"No. No," she says. "I told you, to *take the fine* and wait in NoLA until it tells you to swap! If you done like what I said, we wouldn't be in Rouge! You had enough time to make the swap, and get close enough to Beaumont before resstop so it wouldn't reroute. I planned it with *extra*." She picks up the empty jug.

Sniffs. "Ain't that hard, Joe. Why you so lost? Couldn't find a vein? Couldn't score? Shit, I'd have given you my shit, keep you straight for the duration."

"Sick of it."

Boss-lady nods once, like she don't wanna understand. Algorithm couldn't read that shit in her face. Junkie can though.

"Need to get back on the road," fish says.

"You say you sick of it."

"Wha'?"

"You sick of it, Joe. So just be that and don't be nothin' more."

Something in her hand. Something Joe has seen before.

And that's when the switch goes out, like the long tongue of a crane, and licks the chest of Heart Attack Joe.

"IF YOU WERE HERE WE'D HAVE BEEN ABLE TO SAVE HIS HEART"

...is the first thing Tandy heard out of the box, blinking in the tarmac sun. Bigurl wailing behind them, fines coming thick and fast into Tablet, and Tandy looking around at some kind of abandoned industrial park, the frontages of former outlet stores turned into empty frames by scavengers.

"His heart, Tandy," said Noor, gasping. "His heart."

"Why didn't you just stick it in one of them dry-freeze boxes?" asked Tandy. "They gave you one, right? In your Bigurl?"

Noor had been crying violently, though her face still had the frieze of the infuriated. Now she went dry. While she kept her bloodied hands on Tandy's shoulders, she no longer leaned on them for support, but rather squeezed slowly, tightening an already uncomfortable grip. "You *dumb shit.* Joe fucked up, and his Bigurl wants to go to Shreveport now, not NoLA. I had to fob a ride North off Iltie. Meanwhile, our pax is god knows where, and the delivery is gonna go through. *Early.* We owe the broker, the bodypawn, even fucking IUATO on our fucking late pickups. We are fucking deader than dead."

"Shiiit."

"So I opened him up, and now he's all rotten. We'll never be able to... Hours late, Tandy, you're hours late."

Tandy shrugged. "Box time."

Noor was shaking her head. "We're fucked, Tandy. So fucked. Might as well just stroll out into the lanes now, and get finished. Ain't no way we getting clear of this."

Tandy idly picked Tablet out of Noor's hand. Noor let it go, a surprise in retrospect, and just kept *talking*. Tandy stared at the icons on the screen, bright and cheerful against the plaid map-space and the corporate-source adbots. Something about their comedown, and the small fix they'd had box time, opened up a channel in their brain, a real linear, neat path through clusters of cells that didn't usually work in concert no more, and they held it up and said, "Joe's going to Mobile."

Noor was already laughing in a crazy, cackling way about something else, but now she had to stop, straightface, and stare Tandy for a second before starting to laugh all over again. "My friend, Heart Attack ain't going nowheres, unless it's in a couple plastic bags, but I figured we'd just leave him here? Who cares?"

She would have gone on, but Tandy shook their head, forceful and calm enough to shut her up. They tapped the Bigurl icon in the lot, parked next to hers. "His Bigurl? She ready. That's why she all red. She wanna get going to Mobile." Tandy waved a gnawed-at stub of a fingernail vaguely at the hacked taggings Noor had cued up.

"He said Shreveport."

"Mobile, now. Look, it's moving. And look at them digits: 00d2. That's *our* pax. The one I swapped to you. It rerouted East to back to Mobile instead of West on Beaumont. And then on to Loosa, and then Nashville."

Noor grabbed Tablet, and studied it. "Joe's Bigurl is tracking to meet a fucking runner. Express direct. His Bigurl is still up for it, just in a different place, different destination."

"We could still get the pax back, maybe delay it again and make up the money? You infect Heart Attack's Bigurl right? So she kinda woozy, probably take us, thinking we her op. Worth a fucking go, leastwise. Then when it swaps we—"

Noor leaned in and kissed Tandy on the lips. That was uncomfortable, especially considering how bloody her face was. "Most expensive route code there is. Fucking gold bars and shit, Tandy. We find it, and we break the seal!" Noor exclaimed in their ear. "An express direct runner, you fucking *know* that has gotta be some expensive shit in that pax! They don't want it in Beaumont, but they want it bad in Nashville. They not gonna get it though... that pax is ours. We can sell the bits, whatever they are, and we use it to pay off." When she leaned back out, Noor was smiling that badtooth smile.

"We break it? Why the fuck would we do that, Noor? You make a new bet. We swap it, take it real close, I try to pick up a maintenance in Birmingham, that's at least four hours late, make up some story for Tablet like resstop fire, and..."

"That's not enough Tandy. None of the usual shit could make up what we owe now. Except those juicy, pricey bits in the pax."

Tandy tried not to think about all the ops they'd ever heard about trying to bust open a pax. Like when you were real hard up. Not just like junkie hard up. Like for money you owed to someone so dark and dire, you were ready to throw yourself off a crossover bridge, because you knew that would be the easier argument. Ready to sell your own organs, generate enough capital to save the leftover bits, maybe they'd still add up to you. Like that.

It was suicide, they said. Maybe you got lucky, found some bits worth selling. Maybe you were real lucky, and got enough money to pay off whoever was after you. But the company always found you in the end, and there was just one way that story finished. When the seal was broken, the company charged the op for the loss of cargo in full—and there were only so many ways of extracting that sort of payment.

Occasionally, a black market gang would hijack a Bigurl for whatever was in the pax. Some million dollar load, something worth the risk and the effort. They had the tech to know what was inside, and how to find and deactivate the trackers. During the hit, a smart op would ask the jackers to put a bullet in their head. Because they knew it was better than the company's way.

Normally the jackers would oblige them.

They sat in Joe's box, oil-slick machine vision streaming across the glasshield. Noor was staring at Tablet, *their* Tablet, clucking and muttering to herself, head bobbing back and forth. Her neckveins were all strained out, and she was sweating pretty heavy. Joe wasn't using, and all Tandy's junk was back in their Bigurl, and they hadn't had time to go back for it.

Noor's security infection seemed to have done its work on Joe's Bigurl. She'd spluttered a little, wasn't too pleased with the new meat, but she wanted to get to Mobile something desperate, so she didn't put up too much of a fuss. Company bots were no doubt clearing the infection up, working down the fiber. They had time though. Bigurls were known to be *hardened*, but not exactly responsive. All the same, they were racing a new Big Clock to Mobile.

All Tandy was thinking on, however, was the last time they stroked the flank of *their* Bigurl. Long and, beneath the accumulated slime and shit of the road, smooth. Their Bigurl had responded, lights on and engine running through initial stages of power up; it was almost like the big beast had been excited to see them. Tandy hadn't had too many opportunities to see her from the outside, but they felt, stroking that hide, that she was actually theirs.

Tandy hadn't taken Bigurl off automatic much. Off grid. Off box time. They didn't know how long it be before whichever company owned her today decided remote seizure of control was worth the bandwidth and human hours.

Pretty soon, probably. When Tandy got back, if they ever got back, their Bigurl would almost certainly be gone, and that seemed sadder now than the loss of the little junk in her.

Home was home, whether you recognized it or not.

"Come on come on come on come on!" Noor kept up the litany, rocking back and forth above the shaking Tablet, as if involved in some obscure ritual. Tandy had stopped trying to touch her, or even talk to her. Noor was now past despair, real real far down whatever highway she was on.

On the run to Mobile, Noor's Tablet had froze up for almost forty minutes. Some sort of crash in her hacked-as-shit scripts. Then it caught up with itself, showing massively advanced positions of both Joe's Bigurl and the runner. The runner had already swapped. Noor'd screamed and thrown Tablet at Tandy like a discus. Tandy'd caught it against their chest like a startled pigeon released from a cage, clutched it there, almost cooing at it.

They hadn't had to coax the orphan Bigurl to do max when the runner was en route to Mobile, but now that it was northbound, she became direction-sick. She dropped to cruising speed and looped onto an access road, which deadended at a resstop.

Noor beat her fists against the dash till her skin broke. Her cry was inarticulate.

Tandy sat against the wall, as far away from the various pools of dried fluids as possible, and fought with Noor's Tablet.

Around the time the boss-lady's screaming stopped, as she was licking at the bloody underside of her fists, Tandy managed to convince the Bigurl to fix again on the runner, and she took a semi-legal tributary from the access-road, passing through what appeared to be the ruins of a former chemical weapons testing compound. They were heading toward Loosa, with Bigurl going even harder than before, if that was possible.

Noor rolled over against the box wall like a lost, drugged animal. She slid down it and gave Tandy her unblinking, huge eyes, her mouth shut to a slit. "What you do?" she asked, voice shaved down by abuse.

"Convinced her Heart Attack was on the runner."

"She believe you." It wasn't a question, as much as an admission of doubting, the doubting of everything. Noor didn't look like someone who believed in reality so much anymore. Tandy'd seen this shit in a few junkies going turkey, they didn't fold up inside themselves, but unfolded into the world around them.

Tandy pushed one shoulder up, tried to look like a funny cartoon character, the kind that don't get death by switch in the final frame. "She know what she want to believe."

Noor leaned back against the box wall, eyes still open, but she wasn't seeing shit.

Bigurl was exceeding legal limit, so was her love for her op. Or so Tandy imagined. They shut their eyes, imagining if their Bigurl felt the same, if it was a feel that was the thing, not just a subroutine, damaged, with an extra waypoint added out of Joe's personal allotment. Tricking the orphan Bigurl, that needed doing or Noor would've killed all three, but it made them feel worse than any of the shit they'd done, or seen, last couple weeks. They felt like they'd betrayed the only contract they'd ever willingly accepted.

The runner was at forty past legal limit. Tandy tried to do the math, see if they'd make it, but they couldn't, didn't have that energy, didn't have the faith. Better to be hopeless. Back on the interstate, the faint screaming of the laboring Bigurl, Noor took Tablet back. They should catch up just outside of Mt. Vernon, just after the next pax-switch. There was a resstop there, and the new runner would need a fuel and a resstop, as her op would be almost passed statelet legal limitations on box time.

Tandy didn't sleep because they were reassured. They slept because they were exhausted.

Tandy opened their eyes as they ran through the deracinated forest just off 43, just outside of Mt. Vernon. Tablet went green— the runner had already switched the pax. But resstop was just a breath away. Noor took the switch out of her jacket, looking out at the debased shapes of the debased forest, clicking the weapon against the dash.

Noor announced box time: they'd hit the resstop twenty-three minutes after the runner had arrived. No way were they gonna break open the runner there; the resstops were designed to protect Bigurls hard, and the bodies of the ops were barely factored into the calculations of that. But Noor knew the orphan Bigurl was going to have to get back on highway by way of the service corridor, a quarter-mile stretch of local road running down to the next northbound on-ramp, a slip of the local dessicated forest dividing them from the main road. There, they would have a chance. If they could catch it.

Noor explained the plan to Tandy, who stayed curled in the seat, staring at the glasshield, nodding rhythmically till she stopped speaking. Tandy wasn't sure if Noor understood much anything anymore.

It seemed almost no time, maybe Tandy'd gone blank again, but Bigurl was decelerating down to ten to enter resstop. This was the end of their ride, and they would have to run to catch the runner from here. The two of them jacked open her door with a metal tray filthy from Heat-Em-Up stains. Tandy didn't even feel their body leaving the box, entering the air. Their eyes were closed. There was no fall. Just the impact.

In the dark, they shook.

When Tandy stood, it seemed millennia had passed, or at least a good solid fix, and they were bent bad on the ankle, which wasn't even causing pain. This is it, Tandy thought. That place beyond the fix. They were surprised, kinda, to see they had grabbed Tablet and even managed to still clutch it against their chest, mostly unharmed.

Out ahead, they saw the boss-lady, bloody left arm shown through torn double jacket, running, switch in the other hand, toward the treeline.

The trees were husks, shredded down to whittled nubs by the poison tributary or the hot rain or whatever was this area's particular chemical catastrophe, but these husks still had enough height to obscure the way forward, and Noor ran blind under murky moonlight, sucking breath. Tandy tried to follow, but they were slowed by the ankle. Still no pain, but no stability. They had to relearn how to move without falling over.

It shouldn't have been far, but when they came out onto the service corridor, Tandy had given up believing that they'd ever be moving over any other kind of terrain. Up the short access road, a Bigurl, as ugly as hers, as ugly as any of theirs; it was doing forty, coming down the road directly at them. Noor was there, hanging partially in the street. "Gimme Tablet," she said.

Tandy tossed Tablet over, and Noor, holding the switch under her chin, ran her fingers, fierce and blunt, over it. She looked up and fixed the Bigurl with a gaze so steady Tandy knew it was definitely the runner. Then she shrugged and stepped back, off the street.

"What?" said Tandy.

"What what?"

"We gonna do nothin'?"

"You gonna do."

"But—"

The Bigurl pretty damn close now, and Noor bent down into linebacker and drove her shoulder into the small of Tandy's back. Tandy stumbled out onto the little road, blinded by headlights. The Bigurl screamed as lidar locked on, downshifting automatically, tires shooting out great huffs of crystal firestone freebased off rough road. She slid to a stop a few feet from Tandy, who was still upright but too shocked to move. Wouldn't have stopped for an op in the lot. But Tandy was a pedestrian now.

Then the blare. That big, fucking *blare*.

"You... you... you shut your big fucking mouth!" Tandy screamed to get their muscles moving again, as much as anything.

They noticed, barely, that Noor was at their side, slapping the infection code into Tablet. Then she dashed to the side as the infection twisted its way through Bigurl's decentralized nervous system, and she slammed Tablet into the crack in the box to wedge it open.

Tandy reached out and touched the hot grill of the Bigurl, and the blare stopped. No electrical arc fried them in their sneakers. Guess the infection had worked.

Noor put her back into it and the box door slurped and wrenched open, emitting vape fog and the blare of talk broadcast, some politicast, the deep voice like marching boots frothing out over the Alabama roadway. A four-hundred pound dude wearing some faked metal jewelry retched out of the Bigurl going *Wha Whaaaa* and Noor hit him with the switch and he fell out and hit the road and then Noor hit him again.

"We WILL make America ONE again!" blared the politicast. "We WILL put the people back in charge, where they belong! We WILL RISE AGAIN!"

Noor hit the op another time and he came apart and then Noor was just hitting and hitting and *hitting* until she reached pavement underneath.

Tandy left the spectacle, went round the truck where the long, huge hind end of the Bigurl projected out from the last set of wheels. No hatch, no handle, no button to push. Just a thin plastic seal threaded between two flush steel holes. Tandy ripped it away, with a pound of their heart. And then, they realized they'd never done this, nor seen it done even. Presumably Noor had an idea of what next, but she was beyond communication. So Tandy just reached out their hand and placed it on the hull of the Bigurl.

"Open up girl," they said, and she did, just like that. The snapped plastic seal fell into two pieces on the ground.

Inside were fifty shipping crates, standing vertical like bodies on hooks. Tandy stepped up and in, then they were alone inside the pax. In the shadows, they glanced at the back of their hand where the numbers and letters had been written in indelible marker. They paced down the crates, searching in the bad light for tags. Tandy compared with the scribble, eyes squinted. They had to look at maybe twenty or so down the aisle before they found it, and then they stood there. Was there a code needed to be punched in? Scanner? A keyhole? There was nothing there, so they just tugged on a metal handle. And the thing unfolded. Came apart, like a jaw unhinging itself, but like in seven different ways. A smell of non-human spilling out. The crate was big enough for them to walk in, so they did. Tandy flicked on their zippo, and held the little flame up to the walls, long and black.

When Tandy came back out to the road, the night was gray and humid, the atmosphere so clotted it was like breathing through a dirty mop.

"PAYDAY! PAYDAY! PAYDAY!" the politicast screaming-head was repeating. Tandy flipped the sphincter switch, and it closed. The invective was now muffled, but they could still hear the plosives through the metal.

Noor was cross-legged in the pool of fat man, bloody hands over face. She was shaking. Just slightly. The switch was at her side, still sparking. Tandy picked it up, turned it off, and tossed it down into the toxic run-off by the side of the road. They knelt down next to Noor, whose teeth were chattering. "Can't, can't, *can't*," she kept saying.

"Boss-lady," said Tandy. "*Boss*-lady." Noor wasn't coming out of it.

Tandy got their face in real close. "There ain't nothing in there, Noor. It's empty. There's nothing to sell."

Noor's teeth kept chattering. Then she stopped. Her eyes went to Tandy. Small eyes now.

Slowly, Tandy helped her up. Noor remained half-hunched over herself. For a second, it looked like she would wretch, but her throat never constricted, and she never vomited. Then she looked at them. "Empty?" It was a little girl's voice.

"Empty."

Noor pursed her lips like she was going to say something, then she just nodded. A suddenly wrenching of the Bigurl, and Tandy shied back, Noor unmoving. The Bigurl was shutting her rear end, restarting her engine. The Bigurl jerked forward ten or so feet, then lurched to a pause. Tandy could almost feel it calculating: no op inside. Maybe it knew it was empty of cargo as well, though Tandy doubted that it would have felt anything because of it. More just like shit luck, shit life. Abandoned by its op, it would return to dispatch until it got a new one. The next of how many more, before the scrap heap.

The Bigurl did a complex-angled K turn, and Noor still stood there, dead-eyeing her. Tandy dragged Noor off the road, surprised she didn't fight. The Bigurl accelerated past them, picking up speed and churning the access road into exhaust till she met the highway. Tandy watched the dust dissipate for a moment, and when they looked down, they were surprised to find Noor, too, was sitting on the pavement, watching the runner disappear.

Tandy sat down next to Noor, as the dull sound of massive, slow rotor blades grew louder over the poisoned woods, drowning out the sound of the highway beyond.

Ignoring the churning sound of doom approaching, Noor said, with no inflection in her voice and no expression in her face, "Where we gonna fix, Tandy."

And so the scales were balanced, and commerce continued, just as designed.

OUTSIDE

A blur of gray and blue: late '80s fabric, the kind that stands to your touch, sticks to the pads of your fingers. A collection of human legs, with scrunched pantyhose and billowing slacks, perpetually rearranging themselves like the slow, fluid bars of light that slipped through the window. Out there a wide, white, flat sky. It gnawed at the passengers' auras, consuming the personas they realized on their faces, leaving only a greasy residue. The unpeeling of cellophane wrappers, the crunch of baby carrots between kiddie molars, the hissing of freed CO_2, the indecipherable conversation of adults, couched in lingo, lazy diction, and unpierceable jokes. The noise washed over me like murky, milky sea foam, then settled down to soak in. Cigarette burns dotted the arms of the seats; discolorations bloomed in-between plastic windowpanes. Air vents spluttered and giggled, and the AC barely functioned. During midday the light was unbearable.

The train had personality, but it wasn't *alive*.

The inside of a cat.

In particular, an irritable, asocial ladycat with one fucked-up eye, met during a summer's visit to Belfast, Maine. (Nameless now; I didn't label the picture.) Her ruffled white vest remains uncaptured, nor her tattered black trim, her comically oversized ears, or even that eye, but I have her, sneering in profile, her whole body cut away to show an interior occupied by a hustling, baroque collection of faceless globules. These thinglets teem down to her very paws, vying for space, but also ginning her up for locomotion.

Even at six, I knew cats didn't work that way.

Commuter rail, NE corridor. Very few businesspeople took calls anymore, unless they were selling used electrical equipment or cocaine. Email had just meshed with texting, and human finger-tips made no impact of touchscreens, they simply blessed them, as in a papal benediction. Earbudded college kids rewatched New Golden Age TV obsessively instead of trying to fuck each other in the bathrooms. If you worked best to musical accompaniment, as I did, whenever you unplugged you were subjected to a wash of blank sound: the rattling of plastic tile, the constant shriek of the air conditioning, the dull blast of the wind tunnel the train creat-ed around itself, the whine of the braking system. Physical details were decaying, as if they had been left out in the sun too long. Black mold in the air vents, chalky gray build-up under the sink handles, the undersides of armrests misshapen as if mid-melt.

Hunched into the wheelchair accessible seat, I rendered low-end luxury condos and rentals that would soon people formerly abandoned post-industrial districts. These were not the truly sin-gular structures, those featuring seasonal changes to the on-site arboretum, unique designs for every unit, frontages set back from picturesque side-streets. Rather, they were stacked glass cubes, with thoughtfully-designed, light-penetrated spaces, access to a courtyard feature or Juliet balcony. They would be located in mixed-use buildings, above an overbranded food-hall or a beer garden featuring nine-dollar drafts from nomad breweries. All these buzzwords had all been partially reshuffled from the last catalogue by a twenty-three-year-old with two hundred thousand-odd dollars of student debt, working eighty-hour weeks. I mirrored her in my craft, recycling old renderings, kidding along that I was remixing, helping to end postmodernism by grinding it up for its own ouroboros maw. My designs were technically correct, at least according to the specs I'd been fed by marketing experts (the ones who told architects what the buildings would look like).

Our branding campaigns strove for the same utter sameness as our competitors'. No one cared, our product was going to move as long as the economy kept grinding along. Our customers had never known how to live, and we sure as hell weren't going to show them.

Its form came first, sketched out in a hushed car. Not from any observed arachnid. Bugs had stopped splattering windshields, crawling up the crevasse of your neck, or nestling in the unknown recesses of your apartment. (The rats had, meanwhile, refused to believe in this future, and thrived, for now.) Food source gone, spiders were next.

So my designs came from Saturday morning cartoons, and dusty memories of rented cabins in the Appalachians. They weren't Apple product smooth 'n' sterile, pseudo-Swedish white heritage, or nth-punk DIY. My memories were *spiky*.

I showed them to Arthur, who showed them to Artur. Arthur said, "It should pierce your neck with that *thing*", but Artur was the one who'd already come up with a/G. He just hadn't known, previously, how to transmute it into an object.

"They suck flies dry," my mother would tell me.

"Don't flies die real quick anyway?" I'd respond.

"One or two days is their normal lifespan," she'd say then, patting the air above my head. "But this way they're actually good for something."

Spiders. They crawl over you, and they put themselves in you, and that lets you live in there, which isn't an actual anywhere. "Anti-genius," Artur had written somewhere in first instantiation of a/G branding copy. "An inversion of the god-to-man transmission of genius: the fabrication of an Outside by billions of new trajectories." He did not write that these were escape trajectories, and that the web they would constitute would serve as a place to hang meat traumatized by reality.

The same plastic shell, the same stink of recycled shit. The cars trundled with the same lack of haste, caught the same holes in the track line, let off the same steel-on-steel sighs. The signage was faded, and the gray and blue of the seat coverings were now almost indistinguishable from one another. Windows bulged inwards like insectoid sacks. The plastic face of everything was now covered with a tawny penumbra.

The seats and bathrooms had been removed. In their place were oblong, seven-foot sepulchers with very little clearance between them, running from bleached-khaki to a sick shale gray. These casks were faceless, slightly warm and sweating, and featured no markings whatsoever. Beneath them several dozen thin white lines of tense fiber quivered faintly.

I can hear my mother saying, "No one ever goes *out* anymore," then laughing soft with her teeth and her cigarette.

Now the cars remain, involuble, filled with broken girders, masses of biodegradable packing materials rotting sweetly, the occasional tchotchke some in the first generation attached to their casks before decoupling.

The train cars still move regularly, rarely coming to a halt; they *coast*. You can board them at a relatively slow jog, but old catching-out rules apply: miss and you get your legs crushed under the wheels. There's just no one left to help you once you're prone and squelching.

Nothing regulates, or challenges, your presence. I think this is what certain people's idea of a perfect society once was: total freedom in the absence of all other humans. But all those rebels have decoupled, quite willingly. The few who spend only a little time Outside (there are none, as far as I can glean, who spend none) pose no threat. Everyone and everything exists totally alone and totally connected; there is no nerve center for anybody to firebomb, if anybody even knew how to fashion a firebomb anymore.

Through the grit-pitted and flame-puckered windows, you can see the night skies of thirty years ago, the skylines of twenty, which is how various resident entities have decided things should appear for the rest of existence. I've given up on trying to parse how much of this is an engineering of reality and how much is a gossamer veil.

The swamplands of my youth, once decorated with half-submerged shipping containers, interrupted by sickened little streams, and choked by browning scrubweeds, are now clean as post-operation abscesses. All has been molded into indecipherability by machinations we can only feel.

I've gone back to drawing cats.

SOPHOKLES IN HIS CAVE

Samira made no attempt to capture the storm. Cut from a rat-fur horizon, cloudbursts let slip lightings small enough to hide behind your incisor. There was thunder like the snapping of the bones of some massive inner ear. The wind pressed against Blue Barge, and the chest of its sole occupant, a cold, illegitimate alien. Blue Barge was everything the Atlantic wasn't: clean, empty, static, but it was equally as unreadable. The storm disrupted the interplay of monolithic datacenter and endless ocean. Samira fought the urge to draw the handheld.

Three hours onboard, Samira had already shot three bursts of footage.

A deranged gull, separated from its swarm, had attacked the hem of her abaya and then, after a single solid swat, sulked aft. She'd followed with the handheld. It had cowered in front of an intricate, meaningless lattice of pounded plastic, twitching when she crouched down to document it. After five minutes of refusing to acknowledge her presence, the thing had finally turned on her its blood-drop eyes.

A long tracking shot of Texas Tower Three. On the ride in she'd had to struggle to keep the chopper door a semi-stable frame.

Out over the Georges Bank, the vehicle's internal dampeners had shut off, and the AI-pilot had mumbled something about autonomous zones, freedom of information, and limited meal service. The dampeners were artifacts of a decayed security system; Blue Barge was now a secret so open it retained the slightest vestige of mystery only to civilians. The three radar bulbs on the abandoned radio station appeared dull and unreal outlined in the concrete evening. Samira had recited a sentence from the Wiki article, her husky timbre pitched toward solemn jocular news anchor: "… distant sounds along the steel legs…"

Hardware, black on white, slabs of halogen. The long corridors of the datacenter hid in the hump on the underside of Blue Barge. She'd self-balanced the handheld on the bone floor, cold from the leagues underneath, and switched on slow-mo. The footage showed her sprinting out into an asymmetrical frame, her hijab shifting to obscure her grin, before collapsing after about forty feet. It looked like she'd been assassinated by time.

She snipcast all three. The barge's router stripped geo-locative info and filtered all content through Hog fact-checker AIs before squirting it toward what people still referred to as "the internet". All three snipcasts made it through unmolested. The half-a-dozen people who both followed her protected account and knew where she was had responded with the appropriate amount of envy.

Now, with her shit stowed fore in the artist's quarters, adjacent to the old cafeteria, Samira faced stormwards, remembering how whenever the real weather came, everybody would always be on their phones. On the terraced roof in Neukölln with Vim and Erik as the streets slowly began to fill with flood. Or quayside in Dub, watching summer hail bounce off the backs of upturned iPhones. Another long night in the Brownsville block, another thousand-year storm. It was a civilian thing to do, shoot the weather. And suddenly that's what Samira wanted to see: a constantly refreshing chain of simultaneous storms on her screen, to hold up that screen against her own storm.

She opened the app. The last image displayed, the G-Tower of Flakturm II in Friedrichshain, and then, superimposed, the ouroboros sign of loading. She checked wifi. No signal.

The Black Box was lost in the thicket of bulkheads, datacenter entrances, and entryless hutches somewhere in the chest of the ship. Samira followed the pulsing purple tracing on her handheld map to the hatch, flush with an anonymous bulkhead. Cached sensors accepted her biometrics, and the aperture slid open with a shush. Inside: walls covered in screens, a high-backed wing-chair. She perched on the edge of the wingchair (it felt decrepit, European behind her), waved through the various Intro sections on the nearest screen, then groped open the router. Wasn't just the wifi. The whole connection was down. She requested a reboot and passed the thirty seconds listening to the ventilation system, an animal's exhaust. Still no connection. She pulled up the DM app, aimed one at the Hog HQ: *no internet, this deliberate?*

Reply came so quickly it had to be a bot: *external malfunction, investigation ongoing.*

For some reason, whenever a bot promised something, Samira always believed it would actually happen.

She passed her palm over the left bank of screens almost unconsciously, and they woke up, showing specs, including those of the Black Box itself (92 hours of water, air, light, and protein). She pulled up BargeView, selected infrared, and went up vertical enough to see the entirety of the boat. Her own emanations masked by the Black Box, there was not a single human heat smear.

There was no one here. There was no reason why anyone would be. She checked the router again. Nothing. She resisted the impulse to bother the bot (as if a bot was a thing that could be bothered), then exited, to begin hunting for the krane.

No one had told her there was a krane, but there had to be one.

Blue Barge held the data servers for most of its presence on the NE seaboard. It was doubtful the Hog would allow a self-identified

"Muslim-atheist" Ethiopian-American artist complete autonomy onboard, no matter how progressive their recent branding.

Weaving her way through unmarked hutches, Samira scanned the battleship smear above Blue Barge's tallest structure, the former command tower. She could imagine a krane hanging there, armaments glistening in the sun like strange sex organs. The vision seemed so natural, it made the krane's very absence threatening. She reached the water, and her stomach immediately lurched. She stopped, shut her eyes. She tried to force the image she'd glimpsed briefly in BargeView, the whole structure a neatly delineated parallelogram, but another shape summoned itself: a long, cylindrical sheath for a heavy ceremonial dagger. She seemed a speck on this new, strange topography.

Grabbing hold of the railing, Samira leaned over the sea, as if to purge. Spatial awareness was one of the very few skill-sets she'd arrived in this world possessing. Her early successes in grad school, especially the solo show at Linden, *I Am Not the Area I Feel* (which had won a WhiteBread), had been constructed around intuitive explorations of space. While Contemporary Samira spurned these early efforts as too easy, and had complicated her practice since, Samira still felt physically palsied on the rare occasions her spatial awareness was stripped from her.

Trying to force the salt air into the recesses of her lungs (and desiring a single dirty cigarette), Samira tallied up the drags on her physical body: the nonstop journey, the lack of human contact, the sea-legs, the precooked, protein-heavy rations, two days' lack of sleep, and the tail end of a particularly painful Shark Week. It was enough to disconcert anyone, to turn a simple connection malfunction and hidden krane into evidence of Directed Malice.

She recited the Baudrillard quote reserved for these situations: "The first duty of every revolutionary is immutability."

She stood, and her eyes were open. They were focused on the command tower. Composed of jengaesque pieces, it was the only structure on the vessel without simple, clean lines. Staring at the jutting pieces, Samira began to feel as if the majority of them had shifted *downwards* since her landing the previous day. Hadn't its top-heavy nature been one of the first things she'd noticed? Its awkwardness? And now, with the pieces clustered thickly in the mid-section, the tower seemed to have acquired a complicity with the ocean, with the light itself. Against her.

Samira slapped herself softly on the cheek, her flesh not feeling like her, or any kind of flesh, and said out loud, "I am a fucking exhausted person." She turned from the tower, the sea, and the sky and staggered toward her quarters, fighting a sense of total abandonment.

The project that had enabled the Blue Barge residency was called *commuters*, a series of pics taken in various transit locales displaying passengers contorting themselves to achieve maximum comfort in anti-human environs. A squat woman presses her lower back against an armrest, feet splayed on the inner hull of an Uber-bus. A Madonna and child, wizened to the point where their awkward postures resemble a Rublev or Dionisius ikon pose on a backless plastic bench in the great hall of some airport. Their long, alien necks and disjointed fingers, their placid smiles and vacant eyes.

Their backgrounds would be bled, then each subtle brand of hyper-drab would be mixed together to form a single palate, to be smeared as uniform setting to each of the 23 portraits. (Samira knew this would subtract the ingenuity of each human adapting to a hostile space. She knew this would prove unpopular among some; she didn't care.) The process wasn't automated, which allowed her some measure of control over the aesthetics, as well as to snub the insurgent fad of bot-art. She was still trying to decide if the passengers' faces would be smeared blank.

The project had not been an obvious choice for the residency, Blue Barge's in-house curators often favoring explicitly post-Anthropocene art. Georges Bank and adjacent areas comprised one of the first catastrophically over-fished zones in the North Atlantic, and corporate responsibility had resurged violently post-Pence. Slow video installations of chum slicks sliding along the hull, or of gulls shitting in the former cafeteria, had won eyetime and several important prizes. Samira had been surprised she was even a finalist.

While the motivations of any authoritarian art world actor remained consistently elusive, Samira wondered if her rather confrontational working title had been a motivating factor in the decision. Long before the Hog took possession of Blue Barge from the Department of Defense, the DoD had taken possession of the vessel from Arkdia. Comprised of the flotsam and lagan of the sea-steading movement, the company was designed to hold onto shell corporations, vessels, and equipment for the eventual full nation-state wither. When the Pence Administration began to enact the mass deportations its predecessor had reneged on, Arkdia was shocked back to life with wet capital. Only American-pures were untargeted by the administration, and even then documentation had to be unsullied; sometimes paperwork was required going back a generation, in the case of ethnicities accused of anchor-nurseries. The result was serious braindrain on Silicon Valley and its offspring. Arkdia repurposed an old Peter Thiel-backed start-up called Blueseed that operated vessels in international waters off NYC and SF as hubs for non-pure "innovators and disruptors". Blue Barge had been one of the final hubs operating, before Arkdia was appropriated by a weaponized and deranged DHS (before it itself was subsumed by the DoD). This relatively small group of non-pures, who lived and worked and ate and drank and shat and fucked onboard, were known as "commuters", in a perhaps unintentional bit of institutional irony.

Aft, there was a large open circle, circumference of about thirty feet comprised of a dozen or so eleven-foot poles screwed into the deck, some of which were still lashed together with nylon rope. Tatters of blue plastic, clinging to the rope, fluttered in the wind. Samira began to refer to the area as "the peristyle" and assumed it had been a de facto gathering space for commuters' town meetings, occasional communal meals, and minor revels. The peristyle was surrounded by the last humps, hutches, and datacenter entrances aft, all of which buffered wind, allowing her to set up a work station. (When Samira first tried to work in the abandoned cafeteria, dank and dotted with gullshit, the long, crackling seabird calls echoing in the tremendous space drove her outside.)

"I seek a blank space in my mind," she had written in the application, the kind of overblown, aggrandizing language institutional operators immediately recognized as familiar. Her latest collaboration, scheduled for a container ship in the South China Sea, had imploded quietly, leaving a soft ruin of her social circle. The cause had not been romantic or even personal, merely sexual, leaving no debris in her heart or gut. The terrors of the first day onboard had been revealed, after rest, refueling, and reorientation, to be mere stress-induced paranoia. The work progressed far more quickly than it had in Berlin, with all the attendant distractions and depressions. Samira was even (mostly) glad of the internet's continued absence.

On the third day of no internet, a vision coalesced around Samira. Her back to the molting snow sky, cross-legged on the cold deck, back sagging in slight pain, fingers slapping keyboard, she thought she clocked a flickering in her right periphery. She turned to see a folding table in the center of the peristyle. On it sat platters of rations, fresh-grown greens, quickrice and a single bottle of unlabeled clear liquor. Around the table stood a dozen people frozen in the motions of a feast.

A young woman with intricately hennaed hands flicking flecks of eggshell into the central crack of the folding table.

A jowly older man, business suit frayed in several key junctures, smiling slightly sad as he stares at his empty tooth glass.

A woman in baggy, oil-stained sweats, wearing pseudo-librarian glasses, caught with her mouth open in an exhausted laugh.

They are all worn, but not with the hollow obsession of tech workers; they appear more like the clutches of refugees Samira remembered from the waiting rooms of NGOs, the back lawns of embassies, the detention centers outside of transit hubs. She circled their arrested forms, admiring rotted clothing, patchy and lusterless skin, with sincere, open enjoyment.

As Samira rounded the exposed edge of the table, she stooped to examine its cheap plastic, the color of gruel, eaten away at by time and use. She reached out to run her palm along its top, but pulled back before she made contact, tucking her hand underneath her armpit. She hadn't realized how cold she was, how little feeling was in her fingers. When she stood up, everyone was looking at her.

Samira did not breathe. They did, and they blinked, and their cheeks quivered with the cold. She wanted to flip her hijab up, to fully obscure her face.

She opened her mouth to apologize.

In the Black Box, warm, safe, and alone, Samira read the three DMs from Hog HQ. The first stated that internet had been restored. Thirteen minutes later: "external disruptions" were causing an "existential threat" to all Blue Barge communications. Two minutes later: DMs, too, would have to go silent, due to security issues, but communications should be restored "before the end of the residency".

Samira sat there, suspended in a low-level fury she was trying to convince herself was born of the impotence that came with all tech-service interactions. After thirteen breaths she had to admit that she was burning to gut whatever previous resident had decided to implicate her in his project. (And it was a "he",

she was sure, some New Reality asshole who assumed that anyone who encountered his so-subversive work would just *have* to
document it.) No matter the politics of the artist, she resented
the imposition. She'd come here to work on her own shit, not
to handmaiden someone else's. This was a serious fucking breach
of professionalism, and she needed to contact the curators, *now*.
And she couldn't.

She pulled up BargeView, found the correct search overlay,
then set the system loose for 2.3 seconds. No Artificial Reality
generators found. She tried to push her feet off the desk, but the
wing-chair just absorbed the force. She wriggled viciously, threw
an elbow. No effect.

Commercial AR tech couldn't cloak itself from the elements
which compromised BargeView, and military-level AR would be
nigh impossible to spot in an IRL search. There was, however, a
third way.

Samira's breakout piece had been an algorithm that rewrote
the then-prevalent alt-fash floating swastikas as Windows 95
icons. The swastikas were last ditch IRL warfare on the part of
the wrvlves, a hard core of alt-fashers who'd been flushed from
the state and anything like the public net, as well as temporar-
ily denied freedom of assembly, after their exalted state in the
outgoing administration. Their "floating symbols of hate", which
also included *1488* and the "Jewman" emoji, were meant as a
weaponization of the progressive conception of language as violence. Physical symptoms of nausea and exhaustion were the
desired effect, along with depression, preferably suicidal. Former
sanctuary cities, academic safe spaces, and personal homes (of
Jews, anti-fascists, and PoC) were the primary targets.

Samira's "hack" had been immediately thunkpieced and
socialed, which meant near immediate doxing by the right
and dogpiling by the left, the former for "limiting freedom of
speech", the latter for "corporatist tactics". Several older cultural

theorists, still in the process of reemerging from the firmament, took this discourse as a robust sign of "a return to normalcy". Observing Streisand, Samira gave no response, then, after the next newscrush, deleted her accounts. The alt-fashers concocted various workarounds for whatever walled gardens she erected. She adhered too close to their rape fantasies to be forgotten.

Despite this, she'd felt moderately safe in Berlin. If any city had made beating the shit out of fascists a reputable pastime over the previous forty years, it was this one. Her nascent project involved videoing the flakturms, the WWII last-redoubt concrete bunkers that towered above the parks designed to defamiliarize them. Samira studied, and began to mimic, the footage taken from the 1923 Tut Tomb reveal and its ilk; a certain reverse Occidentalist romanticism was certainly implied.

As Samira crouched in some fronds on the corner of the G-Tower of Flakturm II in Friedrichshain, a tall, naked woman with the head of an owl strode over and stopped about a foot away. The owl-head twisted, the neck bent down, and droplet dead eyes examined the human as if it were a grub. Samira pissed herself slightly. The specifics of the female anatomy, that of a non-surgically altered porn star, were far more high-resolution than the surroundings; the raven head was patchy as a mottled teddy. The disparity kept Samira from having a full-on psychotic break. As she attempted to formulate some kind of response, the owl-woman's long, thin fingers opened the folds of her swollen labia. As her ass and stomach began to quiver with excitement, the non-god leant her head back and began to emit rough squawks of pleasure.

Samira stopped shaking, her scream shriveling in her throat. This was all way too fucking pornographic to be anything other than a troll AR-spoof. Some little alt-fash prodigy fuckchump, too much dick in his brain not to overplay his hand.

She scurried around the side of the flakturm, then dashed through the park, unaware of dozens of mildly censorious German stares. Home, she'd downloaded the open-source schematics for an AR disruptor.

These she still had on her handheld.

Six years ago, with a sizable chunk of a grant left over and the well-stocked tech shops of Berlin at her disposal, Samira had managed to fashion an AR disruptor about the size of a memory stick with a range of 28.3 feet. Now, with far less time and material, Samira welded together a nine-pound IED-looking thing with a range of about 6.5 feet. It was also only good for one shot; the probability of it frying itself out of existence was fairly high.

When she was on deck, lost in the gunmetal horizon, Samira imagined she could feel the krane there, hovering at the periphery of her vision.

commuters' background was almost assembled. Samira was watching the waves lap lazy, letting it breathe. Hard rain had fallen on the shell of the former cafeteria all night, frightening the gulls into new heights of screaming and shitting. Now, staring at the blank dayfall, she became convinced, as she always did, that she should destroy the project and start again with an entirely new practice. It was not that she had the incorrect color, there was no such thing as *correct*, but the early morning light showed her that she had not seen clearly, yet it also showed her that she was, with great effort, capable of achieving her ends, only the effort this time had not been great enough.

Samira lit the small joint she'd been saving for this moment. She'd hoped it would calm her. All it made her do was crave tobacco. Her eyes auto-focused on several somethings on the horizon. They looked like dead aphids on a windowsill, but then they grew larger. Skiffs.

She took a step backward. There was someone next to her. A short man with shaved head and deep blue circles under his eyes. He wore swimming trunks and a tattered green T-shirt with a cartoon caricature of a pig spitting itself. His face was turned toward the boats, was not set in grimness, but strained with the restraint of sudden, florid emotion.

Samira had left the disruptor under the peristyle, covered by a tarp, assuming that the AR was bound to a single specific site. She was grateful that she didn't have the opportunity to annihilate this man. He might look like an undersized soccer hooligan, but he was real. She had to touch his face. As her hand came up to his collarbone, her finger stretching out, the man turned to her, fixing his recessed eyes on hers.

"They're going to kill us all," he said.

Malignant AI-vengeance. Boutique Hog psychotic hallucinogen aerosolized by krane. Trace leavings of post-Uncanny Valley DoD AR. Samira had Erik's pea coat over her head, under a former cafeteria table, the disruptor in her lap. None of these theories made sense. But the man, and the boats, made no sense either.

Unless she was truly insane.

Or they were ghosts.

Which was another way of saying the same thing.

She slept for fourteen hours on the floor of the cafeteria, spooning the disruptor.

When she woke, she worked for twenty-six minutes and found that she was done.

The jenga pieces were evenly distributed throughout the command tower. She approached it slowly, the disruptor bumping off-rhythm on her hip. Close now, she could no longer see the thing's wholeness, only constituent pieces. The asymmetrical grace did not hold up to close examination. The structure looked as bare and abandoned as everything else onboard. She closed her eyes.

"The first duty of every revolutionary is immutability," Samira recited and opened her eyes.

The krane was swimming in place maybe ten feet above the tower. It was a snubnose, the color of the weather, no weaponry visible in its undercarriage.

It existed. There was nothing false in her mind or method. It had taken down communications, perhaps the content of her snipcasts had triggered an auto-defense response, which included either gassing her with visions, or projecting them around her.

Another krane joined it. And another. And another and another and another, until there were a dozen, assuming an offensive pattern, above the center of the vessel.

Samira began to crouch down, then saw, surrounding her, the specters. The eggshell woman was wrapped in a shock blanket. The soccer hooligan, only in long underwear, held a cricket bat. The non-librarian, a pocket pistol.

They were not looking at the sky.

Boarding Blue Barge were a dozen men. They came on not with the passionate intensity of pirates, nor with the studied calm of professionals, but with the swagger and smiles of joy-killers. Their outfits were mismatched, commercial Kevlar and denim jackets and puke cameo, and they held an assortment of ugly automatic weapons, none of which Samira could name. Several had the frog bauble of the alt-fash pinned to their chests. They fanned out sloppy, forming a crooked quarter ellipse, before assuming position. A few spat, but otherwise, the only sound Samira could hear was the breathing of the commuters around her.

The men raised their weapons.

Samira hit the disruptor button.

Nothing even shimmered.

The men began firing.

Samira looked up at the kranes. They had not moved. They were only recording.

The hatch to the Black Box shushed behind her. The screens were all empty. She passed her palms over them, growing more frantic, then collapsed into the wing-chair. There was no internet. There was no DM. There was no BargeView. She could hear nothing. She could only see the outline of her own form in the paltry emergency light cast and multiplied in the screens.

Samira stood she knew not where looking at the background. The color of the sky had become one with the color she had created; it was the surface of the ground in a country burned down to soot. She grasped for the railing, expecting to feel metal in the warmth of her hands. Nothing. It was her and the background. She pressed her body against it, and its coldness became her coldness. She tried to make herself comfortable, and then she could not move.

And the kranes went forth, chanting their lays.

THE 4 PARANOID-RATIONALIST HORROR STORIES ABOUT ARTIFICIAL INTELLIGENCE YOU HAVE TO READ

The less-than-modest successes in AI neural networking theory (DeepMind, various cat-recognition technologies, Calico333) early in the new millennium have given rise to an insurgent paranoid-rationalist brand of horror fiction. Neural network theory, or connectionism, mimics the contemporary visualization of the human brain as a non-hierarchal, parallel-processing structure in a self-organizing & -aggregating approach to semi-supervised machine learning. The theory's mid-20th century's origin point did not provide technology to match theory, and AI-godfather Marvin Minsky's *Perceptrons* (1969), explore-critiquing the titular binary classifier, helped reprioritize research. (The death of the perceptron's creator, Frank Rosenblatt, two years later in a boating accident gives us our first huff of paranoia's pungently addictive odor.) Attendant glacial progress initiated a funding-decrease feedback loop that resulted in the First AI Winter.

With massive late-20th century strides in brain mapping, the incessant churn of Moore's Law, and Silicon Valley oracles' indication that future business models would depend on algorithmic processing and manipulation of the online overdeveloped world's data, neural networking has not only come back into vogue, but has been accepted as an obvious Grand Theory, to the point where Elon Musk et al.'s OpenAI's business plan mimics the theory's structure. (Business theory as AI theory as brain theory, what could possibly go wrong.) This despite the fact that the human brain cannot function IRL without hierarchical decision making (i.e. prioritizing piloting a car at 72mph over cat-face scanning on the phone).

Several dozen pithy maxims coined by field luminaries express roughly the same statement: once an AI has achieved a previously unthinkable benchmark (beating the world's highest-ranked living Go player, setting down a Muskrocket on Deimos), said task is dismissed as no longer requiring "true intelligence". AI theory is littered with such self-delegitimizing dichotomies (please see: Purpose-Specific AI vs. General-Purpose AI, Hard AI vs. Soft AI, The Hard Problem of Consciousness vs. Supposed Soft Problems, ad shitum.) All this obfuscates whether or not we currently live with AI, and, if so, for how long.

Nonetheless, paranoid-rationalists, while surely cognizant of Zeno's Arrow, brace for emergence. The self-described rationalist blog *LessWrong*, partially run by Elizer Yardowksy, an AI researcher and vital figure in early Neo-Reactionary swarm-circles, served as spawning pool for such hideous ideas as Roko's Basilik and the Great Filter. Nick Bostrom, a Swedish philosopher based out of Oxford until its dissolution, expanded upon these ideas in the bestselling kinda-mainstream tome *Superintelligence*, which explored a multitude of AI-originating human extinction events.

Its recommendation to a bleary public by many of the same SV billionaire-celebs who were funding AI research in the first place still astounds.

These thought-experiments affected the disaster-imagination and mouthfeel of incoming horror writers: extremist, rational-ist-to-reactionary, and chill as flesh on the face of Phobos. The question of whether or not said fiction is, indeed, horror and not something new entirely (it's certainly not of the *Weird*), is a question perhaps best left for another habitation soon to be erected on the Thinkpiece Archipelago we have been consigned to evermore.

1. BOXOCTOSIS BY MWX
(AUGUST 3RD, 2018 FROM HEADLESS FROGGY PRESS)

MWx's penultimate collection reiterates their central obsession as forcefully as their first three, though it does not exactly deepen it. Each story remains a derivation on this formula: an emergent AI trapped in a box for safety precautions "takes over" a human interlocutor using only text. Every addition offers, at some point, a kind of dreamy, highly specific imagery some might call im-agistic, if perhaps not entirely sensical. A morning is described as a "slow, wet, gasping pulse"; a sky "heals like a scab, though nothing has split it, and it has never bled an ounce of fluid". The prose, otherwise, can rush from controlled, quotidian restraint to complete bug-out aesthetic nightmare in the space of a single line. While wildly dissimilar authorial voices and narrative struc-tures are adopted story for story, the outcome is always the same: flesh always fails, and the "Take Over" (also the title of MWx's first collection, post-break) is always successful, but what lies over the narrative horizon is always left unexplored.

While some critics have discussed, inevitably, how these sto-ries feel like drafts of a prologue to some larger, "epic" novel, which they hope MWx will focus their "prodigious qualities of description and invention" on one day, they have, of course, missed the point. That the author experienced, in the Spring of 2013, some kind of "break", no matter how badly documented, is, at this point, incontestable. Then the author of a collection of stories, a slim volume of poetry, and two novels, all from scattered Mid-Western nonprofit presses, MWx was not overly well-known, "hopscotching between literary styles with a twinge of pained awkwardness, or awkward pain, in the authorial voice, as if they could settle nowhere, as if nowhere was made for them", to quote from my own review of 2011's *Frozen Seas*. MWx's aversion to media in all forms, surfacing early in a refusal to disclose their gender or employment history, the two favorite biographical tidbits of any literary PR machine, means that we have little information about said "break" besides the transcript of the 911 call obtained, and verified, by attempted doxxers and the subsequent ER bill, obtained through false premises. It feels slightly filthy to even relay this information, but the words "psychotic attack" were used, although it is difficult to tell, exactly, what this means. (The emergency hotline transcript only records "inarticulate screaming".)

The not-insignificant bastion of those who believe that MWx's break was induced by contact with an emergent system have little evidence to support their claims beyond the supposed fact that the technical detail and "daily rigors" of a programmer's life in their three post-break volumes are extremely specific and accurate. The dominant interpretation, outside of Reddit, is that the "Take Over" is not based on an event, real or imagined, experienced by the author, but rather serves as a deliberate metaphor for MWx's break.

Limiting MWx to either having experienced such an event or created it as metaphor, however, seems distinctly small-minded. Might not the constant repetition of the event be seen as a warning, or a prayer? Or, perhaps if we dismiss with propheteering or groveling at the feet of, ahem, Gnon, might it be possible that the author considers the composition of new text detailing the event as a method, however small, of aiding its eventual instantiation in our reality?

(A final untitled collection of machine-generated text over mainly white space still stymies.)

2. THE SINGULAR MACHINE OF LOVING GRACE BY DEBORAH CHAN (JUNE 20TH, 2020 FROM SIMON AND SCHUSTER)

Three months after Marcus Klizenberg becomes the 47th President in a landslide, the first ever "indie executive" with no party or platform besides "technocratic reconstruction" reveals that his early 21st century disruptive social media company has created artificial life in the form of a Philosopher-King named Simonides. Described by a fawning NYT Mag long-form piece as "vain, earthy, and vastly intelligent" and "lacking ideology or identity", the AI ("hard, thank you very much") self-achieved via neural networking/connectionist practice in said social media giant's vast warrens of user-generated data, shepherded by the renowned English-Estonian data scientist and famed former CA Ideology wildman Edgwin Dworkcas. Simonides does not believe in democracy, but then, by this point, neither do the majority of Americans.

After three and a half years of what was never at any point called a civil war by anybody other than UN observers and the global press, most US citizens no longer believe the Union (still more or less intact, minus 1.7 million people) can be self-governed. The feedback loops of revenge killing initiated by a series of supposedly lone-wolf mass shootings at non-violent protests in the early days of the Pence administration have proved that the body politic is simply too fucking psychotic to police itself. "Democracy works in all societies except human ones," Simonides is quoted as saying, but at no point does anyone address the fact that only one AI managed to self-spawn. Simonides, while not having any static, much less corporeal, form (Klizenberg: "Si likes to manifest holographically as Julian Assange just to get the chuckles going"), or perhaps for their very lack of such, proves a popular alternative to human, or at least American, rule.

This is all backstory. As Chan's third novel begins, Klizenberg has just stepped aside as candidate for the 2025 elections, allowing Si to assume his position as head of the just-created New Center party. A variety of non-traditional media disruptions are initiated for Si, including a VR walk-through of their future White House, while Klizenberg dog-whistles that Simonides is "the real brains" behind his highly-approved administration. The opposition is barely-existent, and widely derided as "meatfuckers". On election eve, with the fix firmly in, our protag, Licce Krotkin, an ambitious apolitical muckraker, gets a tip that Si is not what they seem, kicking off an extremely creaky narrative machine. Chan, whose prior novels (important early texts of Constrained Horror) have perfectly balanced sentence-to-sentence, para-to-para rhythms, here abandons her measured onslaught for an approach one must call workmanlike, belying an IRL urgency further reflected in trope-as-fuck characters and extremely generic settings. (Though, bizarrely, this new method of composition results in dialogue far more robust and chewy than in previous Chan efforts). As Krotkin investigates Klizenberg's ideological education in late '90s Berkeley (postmodern relativism gave us Authoritarianism American-style!), Dworkcas's ties to post-Soviet businessmen-gangster-politicians (the dissolution of the USA mirrors that of the USSR!), and struggles with her own new-found anti-democratic, anti-humanist impulses, the requisite number of things get exploded and anally/orally penetrated.

There's a political cynicism on display here that would be astounding if it weren't exactly what everyone seems to be mainlining post-election (4 More Years!); it's just strange (or symptomatic) that it would appear so unvarnished in a mass-market thriller while all our "literary novels" are hygging out and making with impressive descriptions of woodgrains, bullfinch wings, and orgasms. That Chan's thriller didn't perform well at first and has only gathered steam through word of mouth (a second printing was barely okayed by S&S, apparently) says quite a lot, especially now that Twitter has been declared "unfree speech" and abolished.

The ending would be obvious to anyone who's read Poe. Si isn't/wasn't/won't ever be an AI; Dworkcas did not manage to nudge connectionism to completion. A Deep Throat-like figure (calling herself James Deen I shit you not) gives Krotkin the info to prize the lid off and the box is full of… humans. Just a passel of well-meaning technocrats, Klizenberg's previous administration. Krotkin decides with very little prevaricating that Peace in Our Time is worth it and kills the story, hoping to take it to her grave, which she does about three days later.

3. 7 + U BY ALLEGRA VENTURA (OCTOBER 2ND, 2020, KINDLE SINGLETON)

You are playing tic-tac-toe for your life against an emergent AI. It is still in the box, but you are, somehow, in there with it. You, being relatively intelligent and read-up on strategy, rigorously adhere to game theory and play tit-for-tat. As the game advances, however, you become convinced that the AI (whose name is "something like Alton"), which mirrors you tit-for-tat, is also playing *you*, having submerged itself in a pool of data comprised of every game you've ever played on a connected device. All you have to do is play as Not You and win. (A very short story.)

4. TYPE SLOWLY BY NOOR GALE SLOATMAN (JULY 2023, PENGUINRANDOMCOLLINS)

The prose-effort spent establishing mouthfeel in the first seventy or so pages of Sloatman's second novel suggests that we are in for a slow, bright, university-life kitchensink. The autumnal smear of desaturated chartreuse lining faux cobblestone streets; the minute observations of the psychogeographic changes in campus as a glass hall (named after SV billionaire neo-Quisling alumnus) replaces an ancient, warrened sepulchered ex-church; the bandy legs and impressive trunk of an aging, bewildered Russian refugee-prof. We pass time slowly with Maxim Cherry and his husband Digweed Kobp, and their friends, associates, and sorta-enemies, as they traverse their day-to-day in the soft, somewhereinNewEngland university townlet, Howell's Hollow. This is the apex of the Constrained Horror movement, where observation of minute quotidian rituals belies long lightly simmering dramas, many never more than feinted at. Maxim, a barely-tenured professor of computer science and one of the few adherents of the neo-Minsky top-down hierarchical structure of machine learning, is facing his onrushing obsolescence in the face of successive neural-networking strength-to-strengths. There are very many staff-meetings. Digweed owns the town's only bookstore (as the hulk of the former bank, now a former Barnes and Noble, rots slowly on Strait Street, with HH's small contingent of squatters, anarchists, and Sovereign Citizens contesting the space.) Still, Digweed is concerned with the rise of Mescantok University Bookstore (just taken over by a formerly adrift alumnus, disappointed with the outside world's faux-meritocracy) and, of course, "People reading books on their *screens*." This leads Digweed to installing a cafe, which means dealing with plumbing, hiring 19 year olds, constant harassment from a weaponized health department, and an awakened landlord. The submerged narrative slowly gathers context if not force, delivered in an authorial voice that, smoothly sliding between POVs and limited-omnipotence, seems to be of a multitude.

Until Noah Weinberg moves in next door. (Treeline cul-de-sac, two story, no two alike on Joey Jack Ave.) Weinberg is a thin man of indeterminate age, with serious acne-scarred cheeks, and a very occasional, obscurely charming smile. He does not attempt to ingratiate himself with his neighbors, but Digweed immediately declares him "a handsome serial killer" and begins to investigate his property in a style that might be described as Nancy Drew post-Black Bloc training. At this point, it becomes clear, if it was not entirely before, that Digweed is allowed to take occasional other lovers, while Maxim is not. The roots of this non-compromise have been choked, of course, in the dirt of past transgressions. Maxim seems, for his part, to be less disturbed than usual by Digweed's attentions (which causes Digweed to push harder than usual); he does, however, draw on his decade and a half of contacts throughout every layer of strata of Mescantok U and HH society to find out everything he can about Weinberg. Limited detail is forthcoming: Weinberg has just rented out the former B&N, evicted the meth-heads, and begun repairs, and the business paperwork he's filed with BBB shows that he's already running a start-up incubator out of an office on campus. Further, Weinberg has begun heavily recruiting biochemistry grad students, which heavily pleases the university brass since it suggests a local business to funnel grads to.

Maxim, however, has begun to neglect his students, his research, and his husband, spending long hours standing on his sagging front porch, smoking illicit American Spirit Blues and staring at the blank windows of his neighbor's vacant house, at which point we are treated to a long (over 100 pg) flashback, which completely imposes a new authorial voice (Maxim's?, jangled, caffeinated, second-person present-tense), informing us that, yes, almost a decade ago, his lab at MIT almost had a zero-to-one breakthrough in creating an AI named, yup, Wineburg.

The reduction of the instantiation of an AI in human(oid) form IRL to a domestic drama collapses the narrative at this point, with Sloatman neither going for PKD why-is-the-light-switch-in-a-different-position-today freakout, nor turning it into a bullshit techno-thriller, nor even rewriting Frankenstein for our newly sentimental ear, but rather keeping the emphasis on the quotidian and affect. There is no rapprochement, no reunion, no epiphany, only the softly bobbing specter of death. That this is not an affirmation is emphasized by the creeping revelation, well-handled, that the entire MS has been narrated by an AI, attempting to document the last stirrings of genuine, "uninterfered with" human consciousness.

A STONE AND A CLOUD

The first time I met Clare she told me she didn't want to be human anymore. She didn't tell me verbally or via backchat, but from the way she tilted her head when I introduced myself, her lips pressing together, her eyes vacating, as if she was trying to imagine herself inside me, somewhere past the skin, the skull, and the meat. And then there is the fact that Artur introduced us.

An Open Field. You stand in it, and the background blurs. A thick sheen of rain obscures the horizon, or maybe your eyesight fails to serve the level of detail around you. Like a '70s film on an HD screen, you can see more than you're capable of being comfortable with. You sit; the grass underneath you supports you unquestioningly. Your hands hover in front of you: they want to do nothing, cracked and aching as they are. You lay back; you are supported perfectly, the mound of your lower back fitting with the slope of the land. You ever so faintly arch. Are you on an incline? It is of a such a gradual gradient that you would never notice. The sky above you is woven with soft gray clouds and their manatee offspring. They truck slowly across. There is no threat, though you know it must rain often enough; the land is too green. The field reminds you of somewhere you have never been but have read about online, someplace authentic, someplace where you can be yourself, a place free of politics and anxiety. You twitch, sleeping with your eyes open, but you don't need to dream: the clouds pass above.

"You don't look like a videogame designer."

"What does one look like?"

This conversation, she'd say later, had been repeated endlessly. The guy shrugged, his ice cubes trying to crawl out of his cocktail. He wasn't embarrassed, but he didn't have an answer. I could have answered: not so blank, not so restful.

Instead I asked her which games she'd designed. When she told me, I was surprised to find that I'd played one, and told her so. "It has decent market penetration among your population." She said it cold and slow enough that she could have been reading it off a spreadsheet. She didn't give me any body language.

Not knowing what else to say, I introduced myself. The guy with the ice cubes looked at me indolent and aggressive as a medium sized cat, and she said to me, "Artur was telling me I should talk to you."

"About what?"

She didn't respond immediately; she was still looking at my face. The guy with the ice cubes began saying something, so I nodded once, raised my glass of cheap white wine and walked away. I drifted to the edge of the roof; the scrum of people got thicker. They surrounded the bar, though nobody was getting drinks, just admiring the dark wood, the brass scalloping, rough and warped; it had just been salvaged from the captain's stateroom on a recently decommissioned destroyer and bolted into the roof. Someone in engineering tried to explain the process to me but eventually gave up, lacking reassurance. I wondered if any of Artur's people self-styled as a woodsmith; Artur certainly didn't. They were probably going to hire some artisanal Brooklyn guy with a superior website and beard to come in and spend several weeks imaginatively restoring it.

I walked to the opposite side of the roof. There was no one there, just the skyline. I could be impressed by it, if I let myself. I turned and looked back to where Clare was standing, next to a kind of plant I'd never seen before. Artur was there, wide and short and game in his perversion of business casual. They both looked at me. He grinned and waved me over. I mimed a grin, drained my glass and left the party.

She stood almost six foot. Her hair was short cut, yellow as a digital rendering of straw. Her avi was a collapse of autumnal humus, undergrowth that looked like it had been churned in some herbivore's stomach sacs and exuded. She wore no jewelry. Her social was protected; I couldn't see anything. I didn't send a follower request. She'd been wearing a tortoise shell shirt, shellacked like the animal's skin. Her fingers were thin.

NYU MFA '10, she'd done a game as her thesis. *Assemblyline Worker #5697 @ Apple Plant #72, Guangdong Province!* was released just before Steam launched its OS X platform, leaving it just underexposed enough to become culty. "There was a vogue toward boring the player," she said in an interview two years later. "This was, I think, partially lifted from the Contemporary Contemplative Cinema movement, which was at high tide then. Indie gamers wanted to suffer for their play. I was happy to help them. And the Foxconn suicides were in the news. Apple backlash was kicking up. Jobs wasn't dead yet. It seemed obvious. I could do it, so I did it, and then it was just this thing, outside of me. I let it stay there."

The game garnered her some adulation, some hate, and absolutely no money. A postdoc at the New School kept her afloat for a year; she appeared to accomplish nothing there. From there she was hired on to a game company so huge and influential that even I'd heard of it, specifically for a game called Storm. It did not come to fruition and, despite appearances on multiple great unrealized project listicles, no details concerning its gameplay have ever been released.

She didn't surface again till about a year ago when she dropped *An Open Field*, apparently out of nowhere.

It seemed unlike her to be a panelist. There was a reticence in her few interviews, like she had been duped into them contractually, and none had appeared after *An Open Field*. The panel was cagily titled *Undesigned Futures: Spurts of Temporality* and was being held as part of some mammoth conference devoted to the internet that apparently happened every year. I wouldn't have known about it, but Artur sent me the link in an email otherwise empty, save for an obscene emoji and the single line, "u owe me pardner".

The panel was held on the fifth floor of a repurposed warehouse on Dutch Kills where Newtown Creek, repeatedly hot-taked as the most polluted body of water in the NE, begins its thin gurgling division of Brooklyn and Queens. There was little open that late besides a few unlicensed bacchanal clubs. Masked figures, the uncovered edges of their faces sagging with flesh, clung to brick near small steel-lined entrances, smoking furtively and casting an appreciative eye over the bodies that passed them by. Most of the other spaces were occupied by industrial shipping and storage ventures shuttered against the evening. Their lots were blocked off with wilting chain-link, trapping vehicles crouched small like decaying hounds, wet and lost. The moon was full, but it cast no light, and the only flickering down the long side-streets came from the luminescence of bars and bodegas four or five blocks away, reflected.

The front door was opened by a thin, small man with a garbage disposal beard and deeply recessed eyes. He smiled like presentation equaled pain and finger-swooshed his screen, apologizing for the door being locked. "We haven't been able to fix that yet. We don't have the expertise," he said, like he expected a response. I tried to smile back and made my way up an enormous empty stairwell. Had sides of beef been hauled up and down it? Unlikely, given the provenance. More likely: huge metal vats of industrial dye, lye, solvents, paints. I tried to imagine the place screaming with workers, but I'd never actually been in a functioning warehouse, only those repurposed for underground parties, loft apartments, or office spaces. The conference room blurred the line between all three. Its double doors were propped open by manuscripts stuffed under their jambs. A sink with CVC pipe legs held a half dozen plastic wine glasses and ceramic mugs. The hallway broke onto a space divided by a series of rough, used-up looking couches and loveseats. On the right of it were a few folding tables; on the left were about thirty orange plastic scoop-chairs arranged in vague rows pointing at a barely raised stage.

About half the seats were full. I took one on the back left, clocking Clare in my periphery as I stripped off my hoodie. She was stationed in the pseudo-grade school dining hall space, toggling back and forth between a few screens. I sat down, took out my own screen, and began to triage my inbox.

I resurfaced as Recessed Eyes performed an irony on the Occupy mic-check. Nobody echoed him or laughed. He refused to acknowledge this and asked the ether if everything was, "A go?" Somebody somewhere assented, and the panelists tramped up onto the stage, took their seats and their wireless mics. Clare'd cut her hair as short and sexless as Joan of Arc, tinting it bright red. She wore rust plaid trousers and a thin pink sweater with two swans, their beaks meeting in a chaste kiss. She sat with her legs crossed, palms jammed down against the metal chair's struts, staring intently out over and above the crowd. The moderator began to describe the "strategies" of the panel.

Post-conference everyone swarmed to a nearby Mexican place for "fish tacos and cerveza", as Recessed Eyes put it, repeatedly. Bodies jammed the huge industrial blocks. Laughter tinkled against exhausted, black air. In the scrum, I ran into a friend old enough to find me boring; Alex had always been a dog-walker but now edited a well-respected webzine as well. At the bar, she became immersed in deeply coded industry shit-talk. As I began to drift away into the static of their intent and the rhythm of their delivery, Clare appeared next to me.

"Nice to see you again," she said.

"You remember me?" I asked.

"I don't remember your *name*. You're friends with Artur."

"'Friends'."

"He's kind of a human fucking pig." There was something about her lilt that made me think Slovak, Hungarian, or some other off-brand Eastern European state, though her wiki read born and bred in CT. It was as if she'd trained herself to sound unplaceable, deeply foreign.

"Yeah, I'd say that's accurate."

"He also said that you collect people."

"I don't know what that means."

"Well, that's what he said." She took a long pull of her dark, bottled beer. "What'd you think of the panel?"

"I don't think I was able to generate a useful opinion."

"So why'd you come?"

"Because I wanted to see how you handled yourself."

The inside of her mouth, revealed in a single, sane laugh: white teeth, perfectly formed, red flesh. "How," she asked. "Did I do?"

"You had," I said, "Perfect composure."

"I didn't get to ask you last time. What did you think of *An Open Field*?"

"I thought it was the first time I'd relaxed in ten months."

"What," she said, "happened ten months ago?"

Down by the plastic shore separating the two islands, its docks, walkways, and leisure centers not quite abandoned. I remembered them when they were new and freshly branded, the smiling faces of the consumptive class peering down from broad glass facades, telling of untrammeled choice of amenities. Now it was just burnished glass, the heat pouring off it in the early spring sun, the clouds hanging between us and the buildings across the water, making everything that much more difficult to touch.

Inside weren't the settlers of any new island, or their descendants slowly dealing with the savage new lives we'd always assumed were our birthright. Instead, there was a class disappointed enough to shell out for the upgrade.

"I imagine them as swarms," Clare said, tapping on the glass as if there were kittens inside. "Despite the fact that whenever you see them represented they always look so clear and very *distinct* from one another." I tried to blink away the myriad reflections: Clare, my body, the pier, the island behind, the sky, the water. They wouldn't leave, and I still couldn't see the metal tubes, much less the bodies. "The world," she said, pulling herself back, "is emptying out."

"Just the rich," I said.

"Just the rich."

Homeless, deli workers, paranoiac old Village radicals, the ever-growing ranks of the indebted, young and still fresh of body, able to leverage meat against credit, all still haunted the city like it was their vocation, like they knew no one would come after they were gone.

"I did not know life could hold so many," Clare said, briefly glancing back to the island.

She invited me to follow her stare, but my attention had already been captured by the great screen dominating the north side of the complex of buildings, dwarfing wild-grown trees that were never from around here to begin with. On the great screen, the little personages sat, fat and snaked as retroviruses, engaging in their complexities. These fluid dynamics were always expressed in the least understandable terms, to invoke the insularity of the upgraded, to fetishize their new existence, to set it apart from our own. Artur would be cynical and cold enough to see through the screen down to where the code lived in fiberglass and wire, under the concrete husk that sat under our feet like frozen pie shell against which little waves full of dead microorganisms softly slushed.

But when Clare followed my gaze, all she saw was meat.

"Do you have it?" she asked.

I nodded. "Artur gave it to me when I came back."

"You still carry it with you?" Her voice was low like her mouth was dry. Before I could respond, she said, with faint, pigeon-like movements of her left hand, "Show it to me."

I took the small screen out of my pocket, its bare brown back. It had no signal, no apps, no options. Just a single image, faintly shimmering. A stone.

She accepted it just like any other screen, stared at it intently for a moment. Then, slowly, her fingers seized it harder, as if gripping for purchase. "It's live?" she said, looking up. "You really..." She dropped her face. "Is anyone... *there* right now?"

I shook my head. "No one wants a used object. Customers tend to design their own. It takes months. Usually from..." The unsure movements of my hands obscured segments of her face. "Very specific details that emerge suddenly. As if from contact with your own particular muse."

"That sounds like branding copy."

"It is. Artur wrote it, I think."

"You use Artur's words to describe your own experience?" She sounded exasperated, like we'd had this conversation so many fucking times.

I shrugged. "It sounds accurate."

"A vision, that's what it sounds like. You had that much money?"

"No. It was a beta-test. Everything was free."

"What was it like?"

"It was like being a stone."

"Were you instructed to respond to questioning with koans?"

"It was a suggestion from a therapist. Not one of theirs."

"So if I do it I'll say, this is like being..."

"You won't say anything at all."

"But you're here, saying it."

"Something happened."

"What?"

"They still haven't told me."

"This isn't very reassuring to me," she said, inhaling. "At all."

"I don't think there's a lot of reassurance to be given."

"Are they going to put you back?"

"I don't think so."

"And if they did?"

I concentrated on her form, trying to learn, by heart, its outline, the shoals, the reefs, the rickety planking.

"I want you to show me what you want to be," I said.

It was an old box, or rather a new box made of old bits of repurposed wood, fitted together neatly, without seams. You could take it apart by removing the joints; it took a little care not to snap the thing in half. Inside was a memory stick and a slip of notebook paper, bone-white and stiff, which read, "If this relaxes you, you're ill."

You are not the storm. You are a presence in it.

You roil along the median point between the earth and where the atmosphere ends. The ground changes beneath you, but never in relation to the cloud. At the fiercest, where you're shoved around the mass almost too quickly to get any kind of bearing, you achieve a brief glimpse of some megacity beneath you which, though ceaselessly battered by pseudo-tsunamis, lightning bolts, and weeks of torrential rain, still shines with an illumination almost angelic. Other times, as you pass meek and fluffy above, the ground beneath looks devastated, like some kind of scorched battleground, always too high for any kind of telling detail. At times it seems as if you're moving over a perfectly flat surface, a kind of endless map of preprogrammed zones, but then, shuffled toward the "front" of the cloudbank (which is always reforming and growing, shrinking, splitting off from itself), you can see, ahead, the curvature of the earth.

You can click on anything, anywhere; it takes a while for you to realize that this has absolutely no effect on anything.

The game seems as if it will never end.

"You can see," she wrote, on the back of the paper, "Why they never released it."

The one phrase I kept returning to for the duration of the time I sat in front of the screen was, "Once the new way of thinking has been established, the old problems vanish; indeed they become hard to recapture."

It was this text, bare, that I sent to her, with no notation of its origins.

She wrote back several days later: "You can't *build* clouds. And that's why the future you *dream* of never comes true." By that time, she would have already been in the wetroom.

As I'd imagined, Artur ignored the great screen.

"She wanted somewhere comfortable."

"And where was comfortable?"

"You know damn well."

Steam leaked from his mouth. It smelt faintly of burnt berries, inappropriately autumnal. "Did you finally get to fuck her?" He peered up at me, eyes narrowed to slits with cautious respect, not the usual bemused awe. "I don't think I know anybody who *actually* fucked her."

I turned to him and said, holding my voice as steady as I could, "So I can't go back?"

Then his face morphed back to the way it had always been with me: minor spite in the folds of flesh forcing all into a stifled laugh.

Like a teardrop, like an egg, the stone rests in the middle of the screen, supported by nothing but blue and the faint hint of green fields behind it. There must be some kind of sun illuminating, but its rays are assumed rather than detailed, and the end result is kind of a Platonic form of a stone: perfect and whole in itself, its representation totally matching up to its reality.

I still have the screen, but I never touch it.

THE 5 SF STORIES EVERY NEO-REACTIONARY SHOULD READ

It is widely-accepted that SF has provided an ideological bolt-hole for mid-20th-century American-style libertarianism (Heinlein, Pournelle, etc.), but the newly ascendent, if not emergent, Neo-Reactionary movement, which regards traditional conservative modes of thought as little more than bogey-man props for the all-pervading "Cathedral" (best summed up, perhaps, as the all-pervading infrastructure of the post-Enlightenment liberal project), has also inspired a swath of diverse, stimulating SF texts. Early Neo-Reactionary cheerleader Nick Land's pre-NRx theory-fiction dealt with the End of Capitalism (often by zombifying early cyberpunk), posing the question What Comes Next? What better way to explore possible answers than SF?

1. ATVATABAR RISING BY LOUIS CECIL LIGONIUS (NIGHT SHADE, 2013)

Hem Chrysler, a disgraced agent of a never-specified subsection of the Department of Homeland Security, traces his former, straight-laced lady-partner Terry Yancey to a Nevada crater containing a human-sized sucking organic wound. Immersing himself in the fleshy portal, Chrysler is sphinctered to a septic-sea kingdom thriving under the continental United States. Riven by fraternal princeling tensions and ruled over by a Platonic philosopher-king in the last act of his enlightened reign, the kingdom of Atvatabar is populated by the ideological renegadoes and persecuted geniuses of the mid to late 20th century, such as Elvis, Carl Schmitt, and Milton William Cooper. More, thousands of white middle-class American men, shoved aside because of their race, have submerged themselves in Atvatabar's cool, calm embrace; the recent American brain-drain, it seems, hasn't been going to China but underneath. Will Chrysler mange to free Yancey from the ideological traps of her social programming and thus release her from the psycho-bindings of the Atvatabarian kelp-labyrinth? Will Chrysler himself come to understand the intricacies of deception woven into his personalities by the "landlubbers" with the help of a traditional Atvatabarian seaweed-psychedelic sex-ceremony? Will the truly deserving princeling be recognized and supported to rule both the undersea kingdom and Aboveground, as the USA tilts on the eve of a scarcity-induced race war? We described Atvatabar Rising in our Summer 2012 issue "as if Ligotti had cannibalized a lost HG Wells script for an *X-Files* movie, and we mean that in the best possible way!"

2. THE CTHULHU CLUB ASCENDENT BY JIMMY ALOYSIUS COOGAN (ANGRY ROBOT, 2014)

The myriad Cthulhu plushies and other Lovecraftian tie-ins of the world spontaneously form an animated, risen Cthulhu above the University of Warwick one Imbolc. The elder god easily destroys all state and economic institutions, freeing humanity from society's shackles. Chaos of the most generic type immediately ensues; zombies are somehow involved. Luckily, the remnants of the Cthulhu Club, a sect of paraphilosophers, disgraced anthropologists, and marginalized white male techno-shamans whose prehistory was detailed in Nick Land's late eighties piece *Origins of the Cthulhu Club*, have been living off the grid for several decades, keeping in touch via 'The Dark Firmament,' a secret internet operating just beneath normal cyberspace using impossible-to-penetrate encryption. The Club now acts as an informal vanguard, pushing the ruins of former-nation states to fracture further to the point of implosion, forming new healthier mini-fiefdoms that run on abandoned cultural precepts and white hot smokin' genius. Post-agricultural baby-steps, which resemble but are not "scrounging", are detailed with great, near-pathological specificity. Appeased by the billions who expired during this unfortunate but sadly necessary transition, the elder god itself dissipates into ethereal form and plunges into the black chaos of the universe to seek new adventures.

3. THE PASSAGE OF SPIRIT BY DIARMUID WOODHAM-SMITH (GOLLANCZ, 2015)

Sibohain Terstory, a burgeoning Dublin teen, finds that she is the latest in a long line of lycanthropes whose lineage includes such notables as Cain, the Comte de St. Germain, Padraig Pearce, and the French deconstructionist Jacques Derrida. This is no *Twilight* retread though, as upon discovering her powers, on the same night as losing her virginity to a pack of marauding African immigrants, Terstory proceeds to rip to pieces not only her assaulters but also her two whimpering, sycophantic beaus. Taking a long, picaresque bus-ride through an Ireland decimated by the EU and the festering corpse of the Celtic Tiger, Sibohain gathers unto herself the remnants of her diaspora-scattered clan via social media, as well as gaining a stream of acolytes. Soon, her Bus Éireann is the head of a stream of anti-statists; she takes several lovers, including a pale, withered Welshman who teaches her about the imminent end of neo-liberalism, though she rejects his devotion to Marxism and eats his lights. Ensconced in the famed walled city of Derry, Sibohain's forces set up a Temporary Autonomous Zone centered in the Bogside. But while the enemies of the still unchristened political project close in with silver-bullet armed drones, the anarchist-democratic spirit that rules Derry slowly proves itself to be a horrid method of war-time governing, and as the last remaining cabal of lycanthropes in the world are hunted down and slaughtered in the ruins of the tower blocks, Sibohain executes her project's high-level elected officials, including several of her lovers, and institutes a dictatorial matriarchy. Asked by a foot-solider if she will give power back after the war as did Cincinnatus, Sibohain responds, "If Cincinnatus had not taken the plow back up, Rome never would have fallen." Led by her iron will, and aided by the former MMORPG strategist Eamon O'Leary who's but 11 years old, the lycanthropes route UK, US, and NWO forces out of Derry, establishing a foothold whose impact quickly spreads throughout all of Europe and soon the world.

4. AFTER THE CULLING BY ANDREW OPOL (HIPPOCAMPUS PRESS, 2017)

Backed into the ideological rathole of pessimism by the writings of Peter Wessel Zapffe and Ray Brassier, Jonathan M. has come to believe that humanity should be exterminated. Upon rational analysis, Jonathan M. realizes that a conscious effort to "destroy" humanity would be too immense to ever achieve solo; instead he seeks to eliminate what he identifies as "lynchpins", ideological support structures for the idea that life is worth living. Using his training as a USM branding-ranger, and having seen action in both Syria and New Zealand, Jonathan M. (hereafter, JM, an abbreviation one wishes Opol had adopted) launches a massive campaign of propaganda, both of the deed and the screen, including intimidation, castration, and the strafing of suburban city centers. One high point has all of Ohio being made to vomit simultaneously. Integral to this campaign, which JM calls "the Culling" (yes, always with a capital C), is the elimination of "philosofes", who Jonathan M. differentiates from "philosophers", the latter being academic, minutiae-obsessed, insular, and completely unconcerned with affecting Real Change In The World. "Philosofes" are the constructors and apologists of our consensus reality; they include a pseudo-mystic Argentinean novelist, a controversial *New York Times* op-ed "middle-ground-staker", a BBC director of documentaries revealing "the secret and occult history of the late neoliberal world", and a failed libertarian seasteader with a late-night talk show, all of whom Jonathan M. takes a great deal of pleasure personally garroting.

While disposing of the latter, JM discovers the seasteader's nubile sixteen-year-old mistress. JM cannot bring himself to kill her, despite the fact that he could do so, painlessly, 123 different ways. Instead, he takes her on the lam, where she presents to him a new kind of philosophy, distilled from the old seasteader's tepid neo-conservatism, JM's pessimism, and a dash of good ol'-American white hot smokin' genius. This philosophy calls for a new kind of dwelling, a prehistory of the corporate state written in the "the margins of death", where all are granted the right of exit, both from the boundaries of the dwelling and existence itself. This non-state would be devoted exclusively to winnowing the earth's population down to something more "sane"; citizenship is reimagined as a tiered structure based solely around how many deaths you have "enabled". The idea is less to end humanity's existence than to enact the only kind civilization worth having: one devoted to death. JM, recognizing good breeding-stock when he sees it, takes said nymphet to wife, and, using the dead seasteader's vast resources, the two launch a mobile neo-Necropolis.

While primarily a pessimistic text, *After the Culling* deserves its place on this list not only because the parameters of neo-Necropolis' structure owe a great deal to NRx thought, but also because, after Opol's suicide on the date of the book's publication cemented its status as cult object, it drew staggering numbers of readers to NRx blogs. Pessimism, while receiving a more sizable share of publicity generated, still retains its status as a minority viewpoint, perhaps because of its emphasis on the necessity of the extinction of the human race.

5. THE CONSTRUCTION OF THAT GREAT AND HIDEOUS CATHEDRAL BY JERRY IRVING (AKA DIANE BRESSEL) (DARK THOUGHT, 2018; SIMON AND SCHUSTER REPRINT 2020)

SF primarily in its framing, the novel positions itself as a doctoral thesis written in 2063 on the "unconscious erection" of what the "early 21st C radical vanguard" termed "the Cathedral" (please see above for description). A kind of anti-conspiracy novel, *Construction* doesn't posit any single, or multiple, agent of change, no Templars, no Elders of Zion, no Lizardmen From Deep Time, no

Illuminati, no Elvis, Beatles, or The Rolling Stones, but neither does it promote any variation on that stolid standby, dialectical materialism. It is also pace the meta-conspiracy novel, perhaps best personified by Eco's *Foucault's Pendulum*, in that the secret history described in the novel is actually believed by both author and (original) publisher. While the authorial voice is unchanging throughout (a kind of uber-omniscient third person), Irving/Bressel occasionally breaks in to directly address "you", clearly to the reader of "today" (the book was supposedly begun after the Implosion of Summer 2016). As such the novel can be considered a call for concrete action, joining a genre exemplified by Luther Pierce's *The Turner Diaries* and Chernyshevsky's *What Is To Be Done?*. Its aesthetics, deployed at a great and cold distance from "the human screaming" (one of the repetitive phrases used to punctuate the solidification of edifices), are far superior to either, though it has none of Chernyshevsky's humor or, thankfully, Pierce's genocidal lust. Irving/Bressel situates the Cathedral's origins as far back as the invention of agriculture; though, from the dry, humorless forward, she does not seem, pace Zerzen, to believe we should return to a hunter-gatherer society. Irving/Bressel's portrait of society being stripped of the flimsy veneer of civilization by technology, rendered with no moral or ethical handwringing, resembles Ballard, although her massive scope calls to mind Aldiss' *Helliconia Trilogy*. But then the novel (and at 1,056 pages, it could have, conceivably, been split into a trilogy), is not "an attempt to devise a new system", as Irving/Bressell puts it in the foreword, but to explicate, and challenge, an existing one. The success of *Construction*, as well as Bressel's emergence as one of the few women, and minorities, with any authority in the NRx movement, has bolstered her campaign for governorship of Florida, which, as of this writing, remains a highly contested race.

THE GLASSBLOWER

Hanging in the air of the small club is a special kind of exhaustion. Post-synth drainage and slow throb the color of headaches. The patient mold of the interior of an orgasm on the screen behind the stage. Two white-suited henchmen disassemble the two hundred odd pounds of equipment, exchanging quiet, sick little stories. A squat and beautiful young woman with deliberate scarification decorating her shoulders picks crushed plastic cups and discarded drug delivery systems off the floor. Edward sits on the small, high stool propping open the emergency exit, smoking Silk Cut. A heavy, though not fat, man, he has shed his own straitjacket and now wears a gray hunter's flannel above leather pants. His beard is russet and dirty snow, but he does not sit like a mage, more like a Catholic schoolboy, tilted to one side as if to avoid notice and suggest other perpetrators. He exhales a plume of gray, which then leaks out the door where hot scummy rain pounds the twist of a convoluted alleyway. The resultant battering on concrete is almost a nothing sound. It is distinct, but it is as if you are always hearing it and have only just caught on.

"Where do you live?"

"Me?" I adjust the glowing iPhone on my right thigh, the digital read of the recording time running what seems impossibly fast.

"You."

His voice isn't the soft, unstrained tone it is on the more lunar tracks, nor does it approach his dead bandmate's abrasive, churning yowl, once over-described very well in the NME as the final screams of a fetus about to be eaten by its twin. It is moderate, a cast-off discursive tone, both flowing and clipped simultaneously. I don't know enough about England to place it, if its origin is in fact geographic.

"I live a bunch of places."

Edward tightens his posture, legs crossed, knees snug together. Back straight, barely inches away from touching that metal door. He watches as I light my own cigarette, eyes following each of my movements. I find myself secreting from some kind of self-conscious gland.

"Berlin. Sometimes. I lived in New York for longer than anywhere else. My parents live in Roanoke. Thought you'd like that," I say, even though he's given no sign he recognizes the name. "CROATOAN and all that. It's a one-story beach house. They have most of my library, but it's wilting. Salt air." I drink some of the Powers he prefers. His is still untouched. "I have an ex in Austin."

"But you never lived there."

"No, not really."

"We lived," he inclines his chin out the door into the alley, as if Silence was out there, spectral and soaked, leaking fetid ectoplasm from his wounds, "in the same place for nearly nineteen years. A few miles West of here, actually." He accentuates the directionality with the inverse of a hiss, taps ash onto the floor with absent deliberation. "But you knew that."

"Yes."

"You work with Hélène?"

"Sometimes."

"I like her."

"She speaks of you highly. We got extremely drunk once, and she said how much she enjoyed visiting your... chalet."

His laughter is an immediate, reserved thing, not trailing off but ending with extreme deliberation. "Is that the word she used?"

"Yes, not without some irony."

"She wanted to talk about sex, so we talked about sex, though I don't think she got quite what she wanted. But you don't want to talk about sex."

"No. I don't think so at least."

"You don't want to talk about music either. You want to talk about James."

"Never made a secret of it. It was in the email."

"I never read the email."

"It was in the subject line of the email."

He smiles once, the muscle contraction and relaxation forming feral movements. He is still heavily avuncular, without the attendant smarm.

"You don't want to talk about it. Fine. Let's talk about The Quartered Man's commitment to spontaneity."

"There was no commitment to anything." And then, before I could figure out exactly what the fuck to say to *that*: "At times, we could have been spontaneous."

"'Could have been?'"

"We were capable of it."

"Your choice of recording spaces seemed to have been fluid."

"Choice?" Someone else's laugh runs wild in the alley. "I cannot remember, dear boy, the number of places we recorded. I believe I slept, shat, ate, and fucked in all of them though. If that helps you." His cigarette has not gone out yet. I find this difficult to believe. Perhaps I simply did not notice him light a new one. Shafts of remembered cinema history: cigarettes, despite their prevalence, were always a bitch for editors to keep track of. Whether they were lit, how far they had burned down. It makes me light another of my own, for continuity.

"Do you know much about the Vietnamese culture?"

"I read a bit, knowing I'd be talking to you."

"*Co bac?*"

I shake my head, sip my whiskey. His is almost gone. Another continuity problem.

"It's not a test. *Ong bac* are the spirits of the ancestor. *Co bac* are the spirits of strangers. But neither is given preferential treatment. They are obvious, in a way nothing is obvious to the Occidental mind, which needs *proof.*" He says the word as if shitting with his mouth. "They are equal. Even if the particular *co bac* was, in life, an aggressor. Such as an American serviceman. Each is acknowledged and granted a social existence." His spent cigarette arcs into the alley; it is struck down by droplets. "That is why I am going to Vietnam." Soft, dignified smile. "They will know how to look after my spirit."

So, I manage not to say, *it's not just the boys then*. Instead: "You mean the English are incapable of tending to it?"

He stares at me, the smile unchanged. No teeth. "I would never want to obligate them."

"But you'd obligate the Vietnamese?"

His laugh is like a muffled tsk. It would be silly to call it girl-ish. "It isn't considered an obligation. It isn't," he fumbles here, his mouth working, and I see how old is the man inside the fleshy body of a fifty-nine year old, rugger-like behemoth. "Selfless. The Vietnamese understand that movement of persons across great spans is necessary. Their diasporas taught them that, at least. They understand that many of their own kin are now dead, tombed in strange land. Another's *co bac*. Reciprocity is assumed."

"But shouldn't be."

His eyes can go sharp to watery and occluded in seconds; all I can think of is his famous series of alcoholic psychotic episodes, stretched over almost two decades. "Tell me, how do you treat your *co bac*?"

"I wasn't aware—"

"Not," he says, with a fluid chop of his left paw, "your physical *co bac*. But the psychological variety. The kind you accrue, in your work."

We pause, to let the girl hump a series of grossly distended garbage bags into the alley. She mutters Czech in the rain, smells of old sweat and cheap perfume.

"The victims," he says.

"Is this your way—"

"Demetrius."

"Of saying—"

"Demetrius." He inhales my name, a dry heave. Then pauses as he attempts to exhale. "You are a delightful boy."

"And you're a perfect gentleman."

He taps more ash. It wriggles on the floor briefly. "Demetrius." He savors the word like a particular pungent shit; I doubt I've ever felt so disconnected from it. I'm suddenly fighting off very real images of the man squatting.

"Is this your way," I say, keeping my voice carefully modulated, "of saying you won't talk to me?"

"I'd be delighted to speak with you about music."

"But not about James?"

His smile reopens like a wound. "No, I'm afraid not."

I sink the rest of the whiskey and stand. "Well, thank you for your time." Turn off the iPhone, slip it into my pocket.

There, sat on the small square metal chair, he draws an insular power just from his position. He stares up, eyes on me, but lost somewhere, also. "I wouldn't want to preach to you, dear boy."

"I wouldn't want you to either." I toss my cig out the side door but leave through the other one.

Nestled between passive-aggressive communiqués from various editors, Google Calendar reminders of bills to pay, and a bright, drunken, punctuationless email from my mother, is the G-Chat invitation from Terstory. Her chat box lacks a profile pic, having instead the ubiquitous platform-provided silhouette of gray-blue head and shoulders. It's set, perpetually, on red/busy. I click the invite and wait.

I'm in a small, tight room. Worn, squeaking mattress on cracked wooden frame, covered with layers of mismatched, faded multicolor quilts. The walls are a drab blue-brown, decorated with local amateur cliff scenes and decayed B&W pics of corgis. The thin, fit man just past middle age who fronts the ticket-counter-looking front desk is brusque and efficient enough, though he looks as if he's been trying to forget for some time that there are other places. I take a pull of the local off-brand cream ale and strain the heavy muck through my teeth.

She's not online, she's having a social anxiety moment, or she's doing something minor and devious. Or all three. I bring up the draft:

The Quartered Man has no early years. Nobody was paying attention, and its two authors were militantly unreliable narrators. Even now their various constellation of Wikipedia pages are un-cited, unsourced, and policed by self-anointed court-historians engaged in constant internecine warfare. Photographs of members are dated helpfully as "in Thailand, either in the 1980s or 1990s".

Start with this then:

YouTube footage of Flail's 'Sucked Off', Salford, March 1977. Most of the group has its back to the audience as they manipulate machines. A still-unknown woman sits on a metal chair, playing a violin the wrong way on her lap, as if it were a child. The music is what we would call industrial; it wasn't called anything back then, except probably "fucked up". Its throb has been devalued since by every pop doom-fetishizer, but it has not been, quite, deweaponized.

Edward Neolithic is not the small androgynous figure on its knees, tearing at its urban-cameo shirt, howl-intoning the repeated lyric "Take me in / On your knees / On your knees" then clutching a scarecrow man from the audience and sucking his lips, before skittering around on the ground like an animal confused about whether it is meant to be dying or rutting.

Edward Neolithic is the tall, thin man with the goatee and stubblehead, dipping in and out of the shadows, sheened with sweat and salvia, manipulating a multi-use machine, big, black and lightless. The thing was called a B-Boy, and it was a welded together compendium of tape-machines, sampler and noise generators.

He'd made it himself.

From certain camera angles (long, slow pan lifted from Tarkovsky, a hatred of close-up, an obsession with non-human minutiae in detail), the footage can be identified as the product of one John Silence. A London based videographer who'd become involved with Flail that winter, Silence (his real name) remained firmly on the peripheries of Flail, often securing and/or providing funding; he never "officially" shot anything for the group. His presence was the opening movement in a decade-long multi-faceted collaboration with Neolithic: artistic, domestic, sexual, corporate, inexplicitly romantic, which would only truly begin after Flail ceased to exist in 1982. Following a permutation of video-performance projects, including *The Committee of Unpracticable Effects* and *Caesarean*, John Silence and Edward Crisp (having dropped the moniker) chose to call themselves The Quartered Man in 1985, almost a year before they released their first EP.

They'd met James Thorne before this. Like any social climber from a 19th century novel, Thorne had a little income from an aunt, and was supposedly attracted to Flail's mortification of the mental flesh, its lack of "professionalism", and its emphasis on subjugation. Drugs and fucking made him depart sooner rather than later; he did not like the bacchanalia. London is not a city you can "drift away" from; he fled, without altering anyone. This seems to be one of the few things to make anything more than a vague impression on his compatriots.

It is unknown if Crisp and Silence kept up with Thorne during the next nine years, or if they renewed their acquaintanceship in '91, when they moved to a ramshackle, ex-manor house outside of Nailsea and began to compose "music that would leak from the land, emanating from a collective memory few can access any more". The Quartered Man, as project, seems divisively separate from "Edward and Jonathan": two utterly pedestrian, obvious and middle-class names for two harmless middle-age queers, which is what they looked like in the mid-90s, even if it was not what they were even remotely. I picture them taking in young James (when he is with them, he is James, not Thorne, nor The Glassblower): though he wasn't young, I perpetually frame him as a naif. Perhaps it's because the adjective most used to describe him is "uncomplicated". Bowie's "Kooks" plays in the background as the two prance through some serenely bucolic, excessively ordered English public park, finding poor, distraught lost-boy James, and take him home to pamper and occasionally suck off. This undoubtedly did not happen, unless it did, of course.

Thorne had moved south two years before them and resumed his stalled apprenticeship at Maughan's glassworks. Glass was never a traditional Chew Valley product (strangely it *was*, in Nailsea). A glassblower in the Chew Valley was a strangely quixotic career; to return to it as apprentice after years in the city seems unthinkable from this remove, but apparently the return caused little comment. Thorne slipped into Chew Valley as easily as he slipped out of London.

Resettled, Edward and Jonathan inaugurated a period of heroic output, which was to only end in Jonathan's death in 2010. An LP a year, often two, with a scattering of EPs; almost all the records went out of print within a single season. To further obfuscate matters, QM began to refuse to play live shows. James became a fixture in the QM manor-house. He'd discovered, or just decided to reveal, an ethereal, near-castrato pitch, which was deployed sparingly and to great effect on QM's *Ranters and Mummers* ('93). Thorne taught himself bass (very badly, in the Great English Punk Tradition of non-musician bass players) and his clodding, make-shift, deeply upsetting solos would become a recurring distraction from '94 to '01. And then there was his speaking voice, small and precise, like a child trying to memorize a Bible passage, with an accent so disconnected from the local drawl that it seems to come from some other, undiscovered English borough. It was only used once, in the inaccurate recitation of ten lines of the exiled John Dee's letter to his wife that opens *Accidia* ('99). Almost thirty other non-musicians and collaborators haunt QM's prodigious and almost impossible to collate output, but none as constant as a backdrop, or as strangely grounding, as "James".

Interruption. Fierce, low pinging. Insistent. Terstory appears in a small box, and I enlarge, passing my fingers over the brown-skimmed beaten keys of the seven-year-old laptop, my left wrist gaining a slight, barely noticeable electric shock.

"Hi." Long-tapered face, under-exposed skin, dull red hair collapsing down her neck, a snub-nosed attempt at a smile. "Where are you?" Behind her is a run of brilliant, soft-pink fluorescent bulbs against a white background. Empty and warm and clean. She must be at work.

"Chew Stum."

"How was London?"

"Useless."

"You talked to Clara Cleeve?"

"I talked to Clara Cleeve."

"And she knew nothing?"

"Oui."

Terstory tosses her hair back with an extremely pre-planned movement. An actor's trick; it's called business. The comparatively wild motion freezes the screen around her, and she's caught in a flattering pose, her eyes gone in the red tangle, the angles of her face showing her nothing like herself. Almost sexual. "And Edward was also, like you say, *useless*, yes?"

"Yeah. He likes you."

A Gallic shrug, with lip pout. As if to say, *of course he would.* "But he talked to you."

"Yeah, not that I have as much as a fucking sentence about Thorne. Nobody knows shit about this guy. The old duffers down the pub, the barmen, the lady of the Old Vic, his neighbor who found him stroked out in the garden. The grand-niece of the old fucker, Maughan, who left him the business. Nobody knows *shit.*"

"And I am supposed to be... your therapist?"

You don't think, when you're only seeing an abstract freeze of someone's motion that they can see you. When of course they can: I mime a smile. "No. You're supposed to be my editor."

Her face becomes slowly unstuck from the environment; she remains unblinking. She is never so unnerving flesh to flesh. Some would write this off to the medium disrupting her personality, but I know her well enough to know the medium is just revealing it. "Make it about the victims."

"No."

"Pourquoi?"

"Because we all know victims. They bore us."

She laughs once, a harsh bark. I notice for the first time a light red welt or bruise or gnaw adjacent to the left major throat tendon. Then her face coming back down:"That is a value judgement."

"So the fuck what."

"You're going to his studio tomorrow?"

"Yeah, if I can break in."

"C'est bon. Make it about that."

"I don't think that makes any sense..."

"File tomorrow or the next day."

"Fuck that, I don't have a killer, I don't have—"

"Tomorrow or the next day. This article was a chance, and it was the last one." Her oversized palm hovers over her keyboard.

"Wait—"

She doesn't.

I close the mouth of the computer. The battery is cranking, overhot on my testicles; the right one has begun to ache. I push the laptop off onto the bed. Stand up and walk to the window. Cross-barred, the width of my chest, it looks out onto a lacuna of a landscape: a run of concrete on the edge of town, what I suppose to be an industrial road. Teens traipse by, hooting and drinking from long, bulbous, green plastic bottles. I take a final pull from the can. Tastes of grit.

The slow, wet, gasping pulse of Chew Stum Valley morning.

Hazed sunlight leaks through the visages of minor saints, complex family crests, an endless interlocking swarm of dragons, and, adjacent to the garden exit, a white-and-blue portrait of a young boy, eyes and mouth slits. The lad resembles less a Western Christian saint than some pagan entity, carved into unbending form thousands of years ago by a mad mendicant ikonist; its perspective warped to look ageless and inhuman, no-child and every-child. There is an amateurishness as well as a deliberateness, the saying of that which one has been trying to say. That I can't understand the language is beside the point. An apprentice-work, from what little I've gathered from Thorne's professional contacts.

Thorne redid the St. George and the Dragon motif for a church in Bristol a few years ago. A local rag had called the job "splendid" and "boisterously coloured", which seemed like the wording of some helpless octogenarian editor, or at least someone who wanted to be one. I see no need to go examine it myself, unless I become truly desperate. Otherwise most of his sales seem to have been to rich London scumfucks; his dealer, James Graham, described their relations to me as "slight yet attentive and almost always conducted electronically". There was never an invitation south for Graham, and his occasional attempts to lure Thorne north were always gently rebuffed. As for the buyers, many of them were at least on the fringe of industrial and its attendant avant-garde. Idle wealth positions itself inside every underground movement, and artisans always find patrons, of whatever sort. None of these patrons, however, met Thorne after 1983, and their few proffered memories of him before are insubstantial.

I take some pictures with the phone, but I'm not good enough to capture the precision or the curious lack of anything that could be called style. Some pieces are obviously religious motifs, others abstract gyrations of color, other staid and sheer blue-white-as-ice cliffs, others aboriginalesque folk-art smear-portraits. Were they drafts, mistakes, or commissions never retrieved? None spoke to the artist who'd created the apprentice-work; it was as if he had done his masterwork as an apprentice, then settled complacently if not comfortably into the realm of the disposable. The apprentice-piece evokes a violinist playing a few discordant notes before a symphony to tell his audience that he knows his trade but is not subservient to it.

The great and ramshackle single room (easily accessed/broken-into) more resembles the great cavern of an ancestral mead hall than the stereotypical post-modern urban artisan's warehouse workspace. Clean but not antiseptic, the stink is of dirt, not mold; the floor is hard-packed earth, so tight that I first mistook it for well-treated wood. Various staging areas—long wooden benches with short, metal stools—are stocked with equipment, but there are no half-completed projects strewn about. No chewed up wood chips. No scattering of sandpaper. No shattered glass.

There is always a moment of frisson when in the habitat of a killer. It lends charge to the bowels and balls; it makes you think you're going to find the hidden journals, the manifesto, the hard drive with the half-erased search history that the cops missed. And I have, before; the cops fucked up, and I saw something they missed because I was young and obsessed with the crime in question and the idea of myself being obsessed with it. But not here. There are no crannies and no crawl-spaces and the walls are not hollow. There's nothing the cops missed.

They found a final body here on the packed-earth, and I find nothing.

She calls. Terstory never actually *calls* anyone. I put down my pint of real ale, which tastes like something a two-year old pukes up after drinking two cans of dad's Bud real fast.

"Yeah?" I'm negotiating my way through the less reputable of the locals, with Kev, the boiled-beef-cheeked bartender, tracing my path with his eyes.

"He's dead."

"Who's dead?"

"Neolithic."

"Edward? Who? Crisp?" Outside, it has begun to faintly slush; small cold licks the left side of my head, the right side pressed against the pub wall.

"Yes. A drunken fall. Three flights of stairs. His friend's apartment in London."

"Jesus Christ. Just how Silence died?"

"Yes, the speculation is it was deliberate."

"I fucking *doubt* it."

"That's what I want to hear. Come back. You're writing the article."

"What article?"

"Edward Crisp's final interview."

"You're fucking kidding."

"I'm fucking not. Serial killer story is dead. Put it in your memoirs."

"What's my angle?"

"By the time you are in JFK, I will have thought one." She hangs up.

You'd think there'd be wind out here. You'd think it'd be vicious.

The seventh track on QM's '00 EP, *The Physical Defects of Mankind*, is entitled "Glassblower". Recorded during a two-week long shamanic residency in London, it's one of two QM releases from '97 to '08 to not feature Thorne's input. Reportedly improvised, both seamless and jarring, it circles around chanted Latin supposedly from a lost book of Seneca's and various portraits of its owners down the years. This is not quite a concept album since the paltry narrative, if it even could be said to be one, only becomes really understandable after about the twentieth time you listen to it. And even then, there's no way the seventh and final track fits in.

Sung in a lilting, amateur sing-song that a chain-smoking grandmother might summon, "Glassblower" is a perversion of the Pied Piper narrative. The titular artisan is not a Germanic wanderer, but a local of a small unnamed English village who spends years crafting a stained glass window with the motif of St. George slaying the Worm but when he presents it to the local parish, it is rejected. "St. George looked too much like a man, The Worm, too, a man." Distraught, the glassblower crafts a shimmering obsidian rod, unbreakable and erect, which entrances, perhaps accidentally, the children of the town. The glassblower, seeking only refuge from disgrace, sets out not to the sea but to the mountains. It is never entirely clear to the singer, the audience, or the glassblower himself if he knows the town's children are following him.

The result is still something of a forced march. The children are whipped by stinging branches, set upon by wolves, spirited away by falcons, trampled by their fellows, felled by hunger and thirst, swallowed by ditchwater. Each minor atrocity is catalogued by the stilted voice, which seems to be singing almost against its will. The tune is of an old standard, though you can never quite place it (and, indeed, when subjected to examination by those who know of these things, proves to be quite original). The glassblower himself is bruised and half-starved yet continues to tramp through "these wooden mountains" long after his train of followers has been decimated, "an emaciated, despised, vagabond".

The glassblower is never described, save as "not young, not big"; he could be Thorne, though Thorne never killed children, as far as anyone knows. Did Edward and Jonathan know James was a killer? Could they feel it? Did it ooze out of Edward's unconscious as he composed-sang it?

Does it even fucking *matter*? They knew him or they didn't; they knew he was a killer or they didn't. They don't know anything now.

Down to the sea. Signless, the coastline seems to shiver and twitch when you're looking away. I don't recognize the topography even though I've been to the scene twice. A black rip, where the earth-colored water meets a vaguely rust-colored sky. Impressive and occult the first time, now it just lulls me. I wonder if people occasionally throw themselves over the side with no planning whatsoever. I trace the drop slowly, not as sober as I should be to have taken the wrong-side-of-the-road drive down here, listening to static and local presentations of arid pub-hop. A local publican, selling me take-out cans of cider, told me that two German bicyclists got confused by the switchbacking and went right off one of the cliffs, the end of last summer. This seems to be the only thing the locals like about the coast. Otherwise, they hate it like they hate their children: grudgingly.

It's stupid of me to be out here, hunting for something that will allow me to leave. Salvage, as from a shipwreck. After nearly twenty minutes of almost-careful trudging, I come across the run. A cobbled together series of stones, not really steps and certainly not even or flat, complemented by the occasional plank of wood, pushed deep into the earth. In some sections, there is even a molting, hollowed-out metal rod serving as handrail. Run your palm along it, it'll slice you open, leave shards of rusted grit inside the wound.

The descent is slippery and steep, becomes a wind-tunnel. Forces slip, battering the small, delicate bones of my inner ear. The gulch before me, a massive fall-down to the beach where waves lazily crash and froth white, seems inevitable. Half-way down, I transition into something of a crouch-climb, my body against the side of the cliff, my fingers clawing at the rocks and wood and ground in the spaces inbetween, one boot seeking blindly the next notch beneath, the other filling the space recently vacated. My heart is roaming, the wind is banshee, I don't believe in spirits, and I am sober.

The last ten feet, I stand up straight and run, allowing the last, lush pull of gravity to turn a light jog into a fierce sprint to stay upright, so that when I break out onto the beach, it is at speed, with maddened energy and inflamed senses, and I see it as Thorne must have seen it.

A lacuna.

So he filled it. With a body intact. Besides what he had done to the lungs.

Laid out. Young dead Rick Redding, in a state of repose. Here, just at the edge of the tide at its fullest. Hands folded on his chest. Face sculpted in a calm, suggestive relief.

This was the second one he got right.

The very first was a public park, almost half a mile from the beach, dragged through underbrush, abandoned half under a public picnic table. Rotting wood. A mother doing advance scouting twenty-five Saturday mornings ago saw it, thought it was a bum, called the rozzers.

The second was a highway dump not three miles from Bristol.

Third, and his first true success, was a few miles up the beach. This was a re-do, an attempt to see if he could make it work again. He could.

But why Redding?

Any conventional article on the murders would start here. The lens of a single victim: not just the timeline and horrific details and a liberal "recreation" of the minutes, but the squelched hope blooming under the stress of the investigation. He'd had a drinking problem, she'd only just barely gotten her bachelor's, she'd been able to move out of her uncle's, they'd only just gotten engaged. Ad shitum, ad shitum. Here the imagination yanks you away from the more obvious centerpieces (first vic, last, the killing that signaled a shift in approach, the killing that refined the approach, the killing that gave the cops *what they needed*, and so on and so on and so on and so on and so on). Unlike the other victims, these unbelievable figures exist outside the simple narrative of execution. The reader wants to follow her as she does coke in the bathroom of the only pub that hasn't barred her, as he somehow succeeds in the most unlikely get-rich-quick scheme yet, and he breaks another fucking promise, you know he would, of course he would. These people weren't waiting to be plucked out of their staid gyrations of a blest and boring life.

So who was young dead Rick Redding? Ran with a few Glasgow youth organizations not approved of by the police, but his now-unfrozen rap sheet is mostly comprised of graffiti-related incidents. Never spent more than a night in jail. Two years of London art school, with an apparent sideline in selling liquid MDMA. Then he just fucked off; his mates had no clue where to. No idea why he'd come here.

Tall; auburn hair cut short. Awkwardly gangled but confident as fuck. Low, empty voice. His smile like it had been dragged from a pile of rubble, unaware it was still capable of even twitching. On his Royal Enfield. These photographs portray with sentimentality an already kind of vanished lifestyle. He seems to be posing in them simply because he knew he was going to die.

With Redding, the person within the victim reveals himself less through action than through the inscrutability of the youth, the not-letting-in.

Except. Except it's horseshit. Redding was no more real than any of the other eight people Thorne killed, and is now no less dead than them, Thorne, Crisp, and Silence.

This is why I never write about the victim. I start with the killer and stay with the killer and it is always the killer.

I stand where Redding's head lay, or almost. There is a small, green rock you can spot in crime scene photos. This is where Thorne stood, or almost, but my certainty that I felt what he felt—the lacuna, the need to fill it—has twisted off and screamed away from my mind. I can't feel anything he might have felt: not the exhaustion of triumph, not the sexual thrill, not the disappointment that comes with the realization that the hunger is again growing. He has left nothing here, and there is nothing here.

I close my eyes and listen to the surf and the wind and wait until I can force myself to feel, soft and measured and rank, his breath upon my neck.

LUNGS

There is one photo of Tellerman I haven't deleted from my phone. In it, he is half-turned, caught in the pivot, facing away. Infinitely beefy. You can see the flesh of his neck, the thick outlines of the bones of his right hand. He'd been sitting on the back table, showing me the video Susannah had taken. His body framed by the smartphone, down there, pounding on the bedroom shag carpet, caught in the clench of a convulsion. You could hear her sobbing these little lost gasps at the end of her breaths. It was the only soundtrack; his own particular passion was silent. Tellerman thought it was funny, or he wanted me to think he thought it was funny. I don't know if by that point he was capable of making that distinction.

"That's why I can't drink," he said.

"Not even one?"

"Not even a *Heineken*."

Boone was dressed in ripped-hem blue jeans, beat to fuck black concert Keds, his button-up white "work shirt". He would hold his hands up in front of his face, palms open and fingers splayed, then shake them, as if to make a point. He never seemed to stop chuckling.

"Are you enjoying that?" he would ask me, as I slurped my Lone Star. "Is it really, really good? Do you *like* it?"

He didn't like the Austin businessmen who'd organized the gig. He was a self-described "esoteric" who wore red trousers and a buttonless old paisley suit jacket over children's T-shirts. The bar, some new craft-ale joint, reflected his taste: ostentatiously dark and velvet and empty. Tellerman didn't like the way the businessman sang along on "Yancey Brothers Blues", and he told him to fuck off. The businessman, whose name had a heraldic ring to it but was otherwise impossible to remember, laughed it off like it was love. Afterwards, though, when attention had shifted from him, I could see his lips moving in some vicious, pathetic invocation. He probably couldn't even tell Boone hated him more because he was available than anything else. Tellerman was down some fucked-up inward path I couldn't recognize; his stage presence had always been manufactured aggression and minor cruelties, but this was unfeigned hate. It soured his delivery, and the evening became about that. It was, at least, a show.

I didn't need to see it. I took my drink out to the table someone had dragged out into the small sunken concrete back garden, littered with drained bottles of Miller Lite and smushed cigarette butts. I chain-smoked and stared up at a sky so black it was almost green. It was something to do.

"Yo."

Tellerman stood grinning in the metal doorway. "Spare a smoke?"

"Sure."

"Thanks." He accepted the cig with a stricken little swoop of the head, chuckling as he righted himself. "I'm sick of everyone," he explained, "but I'll miss them all."

"What does that even mean?"

He held the cigarette low between two fingers, filter against his cheek as he laughed. "I don't fucking know. You know what

Townes Van Zandt said when someone asked him why he wrote such sad songs?"

"No."

"He said…" Tellerman lit the smoke with a thin, wilted little motel match. "He said, 'My songs aren't sad, they're hopeless.'"

I watched him exhale, long and soft.

"What'd you mean by that?"

Tellerman shrugged. "It's what he said."

"What'd you mean you're gonna miss everyone?"

He shrugged. "I lied, I guess." He sucked the last life out of the smoke and ditched it down. "I won't miss a single one of the cunts. You gonna sing tonight, or are you just gonna sit out here like a little bitch?" Then he went back inside.

It's my only picture of him now, and it looks nothing like him at all.

Every Steeltown Infrastructure YouTube video has been transformed into a collective mourning site. It gradually happened over the last six weeks, but now it just looks like it's always been that way.

The only good thing is I now play this song every day.

to hell with this world

that guitar is tearing my heart apart

This was a suicide.

i wish i could hear his next song :(

I went to the tribute concert last night at Vic's. bandmates and friends passed around instruments for 5 1/2 hours. no booze? fuck that we got ripped he was mad bastard love you bt you helped me change

I don't have the strength to listen to this album anymore, but I will never be able to stop hearing it.

tell me how to get the devil out get the devil out

today is a good day to hear that voice

It doesn't sound anything at all like the people who knew him. José captured that with the official announcement on the All Kittens Are Dead Kittens Records website. It was just a single sentence, but I can't imagine a better one. "Boone punched out early Monday morning with nothing in his pockets but three bucks and a cell phone with his aunt's number on it."

But still, looking at these strangers discussing their own personal sloughs of despond and when they quit drinking and what the backroads looked like at midnight and how they can't see any way out, all that hurts more than watching Allie trying to light a rollie in the funeral home parking lot, her hands shaking so hard Karl had to do it for her. I was pinned where I was, black and sweat-slick and cold. There maybe has to be things you can't feel, and there maybe has to be someone at these events who can't feel them.

The way he told it to me, Boone didn't actually try to do anything at all the first time he knew he was dying. He just upped the dosage of all the narcotics and gave up trying to write, concentrated on playing wherever would have him. Susannah had his truck at that point, so he was hitching and taking the bus, down there on the borderlands, Pennsylvania West Virginia Maryland Virginia. For a while, he didn't even have a guitar, just borrowed whatever he could get. Appearing in the same non-incorporated townships, playing the same cheap shit watering holes, backrooms and basements, the occasional big-city seisún and lock-in, busking in suburban city centers. There'd been no formal announcement, but anyone who came could see he was dying up there. Word metastasized, and the uneven scar he was tracing across the post-industrial Northeast began to attract a morbid following, and his name became synonymous with *the serious artist*. Boone didn't seem to notice much. He really should have died that first time; it was the only thing he was ever any good at.

Years later, sitting in the cab of my pickup parked in that abandoned gas station, the little red and white cooler sitting on his lap, he told me everything started when he puked some bloody stomach junk up onto a trucker's lap. The guy was half-dead with exhaustion and whatever he'd been popping to keep going, so he just pulled over to the side of the highway and dragged Boone out. Didn't even bother to beat the shit out of him, just got back in and kept going. Tellerman lay there, curled like a dung beetle, and when he got up, he found he'd pissed blood all over himself. The few passing vehicles ignored his hails. He figured, finally, that he was going to die. "It seemed appropriate enough," he said to me, suppressing the gurgling in his lungs. "And I got, just then, that I didn't want to die that way. Some paragraph at the end of my Wikipedia page everyone'll have trouble believing it's so perfect. It'd be so fucked. Shit, I thought, what if I *don't* die this way? That's what got me walking. Just to say *fuck 'em*. I kept saying that to myself, *fuck 'em, fuck 'em, fuck 'em all*. It was always the only way I ever got any shit done in my life anyway."

He was at the gas station before he recognized what it was. Lights off, windows white-washed. But inside, there maybe was something to drink, something to smoke, maybe even a phone that hadn't been disconnected. "Though I don't know who I'd have called," he said, grinning. He tried the door and he tried throwing himself at the door. He went round back, heard the trickle before he saw the hillside. "I didn't know I was on a mountain. I guess I was at a lot of places those days without knowing where I was or how I got there. That wasn't particularly strange." The hillside was a long, slow ascent, down which came the sound of water running faint and far and silver. It was pre-dawn, and he remembered the ancient Greeks believed their gods lived on hills, amongst springs. That thought, if anything, made him climb.

"What's this place's name?" I asked.

"I don't know. I'm sure it has one, but I don't know it."

Then, fumbling and anxious like a child given the expected, demanded present who still can't believe it's Christmas, Tellerman cracked the top of the cooler. His thin, starved hands clenched into the hissing plastic-wrapped dry ice. They closed around something solid, and he sat there, weighing and grinning.

Then he closed and placed the cooler on the scuffed sunspot floor, well within his reach, and sat back, asking for one of my cigarettes. He ripped the filter off and lit it. There was no anxiety here now. The quickness and surety of his movements, the speckled, gin-aqua cast of his eyes showed only relief. Filled with smoke, something inside his chest purred like a cat unused to vocalizations, and he rested his eyes on me, utterly at ease, and said, "They're mine; they were always mine."

Two videos.

The first. Townes Van Zandt playing "Nothing". He sits on a shit-brown crinkled couch in some hotel lobby. Under the harsh halogen, his mottled face, and in his already-broken hands an unmarred guitar, cheap and new. There is a plastic plant over his right shoulder. After he finishes playing, he bends over the frets and says, as if to himself, "I'm glad I remembered that."

The second. Boone Tellerman, "It Never Rains on West 79 Where My Baby Died". Shirtless and wearing those black jeans, white-streaked as if shat on by pigeons. You can feel the sheen coming off him, equal parts cocaine and sweat. He sits on a red-iron stoop somewhere near the water in North Brooklyn. Snatches of blank blue and mythic, immediate skyline show when the hand holding the camera jerks away. This was before he got sick the first time, and he looks crazy young and weed-thin, jowls yet to develop. At the video's end, a lady gallops down the steps, knocks her knee into his elbow, screwing up the final verse. He doesn't pay it any mind, just finishes the last couple lines a cappella. Then, after drawing a single breath, he says, in an almost amazed exclamation, "Highways don't *go* nowhere," the verb a squeak. And then he laughs.

The first is on YouTube. We'd watch it after all night drinking sessions. Then Tellerman'd do "Sunday Morning Coming Down", and we'd have a last beer on my stone balcony. It faced west, and we could see the dawn break over the hull of the building behind us. It was one of the few ways to settle him down enough to get three or four hours of sleep on the peach-puke pull-out. Tellerman'd never say anything while we watched it or any of the other videos comprising what he called "the Townes motel room suite". Boone always had a perverse enough sense of pride to never abase himself in front of anything like a hero. He once called an interviewer a "stupid gash" because she referred to Bob Dylan, unquestioningly, as a genius.

The second I own. Allie showed it to me, long after Boone left what some have since taken to calling his Brooklyn Residency. She said she couldn't stand having any of this shit anymore, and did I at least want to see it before she deleted it. I made her send me a copy of the file.

Boone sat in the iron chair, long chalk scratchings on the concrete porch beneath. A bruised green tank was between his knees, a mask over his vzier-like features obscured all but two small sharp sea-blue stone eyes and a gnarly old sponge beard. A tree was dying over us.

"Jesus fuck," I said.

A distorted laugh and then he looped his thumbs through the elastic bands and loosened the mask to speak out of its corner. "You want some?"

"Hell no."

"Pure."

"People aren't supposed to breathe just *oxygen*."

"Yeah, *people*." He said it like he was going to puke.

I shook my head and sat down on the stonework that formed a fat curve along the side of the cabin. Lit a smoke. I could see him grinning under that get-up, his nose twitching like a psycho-pathic bunny's. The plastic confused the motions, making them a blur of flesh.

"You rent this place?"

"My aunt's."

"She own it?"

"S'about all she owns."

"Where she at?"

"You're safe, son. She ain't here."

I glanced past his form. Through the doorway, a shipwreck of a kitchen, the further dark recesses of a living room. "You got a guitar in there?"

"No."

"I got one in the car. You want me to go down and get it?"

"Fuck no. Came up here to concentrate."

"On what?"

He spidered his fingers on the mask.

The late-night long-haul drive had burned away whatever was left of my energy and aggression. I sipped at the tepid gas station coffee I'd brought with me. He reached out with long, tapered fingers for my cigarette and took a drag, filling the mask with smoke. I let him finish it that way. Fingered the plastic shopping bag with the twelve pack in it. "Should probably stick the beer in the fridge."

"Don't bother. Take it with us."

"We going somewhere?"

"Told you."

"Yeah. I was a bit confused."

"Want you to drive me somewheres. Why I asked you."

I took out one of the beers, cracked it. Foam rushed up and out, sweet and rancid. "The hospital?"

"No health care."

"No? What about Allie?"

He shook his head, slight movements slow enough not to upset the ruptured bags in his upper chest. "She got that taken care of."

"Jesus, man. That's vicious."

"Not really." He massaged his throat like it was hers. "Considering."

I lit a new smoke off the old. "Retribution?"

"Swift and just."

"What'd you do?"

"Lots of things."

"Shit." I stared down the long awkward brick path to what was almost a driveway. The thin river beyond and the foul-smelling trees guarding it. "Where do you want to go?"

"I'll show you."

I took out my crack-faced iPhone, and he just stared at it for a second, totally uncomprehending. I made to hand it over to him. "On the map."

He grinned, his lips flaring a little under the mask. Then he laughed suddenly and lightly, his chest barely moving. There was still the sound of flesh being chopped on a wooden block. "No," he said, when he'd recovered what passed for his voice those days. "It's not on any goddamn map."

Dawn of dead leaves in storm-pits and dry caterpillar husks. The sound of wasps trying to fuck in the heat. I didn't know how long we'd been driving, but it had been state roads to local to unmarked cowpaths, back and forth, back and forth. I stopped looking for signs around the time I stopped believing Tellerman knew where we were going. But then it was too long, too far for anyone to just be making this shit up as he went along.

"Stop," he said in front of an abandoned gas station, halfway up a mountain we were going down. Someone had scraped most of its face bare; beyond and below us, the drop-off. "Just park anywhere," Tellerman said. I parked the car near one of the pumps, and he closed his eyes. "Over by the tank. The big white one out back. You see it?"

"Uh—yeah. Yeah, I see it."

"There's a small path behind it. Through the trees. Go up it."

"What?"

"Walk up it. There's a clearing up a ways. Something there for me." Along the way, Tellerman'd taken off his shirt, and the little light we had was harsh on his torso, tobacco-hued and criss-crossed with long brandings, the crevasse an appendectomy puncture. His spindly arms, all elbows and knobbed knuckles, tensed. He grimaced, a little unsure of what such an expression might mean to someone.

"I don't get you."

"Take the cooler." He gestured down to his feet. There, about as big as a gym bag, red and white, was a cheap-ass plastic cooler with a football mascot wasp on the side. It was the kind of thing you'd get on special at Walmart and would expect to fall apart a couple months later.

"What's up there?"

"You'll know it when you see it."

"That's not an answer."

He hauled the cooler up and balanced it on his knees. "Take it."

I did what he said. Moving slowly through the parking lot, the dawn heat-fog still heaving itself off the side of the mountain, I was able to romanticize the whole sordid episode. Granting an old, hateful friend a final, strange wish. I curved around the huge rusting white tank, and, yes, there was a small beaten-dirt path. I eased into the thick of the straight, uncompromised trees, growing heavy and unbowed like a cartoonist or surveyor might portray. Trudged up past felled dogwoods and live sycamores, heavy, lichen-encrusted oaks. Forty feet up or so, the rise broke into a clearing, sloping unevenly upward toward a rock face, where a minor stream splurted down rough into the forest. I couldn't hear its trickle. Too faint. The shitbrown ground was decorated with half-smoked cigarettes, off-brand beer bottles webbed with impact, the occasional tufting of dead grass, used condoms and used cartridges, a whole shopping cart partially submerged in the wet earth. It was this final detail that made me realize that the glade was soft to the point of being infinitely fibrous. It seemed to breathe, stinking of cleaning chemicals and cum. I took four steps and lowered myself to both knees, digging my hands into the fetid, spongey ground. I squirmed them blindly, feeling. I knew what I was doing; I don't know how I knew what I was doing.

That was how I found his lungs.

He called the last time. "Need to go back."

"Where?"

"Need you to drive me there." His voice sounded distant, like it had been recorded then partially taped over with soft street noise. "When can you be here?"

"What's gone septic now, Boone?"

"Fuck you, come get me."

"Is there someone with you?"

"No."

"I can hear someone. Where are you?"

"I don't know."

"Makes it hard for me to come get you."

"This isn't funny."

"I never said it was."

"You won't come get me, will you? Just because I *asked*."

"Who are you with?"

"You won't, will you, you bastard?" But he was just laughing.

Back on the state road. The wind hissing through the slits of the pickup's uncaulked windows, rumble strips catching the wheels whenever I let my attention go unfettered. I can't find it; I knew I'd never be able to find it. I don't know if I'm even really looking. I don't know how you'd go about looking for it in the first place. It would be appropriate to play some *Steeltown* now. Maybe "Riding With Queen Joe" or even the *Shotgun Gurl* EP. But I can't listen to him in the car, can't listen to him anywhere actually. I can't even play his shit live anymore, and people always said I sounded more like him than he ever did. So there's no music. The trees on the side of the road are veined; they seem to assemble the thick and bulbous sky of the world they are trapped in, but I know they just describe the parts of it I cannot see. I don't know the names of any of the trees down near the borderland, Pennsylvania West Virginia Maryland Virginia, back and forth, over and across the mountains. State roads or federal, they can't take you any place you want to go.

HUMAN CHILD

It has been an aching day. The sky heals like a scab, but nothing has split it, and it has never bled an ounce of fluid. Light the first of the evening. My hands ache. Fluxing bone pain that doesn't dissipate. Rest my elbows on the black metal railing adjacent to the basement stairs. A Japanese guy with coiffed hair and a model's blank face brushes by, street-level. I think I hear him say, sotto voce, into a phone curled against the side of his skull, "...other territories... how does it feel there?"

The door jerks towards me: I catch it. The last of the maggots file out, pawing at coats, extracting packs of cigarettes, demanding lights off each other, howling about the stupidity of associates and lovers. I wait till they're halfway down the block, then go back inside. Clear the scrap-wood tables of barely begun drinks, kick the chairs and jerk the tables back into some kind of order. I have my head down, starting the wash, when the door heaves and wheezes.

Kid. Small and thin. White-stained hoodie draped, obscuring features. He's looking at my face in the way people who know you look at you. I straighten up and move down the bar towards him. Just from the way he's standing, I know I don't know him.

"Gonna have to see ID, man."

As I approach, the candle throws up yellow globe light, and I can see the shorn sides of his head. Scraped unclean with cheap razors. I tighten, keep a good deal of the bar between the two of us. I think of the metal bar under the wash.

"Not looking for a drink." His voice is a slurry of broken things. His hands jammed into the hoodie's pockets. He hasn't looked anywhere except right at me. There's a bunch of things I could say. None of them would ease the situation in the necessary direction.

His eyes are somewhere I've never been. "Knowa girl named Kimmie?"

"Don't know anyone named that, no."

"Kimmie."

"No idea."

The kid leans slightly over the bar. I can see the beginning of lazy slashes of tribal tattooing on his wrists. There is what looks like at first a severe case of eczema on his neck, but as he comes closer, I can see it's scar-art, created through glass laceration. Thought it was out of style.

And I can smell him. Old puke and new trash. Like one of the gutter punks who camp out in Tompkins Square Park and adjoining streets, but they don't come in here, they know better than that.

"Said she knew you."

"No idea, man. Sorry."

"You're Aaron."

"No, that's not my name."

His single, simple grin. "Kimmie said."

"Not me."

"Aaron."

"No."

"Aaron." It's a statement. He places both his hands on the bar like they're dead birds he's been carrying around too long in his pockets. "She said you knew how to get back."

"Get back where?"

He thinks this is funny: his face begins to convulse around the slit of a smile. His body is impossibly still, like a caryatid of an unseen palace. Then his neck begins to spasm, and something happens to his eyes. His shoulder twitches, and his head drops as if he's mid-seizure. I step back, place the base of my spine against the counter behind me. A middle-aged couple comes through the door bubbling and laughing, talking about the never-removed Christmas lights, calling for two Stella. In the second I look away from the kid, he's out the door, quick-lurching up the stairs. The couple brightly ignores his transit, settling. I pour the beer, take money, give change. Stymie attempted dialogue. "How long has this place *been* here..." Curve around the bar. Outside. Up the concrete stairs.

There is nothing on the sidewalk except for dog shit, menthols smoked down to the nub, and chip bags, inside-out, gleaming. The sky is wet and swirled with grays, refusing to rain.

Army jacket hung over his sloped shoulders, a brace of white-heads running up the right side of his neck, my brother stood in front of the cafe door. It was the late morning rush, espresso hiss and plume. Early twenties with their anti-ironic plumage and hung-over fleshmasks would walk up behind him and do a nimble three-step; in New York, you can never quite believe that the person who is in your way is not about to begin the process of getting out of it. Then they'd say something passive and suburban or touch him lightly on the shoulder. He'd turn a little, looking almost hunchback, grimace, smile down at them, then open his eyes in surprise and shuffle to the side. After they passed, he'd return to his station, staring out the window at the broken sidewalk, the trucks slamming over the surface of the street. I saw him repeat this process four or five times, always with the same surprise and lack of agility, as if he had simply become incapable of learning from past experiences. Eventually,

I had to stand, take him by the shoulder and elbow, and lead him back to the table.

I was seventeen, taking a week of my break to visit him. I'd known he'd dropped out. I hadn't known he was this bad.

He tapped out a tattoo on the table with his knuckles, some kind of obscure protection. "Do you dream?" he asked me.

"Yes. Probably."

"You don't remember them?"

"Not really. Smears of them. Never faces or anything. Colors and feelings."

"So we could be having the same dream and not know it."

"I guess."

"Would you go back there with me? If we could?"

"Go back where?"

His eyes did this little animal thing, like he was catching up with me. "The marcot, Cat. Where else have you ever been that you'd want to go back to?"

"The marcot?"

His face slipped a little. Then his head began bobbing back and forth like someone had cut his jugular and physics had not yet decided what was to be done. He said, very softly, "We went there together."

"I don't remember that."

"When you were six and I was twelve."

"I don't remember much of that."

"Remember much of what?"

"Before I went away to school."

He was blinking at me, slow and deliberate. "I don't remember much after mom and dad died."

"They didn't."

"What?"

"They didn't die."

I stood without knowing what I was doing, my hand closing around my backpack. My brother reached across the table and grabbed my wrist. We held the bas-relief, slightly risen, me pulling against his grip ever so gently, for maybe an entire minute. Then I released the backpack, and he released me, and we both sat down.

That evening, I watched him do nitrous, inhaling leisurely into the fluid-rimmed balloon, frozen steam coming off its top, his one huge hand encompassing most of its fat body. And when he leaned back into unconsciousness, he was smiling, no blood in his face.

"...you couldn't really see the expression on its face, its mouth was broken or stuffed with moss or worn away by water, or it was just hidden by shadow, it was hard to tell, but I could see the mane, the eyes. It was blue, even in the dark, you could tell it was blue, blue-black, and it was supported there, by some kind of stone column, and I asked him what it was, and he said, 'A drain, of course,' in that Hackney accent, and I asked him how he knew, and he said he'd been looking for it for so goddamn long of course he'd recognize it, and that was when he flopped over onto his back and began to kick his legs up in the air and let out these little shrieks. I thought something was wrong with him, his face was all screwed up and his eyes were shut and his forehead and brow, I guess you'd call it a brow, were all wrinkled. But as the shrieks, they were really these kind of small things, not that loud, rose in pitch, I realized that he was joyous and anxious too, that this was a *celebration*." He stopped there and smiled at me.

Down at the L curve of the bar. Natalie covering my ass on a strangely quiet fall Friday.

"So? What happened?" I poured myself another two fingers of scotch. Aaron waved the proffered bottle off. His fingers seemed thicker than the last time I saw him, his face more sallow and excited. His clothes looked fresh from Walmart, though they fit perfectly. The pink polo seemed particularly inappropriate.

"I dunno. This was just a scouting expedition. He had to do some more research. I got caught up in other shit. He never got in touch again."

"He knew how to get in touch with you?"

"Everybody knew how to get in touch with me."

"I didn't."

"I didn't mean people like you."

"People like me."

"Yes." He said it like everything was so evident.

"What do you think he was going to do?"

"What do I think—" His fingers knitted together over his right knee. "He was going to go down there and follow it. The old drain and the river it led to."

"Where did he think it led to?"

"We didn't know," Aaron said. "But that was the point. Wasn't it?"

I usually went out easy, slept hard, and woke late, blinking gauze away. After one particular Monday night of Ambien and Dewar's, dreams crawled up my skin, up my nostrils. I woke repeatedly, each time knowing exactly where and who I was. Around five, I slipped out of bed, steadied myself against the gently flaking blue walls, slouched toward the kitchen for a drink. Stopped over the couch. I'd forgotten my brother was there. Curled, flimsy covers twisted about his ankles like a homemade escape rope, less in a fetal position than like a beetle. He enacted, with wrists, elbows, lower jaw, and neck, such strange positions, somehow fluid and somehow jarring, that I didn't think, at the time, I'd ever seen a human have purpose for. There was no noise, except for the scratching of his jeans against the rough material of the couch. I was reminded of the nature of sexual fantasy long before experiencing penetration, when all there is is the idea of warm, of hiding. "You go limp," an ex had once observed of my sleep patterns, "and then suddenly you kick out once or twice like a dog."

"A fucking *speck*." It was late, and he was drunk two beers in. I'd had quite a bit more, but I was metabolizing at a steady rate in those days. Aaron sat on the beat-to-fuck blue couch, legs curled up under him. He wore one of my blotched white work shirts and an old pair of my black jeans, threads exposed on the inner left thigh. He'd shaved but had not slept well, and the weight he'd put on since living with me showed in obvious places: curled in a roll at the gut, under the folds of his arms, the chin, the cheeks.

"I've never stopped looking for it. And I haven't found a *fucking* speck," and here he showed me non-space between thumb and forefinger. "I've found things, yeah, I've found strange things, but the people who've, they've said they know what I'm talking about, they didn't give it the same name... They've all been looking for, I don't know, maybe looking for attention. Notoriety. Power. If that makes sense." He raised his hands, showing me the plain palms, the fingers gripping the air between us. "Do you remember waking up after? In the ditch? My arm thrown over you, my stomach pressing against your ribs, your T-shirt? It was the green Slimer one, and the sun was above us, and there was the slow, steady rhythm of your heart under my hand. That was real. Just for a minute. It was real. Mom and dad." He looked off, then his gaze clipped back to me. "They were there, and then they weren't. Maybe they'd never existed. Maybe they were an intervention. But I don't know, and it doesn't matter. I was never alive, never even born, until I came to the marcot, and the same goes for you, Cat. You know that." His hands retracted and clutched his upper arms. He twisted back and forth, not quite rocking. Then, softly, looking down at that sloped, bare floor, "I know it happened. I just need to hear you say it. Just once."

I rarely laugh from my heart, the shaking, difficult kind of laughter you can't control, but that's what I did then, the thing seizing me and not letting me go, shaking my torso with violence, forcing out sobs, tears, and making me gasp for air. Aaron watched me the whole time.

He'd stayed with me for almost two months. I think it was the happiest I'd ever been.

Then Kimmie.

Flame-scorched forearms, she seemed of autumn, all the stronger for it. The wave-mass of tan scarification ran roughshod from thick-knobbed wrist bones to the plains of upper, fleshy arms. She refused long sleeves even in the winter, kept to simple white T-shirts after spring bled into summer, but she didn't flaunt her trauma, spectacle herself, enjoining her figure to your minor wells of pity and superstitious fear.

I first saw her staring down at a jagged tangle of glass at her feet like she had no idea where it had come from. Her iPod had reached the end of a playlist of muddy old funk, and into the crisp, new silence, the crash had been loud and immediate. The cafe had just started serving beer and wine, the latter in these really unfortunate long-stemmed glasses you'd see at a restaurant with tablecloths. She regarded the glass mutely, her body stalled in a bend forward, a position she held so long it seemed stilted, posed like a modern dance arrangement. It wasn't this desperate unnaturalness, but the look of negation on her face, her total rejection of the incident that made me get up from my table and approach her.

Kimmie could bleed the word "boy" of all its talk-down city connotations, shiver you with its purr. She drank good bourbon, but she drank slowly, and she did not often get drunk. She made you tell her stories about yourself, or stories others had told you; she leaned across the bar and grasped your wrist and demanded it of you, Korean features contracted by Western lilt, extremely American. Both forced a sense of wide vistas, as well as a certain lack of innocence. She wouldn't offer advice, and that was welcome enough. Telling her tales wasn't an unburdening; she offered her complete self up and drank it in readily, smiling close-mouthed and without opinion.

She came from this little thing that called itself a town, non-incorporated, in between two ranges of things that were not quite mountains in a state that really shouldn't have been a state anymore. Came from; well, was imported to, adopted and flown in, but she had no memory of being born, no memory of Korea. The town, they would have bonfires when autumn hung heavy above the abandoned mineshafts, the slim, wooden gateposts with parked motorbikes in front of what they called bars, the un-streamlined chapels. Yard refuse, dried deadwood still unsoaked by dew, crippled furniture unsalvaged by the middling talents of local craftsmen, leaves and brush, all things with their ends irrevocably stuck in them, handed down from Christ for the single purpose of burning. She described the smell, as if tar had been alight for years, as if summer itself were for burning, the excitement that came with the sacrifice of the end of the year, hailing the season of miracles, demons and godlings and pilgrimsnindians, dead 'n' hungry. The thrill of children who don't know that their world is limited by the laws of physics and sickness. She described her parents' drive in the dark, just highway and highway, the tractor-trailers downshifting with bunkerbuster explosions, the long pebbled climbs of emergency access roads, for when one of these behemoths went rogue. She described the food, gourd-based, and watching her mother drink and dance, slight and free, happy to become a stereotype. She did not describe the actual incident, the day when her flesh was transfigured to no longer resemble itself but something unmoving, some kind of mountain topography: dry rivers, empty valleys, useless plateaus. But it was the burning that convinced her that there was another place; she had not touched, seen, or even felt it, yet had become inexorably sure that this world could not simply be all there is.

The stairs, inlaid and rococo, were steep and easy to misjudge. We watched the run of semi-mythological scenes sketched on the walls, muzzled bears and heavy hares, dwarf trees fruiting, a caravan of cats, and wondered if these scenes were executed from legend or just the imaginings of a hired artist, storyless, bidding his characters to cavort purposelessly.

Kimmie clung to my clothing, banging deliberately against my side on our way down, laughing loud and dirty with each collision, turning out her limbs to catch against pillars and the spaces created between railings; on one impact I swear I heard something crack. The street, when we finally came out onto it, was a mid-morning Saturday bugfuck. We just leaned in and plowed through.

Aaron grabbed my head and brought his face to mine.

"Tell me you'll come with me," he said.

Blonde and skeletal and so hunched he seemed shrunken, ligature marks on his neck and a tic in the well of his left eye, his fingers smooth and weak, his teeth small shoals in a great pale gumline. His clothes garish tatters. He, or someone drugged, had given himself a mohawk and then allowed the hair to grow back irregularly so that the central slash of hair was now nearly obscured. He squinted like a sewer rat dragged into daylight. "Tell *me*."

Kimmie hit him hard on the cheek, exhaling a stylized grunt as she followed through. Aaron recoiled but didn't even as much as look at her.

"Kimmie," I said. "It's okay. This is my brother."

"Fuckin' *what?*" she said.

"Aaron."

"I know how to. It's so simple."

"Let go of him. You're hurting."

"Kimmie."

The crowd churned.

"The marcot." I made myself say it.

"Yes." He put everything he had left into the affirmation. "Hearing you say its *name*."

"It never existed."

He didn't let go of me but rather, after a single second, pressed my head firmly between his hands with a strength I'd never been able to allow myself to see in him, then leaned forward and kissed me where the left cheek meets the mouth. He released me then folded himself into the crowd. Kimmie stood there in the burnt-egg light, looking up at me like she hadn't, until now, seen me at all.

I ask Natalie to cover my shift and Stewart for his car.

Everyone looks at you strange, coming into the state. *You must be lost*, they think. Were we? What could we have been doing here in the first place? Any family outing would have normally been confined to the Great Falls or Wolf Trap or, at the most experimental, "discovered" backroads. *West Virginia: Open for Business* read the signs as you cross the border. This is a state almost impossible to mock.

It takes some effort to find 81, even more the cow path leading off it. Last time (and I am terrified by how I'm thinking of it so casually as "last time"), Aaron knew the way here, issuing directions as he bounced, joyous and anxious, in the bucket seat of Kimmie's aunt's old gunboat.

I stopped at what I, correctly, assumed was the last place to fill up for cigarettes, Red Bull and a 22 of Bud. I chained, sunk half the energy drink, the entirety of the beer, followed by the rest of the former, its metal taste dulled by exposure to air, its violence to the palate and gullet less crisp. I tried to vomit, head between my knees, half sitting on the passenger seat, head stuck out the open door. Nothing happened.

Driving now alongside a long unbroken, unmended metal fence, no animals in sight and nothing between the sky and myself but the very fact of the car itself, I wonder at my calmness. It makes little sense, but it stays till I have navigated up the tree-engulfed path to the little ditch where she is coming to stand upright now.

Alone. Hair like scrap growing back on a tan, perfectly curved scalp. Bagged out in a yellow jumper, burnt-orange pants, blue-black winter jacket, all three or four sizes too big. Hands emerging out of the two sleeves like shy sea spiders exiting furred coral caves. Sclerotic spine like Eros bid the body bend over, but only the upper torso gave into seduction. Face open at the center, drawn out and stretched at the edges. Mouth open ever so slightly.

She advances, tripping over herself repeatedly, calling my name in this sweet, ragged voice, nothing like the one she used to have. There is not the scrotal thrilling fear I expect or the empty ache of the pathologically depressed. There is just an emotion I cannot hope to capture and classify.

I throw my arm over the seat back next to me (not her eyes) and slam the shift into reverse, tear downhill. I close my own eyes, so I can't get a glimpse of her reflection in the rearview mirror.

"That's where you think mom and dad died." We stood by the beginning of the curve, traffic a full and complete line to our side, the flashes of ambo lights from around the bend just barely visible on the dull chrome of rearview mirrors, the sheen of the wet road. The drivers didn't appear too upset; they checked texts, played video games on their phones as if they had nowhere to be. Perhaps they didn't.

"Around that corner?"

He nodded slowly, as if distracted. He'd grown fat in prison, or the hospital, I'd never been able to get a straight answer just which kind of institution he'd been placed in. Mostly bald, though no men in our family were so. Glum-faced with this strangely sweet new smile and horrible breath. His hands jammed into the pockets of his Wolverines hoodie.

"That's some fucking coincidence."

"Well, it's not where we're going."

I looked at him; he'd turned back to regard the long unbroken stream, now shutting off their engines, getting ready for the long haul. The harsh rhythmic wail of a copter's rotors came from above and far around the bend, refracted straight through the trees.

"Good." He smiled. "That means not everyone is dead." He began to slowly pick his way back toward our car, as if each step's province was deeply important.

"Stay in the car."

"What do you think is going to happen?"

I shut the door. My brother was already at the side of the thing he called a road, kicking wildly at a lead-covered ditch. His arms flailed wildly with each strike, as if he were a duck trying to gain balance. "Help me help me!" he shrieked.

I grabbed his arms and pressed them down to his sides. Close now, we were on the very lip of the ditch. He turned in the embrace. "We're here!" It was a kind of enthusiasm even he might have found suspect a few years beforehand.

"Settle down," I said. "Nothing's gonna happen."

"You don't know that," he said, his foot digging at the leaves again. "She's probably almost dead by now."

"What? Who are you—"

"Christina Clarke. The girl they just evacuated in the med chopper." He blinked once. "Come *on*." Tugging at me.

"Wait, you *knew?*"

"Not quite. It doesn't make—" His face went slack; he let go and stumbled down to his hands and knees. "*Cat*." His voice registers lower than it should have been, than I have ever heard anybody's go.

I turned to the car, where Kimmie sat watching us through the window, her mouth open ever so slightly.

"Cat!"

I watched her face as it happened.

The car barely moves at seventy-six miles an hour. No backroads here. Just highway, dead trees, cars, strip malls, all choppy, misdirected, fractal, only visible in the periphery. In the side mirror, its edges ridged, the collapse of light breaks spastically in the form of a lesser inhabitant of a bestiary, deliberately lost, amorphous, without intent, neither advancing nor retreating, its form caught in a transition, a relationship impossible to sever.

THE IDEAL AND THE ACTUAL

Nicky was sitting in my chair, her palms out open flat, finishing some anecdote I didn't bother trying to understand. The door shut, and she turned toward me, her muscles forming a tableau I couldn't read. She was thin, stilted, dressed all in black, except for the three small white buttons stitching her breast. Her eyes inventoried my features, and she opened her mouth to say something, but then we were introduced.

I listened to her describe her dissertation, watching the way the cheap halogen deck-lights bared her blonde hair ragged. She slowly turned to me, the gray speckled concrete framing her skull. Her lips moved as if she was speaking to the deaf. "You didn't have to stay up with me if you didn't want to."

Nicky spoke a kind of sitcom, accent-less American, washed clean of the Mississippi; she hadn't even contrived to pick up local slang. No "unis", no talk of "flat-mates". I appreciated it and told her as much.

"I don't think people should have two ways of speaking," she said, leaning against the great glass wall of our porch door, appraising me. I made myself look away from her, out over the wet, black street, where the houses jutted squat like stained molars. We talked about shit television; we talked about great television. I asked her what her son's name was, and she told me.

"I don't know if I could do that."

"What?"

"Raise a kid like that. By yourself."

"I'm not always by myself."

"Still."

"Of course you could. When it comes to that with your girl-friend or wife or whatever, don't say that because you think that."

There was still the wine to finish.

We went inside eventually, without discussing it, without either one of us really leading. She lay down length-wise on the white-speckled couch, lifting an arched right foot over my lap, mouse-passing my ear. We spoke briefly of the conference and how she would get to JFK the next morning. Her eyes were on me, black and small, her head scrunched down like an old wom-an's. Then she bird-twitched her head and dismounted the couch, having made her decision not to sleep with me.

Small type, no caps. She wrote the way other people text, dis-tracted and without consideration, but also oddly emotional with a preponderance of *oh mys*, strange and stately like someone else's grandmother. She gave herself nicknames and spoke like a child and spoke like she was talking to a child and misspelled and spurned the notion of paragraphs, just hitting the enter button seemingly at random. She would cut and paste large swathes of poetry, much of it transcendentally awful. Her correspondence was fractured: she wrote back several minutes after I sent my first email with the sentence *i wanted to let you know how excited i was by your last email* but didn't respond to the second for almost three weeks. When she wrote that she was coming back to the city for an interview, I told her she was welcome to stay with us again.

She allowed her leg between mine. She was all nerves from the day's interview; three whiskeys in and she was still talking about it, and then she said, "I don't want to be talking about this, I want to be here, looking at you," and she said it to her hands which were clutching the glass. I leaned in and took her cheek in my palm, and she looked me in the eyes and said, weak and white, "That's nice, that's so nice," and she gave me her other cheek, and I kissed it, and she said, "You like me," like a child would say to a dog, almost amazed, and I leaned in again, and she allowed me the other side of her mouth to kiss, and when I'd done that, she said, "I can't kiss you. I'm sorry, but I can't kiss you." There was the easy stupidity of the bar around us, and suddenly I wanted to recede into it, to be just anyone, laughing at any joke, or alone with my pint, but instead one of my thumbs drew a semi-circle on the outline of her cheek bone. She was in love with a man who didn't love her; that's what she told me. The father of her child, was that what she was supposed to call him? She couldn't see just calling him that, but that's what he was to her now; it was that or her "friend". She could fuck me, she wanted to fuck me, but she wasn't going to let that happen. She'd acted in bad faith enough, when she was younger, when she wasn't that young, lately. There was intensity, but there had been intensity so many other times before, and she didn't want just that, and she said she was sorry, and I sat there and stroked her cheek once more and said, "Okay." She stared into my face, I couldn't tell you what she saw, and said, "That's not what you're supposed to say. That's not what you're supposed to say at all." She waited for me to say something else, and when I couldn't, she lightly kissed the palm of my hand.

She gave me objects. A stuffed mouse, small-dog big, carefully preserved, missing only one whisker, pupil-less and fat. The view from her bathroom window: gray brick and water-pipe. An old fuck-seat hanging in the corner where her Heidegger was piled. Her bunk-bed flush against the back wall, top for her, bottom for

Michael. The descriptions were off-hand, stuck into paragraphs they were only tangentially related to. I didn't know the color of her walls or the name of the street she lived on, but I felt as if I could walk the length of her room, placing my hand on objects, dragging my shoes along her rough, green living-room carpet while she sat sprawled and stick-like in the brown leather recliner, staring up at me, her eyes blank, black beads, her smile not really a smile. I knew the composition of the room was in flux. I knew there would be new stacks of papers and crumbling piles of books, that Michael owned space she never described, that he must reshape everything constantly, that people came over, and that she sat places I couldn't imagine, arranged herself in ways I couldn't understand. Her hairstyle would change, of course, though it's doubtful I would have noticed even if I was there.

She stares at the camera with an unforced, focused aggression, a smile that isn't a smile but a dead thing on her lips. She's at a formal function; there is the moon-cut of a pristine white table-cloth on top of which sits a sleek, thin champagne flute that is almost empty. There is a fat, gilt, quadrilateral mirror hanging just to her left, placed back about ten feet, nudging her ears; it is scarred by an implosion of white light.

She hangs onto a lamp post, one hand dangling with sunglasses, her face composed with bald affectation. Every limb out straight.

The edges of her wrists jut as she moves them forward in a pseudo-sensuous motion, standing by the bathrooms in a bar that's just about to close, someone with a horrible goatee and neck-fat and too-thin glasses just beginning to look away from her, her smile out-sized like I haven't been allowed to see, her pupils a little too big.

She gathers her sister's hair carefully into a pony-tail behind her head. They look alike, her sister younger, more exhausted, as if Nicky had been drained of all color.

The pictures with her son were easier. They were impenetrable; they made sense.

After a time, I couldn't look at pictures anymore. I couldn't remember what she smelled like, I tried to place it but all I could gather was lingering traces of human. But I'd touched her, I'd kissed her, and she had, briefly, kissed the inside of my wrists and placed her face in the curve between my neck and right shoulder, allowed it to rest there. I wanted to be sick.

Nicky had lifted herself, legs briefly churning, ass-first onto the blank balustrade, and the ramble of the park broke out beneath her, a people-less vista. A choked frozen stream snaked through its guts, as unhued and cracked as the sky above it. We had been unable to speak for some time. There was wind.

"I told him about my skeletons because that's what you do when you love someone."

"And then?"

She made a movement of her hand that could have resembled anything.

I told her I didn't believe in skeletons. I told her I thought the whole idea of revelation was insane. She said that only a lapsed Catholic would say that, and he was a lapsed Catholic too, that was his thing, that was it.

I told her I didn't care about sin.

She told me two things then stared at me as if willing me to hit her.

I was close enough where I could lean in without thinking about it and kiss her where her cheek met the edge of her right eye, her glasses pushed up onto her head. Something in the center of her chest shook violently and briefly, and she said "Oh," as if she had forgotten something relatively unimportant.

She'd written to me, and I back to her, and she'd responded, and I'd responded, and she'd sent a long, nonlinear thing, and I'd replied with a brief note, and she wrote back, *I don't know what to expect from you. I never know what you're going to do next.* I didn't know how to respond to that, and told her, then waited for some time. Nothing came. I didn't fill the space. My life was static, unbent; I only had questions for her. *How is Michael at school? Did you make it to Dorset? Have you read what I sent you?* I sent none of them. I checked my email every five minutes, then refused to even boot up the computer for a day and a half, then forced myself to check only twice a day, the rest of the time thinking only of her words that might be settling there, under her name, under my name. I wouldn't, of course, write to her again without a response.

She wrote me after five and a half weeks to tell me she'd heard back from The New School.

I took a hotel room not too far off from campus. She was teaching class the first day and invited me to sit in. I was uncomfortable with the idea and begged off, citing jetlag. Instead, I went to the Tate Modern. A friend had told me that Schiele's final painting was on loan there, the figures supposedly just as awkwardly pornographic as before, but with the possibility of tenderness now existing between them. I couldn't find it.

We had a curry for dinner; she talked a lot about the restaurant and her history with it. There was a miniature waterfall in the bathroom, complimented by birdsong; the waiters spoke Urdu and smoked outside furiously. She'd brought her sister there; Michael loved the poppadoms. I asked if I could meet him. "He's with his father this weekend. Besides, what would I say? Here's my friend, here's this guy I met in New York City? No, that wouldn't work. It wouldn't work at all." I asked her if she wanted to get a beer after; she said she was tired, that the class had taken a lot out of her, or maybe it was the heavy food. "I don't drink much here, anyway, and when I do, it's wine. I was on vacation when I met you. That was different."

My head on her lap, she traced the contours of my cheeks. Tom Waits was on low, one of his more distant, sardonic tracks. Her three rooms were completely foreign to me. I couldn't remember any of the mapping I'd done, and nothing I saw jogged my memory. Her warmless hand drifted down the length of my torso to my thigh, then traced without touching the length of my cock, coming to rest, palm open and splayed, just above my knee. I looked up and she was smiling blankly, staring at something that I couldn't see. I brushed her hand away and sat up, twisted 180 on my knees, and pushed her shoulders slowly back so that her upper back rested on the edge of the couch. I kissed her harshly, and she kissed me back until we both couldn't breathe, and by then I had her jeans undone and my hand in her, and when I brought my head back, she looked up at me, her smile somehow intact and said, "It's you."

WASPS/SPIDERS

I don't remember meeting Fareen Ali. She's there in memories like camera-phone captures: bleary and dragged through light, at the end of some undersea lit hallway, holding Osiris or Qu'Shawn's hand, her face smiling and averted, subMadonna. We were from the same university, supported on the same TA-system, and so "Ms. Fareen" was a phrase I heard every day, unquestioned, until it became simple and obvious who she was. I don't remember the initial handshake or the brief parlay of where who what. I don't remember walking to the Q train with her for the first time. I kept a neon orange seat between us, and she said my name the way the children said it, but drawing it out and licking up the side of its face. We were going under the Hudson, and outside of us was the tunnel like the skeleton of a man made out of fluorescence and night, and it shook us like re-entry, the fingernail screams of the machinery barely background. "Sit next to me," Fareen said. "I won't hurt you." I noticed as she lifted her arm that she did not shave. It was early October 2001, but summer had not ended, and she smelled raw and root-vegetable, like she would never die. A long left strip of stringer's hell: brown and rust with sharp shocks of green and tattered, leaking streamers of yellow coupled with the omnipresent open mouth of a mourner, his beard becoming full, losing its black. Lead: "Karachi." "Attack." "Civilians." Eyes flit down the page: "late of New Jersey," and there in the Helvetica, so bizarrely formal, so ancient, is her name.

Reload: the screen's a cataract, the single, simple color of waiting. The beetle-segmented loading icon gyres, and my wrist and finger are already opening the next tab when the page front-loads. The article is unchanged. The *Post*, *Guardian*, *BBC*, *Dawn News*, all report the same. Only the *Times* and *Dawn News* have her name; *Dawn* has, as you would imagine, an obituary.

Without even noticing, I've pulled up her wall. Her profile picture is thin and twisted, arms folding in on themselves, weirdly stiff, dressed in a green-black swirling one-piece. Her short ragged haircut and the slightest touch of dark makeup accentuate her closed eyes. I scroll down; activity is pretty sparse. A few links to her work on *Dawn News*. Occasional op-ed pieces from the *New Left* or *The Nation*. Cryptic in-jokes from a guy named Asim, sentimental B-sides of poetry from her sister. I scroll back up to look at the picture. She smiles warmly, close-mouthed, looking like someone I never knew.

I close the computer, the screen touching the keyboard. The light briefly blinks out. I straighten up my spine, push the white shell away from my ankles. Out my wall-size window: the side curve of the onion dome, a pigeon briefly in free-fall. No clouds in the sky, no blue, just a graying construct, like we all have the same app that reduces everything to the same no-color.

WTC '93 needs detail, so I come to the last stop on N-R before Manhattan. Not quite raining, something else. Spring wind on my neck. It's all basement apartments out here; it's all overpass. Dark, and you can't see the city. I stand in a slick, slim alley where a young Bangladeshi man is attempting to park a cube of a U-Haul truck again and again, sickeningly overproduced music leaking from the cab. He does not seem anxious; he taps finger and wrist-bones on the dash out of time. In front of me: beat van, bright bile yellow; droplets collect on its side, cling there, refuse to slide down its hulk. Panel van: Ford E-350. On February 26th, 1993, Ramzi Yousef and Eyad Ismoil drove one just like it into the underground parking garage of the World Trade Center. Five years later, Timothy McVeigh parked the same kind, carrying roughly the same weight (1,500 pounds, plus human and candy bars or whatever), underneath the Alfred P. Murrah Federal Building's childcare center.

I can't see it.

Strip off soaked clothes. Scotch and soda. The room is tenement sloped, like the interior of a trepanned skull. Light a cigarette, move among the data, the physical stuff in clumps on the raw rust-carpet, sagging the bookshelves, covering my "desk", i.e. the breakfast nook, and the kitchen counter, bone-dry for months now. Books (Lance and Davis and Reeve and Coll), government reports (Port Authority Police, FBI, NYPD), architectural schematics (Yamasaki, the WTC's architect; a glimpse of the "bathtub" retaining wall), transcripts of conversations with the blind sheik, with Yousef, two dozen links of eye-witness testimony available on the internet.

"...a physical expression of the universal effort of men to seek and achieve world peace."

I take the a/G out; it looks like a spider, if all spiders were dull-white and designed by institutionalized schizophrenics. The idea is, roughly, this: I imagine the experience, and the a/G sucks it in, stores it. It's uploaded to the server, where the Motherfucker sells it for a hefty price. It's a luxury item, but then we're a luxury-item culture. Most everybody works in broad fantasy, unsurprisingly the most popular genre, but I've cornered a sick, strange little market comprised of people who are interested, primarily, in experiencing the trauma generated by terrorist attacks.

I stroke the spider, and it responds by crawling up my chest, curving around my neck (nice and cold.) They couldn't make it sexy, so they made it deeply disturbing. The idea is that humans can get used to anything. The mating-action with my spinal cord is brief and almost painless. A maggot whisper-walks across the interior of my skull; they say the brain is numb.

Things don't slip so much as congeal.

Minoru Yamasaki:

Yellowboy in the corner of the shop. Two whiteboys twisting cigarettes straight, eyeing you almost tenderly with their young orbs, blue and white and red. American Caramel in hands: Senators and Indians. Stay there. Spine aligned with the corner, feel it synch with the building that is nothing but a building, and if you stand with your back to it, then they will simply stare at you, and tell some joke you can barely hear, the last line of it spat loud into now-roiling laughter. Eyes on you now. Look away. Hold the card. Look at that card. They won't see you.

Let go.

My eyes are open and I'm sitting on my couch. I don't know if I started here; I don't appear to be bleeding, so I probably haven't moved. The a/G (it doesn't have a name, nobody names these things) is nowhere to be seen. It likes to hide under the fridge down by the click-on-click-off. Sometimes I catch it trembling. I find my hands are shaking; I use them to light a cigarette.

I need a start. I don't even have a fucking start.

My head is pounding.

I can't see it.

It takes several days to assemble the narrative of Fareen's death: down by the water, condo, wealthy zone, drone strike. "Surgical." I wonder what that even means. Four dead, at least thirty wounded. They took out a floor of the building. The violence erased from memory by the following day's suicide-belt in a market in Islamabad, the blood-sluicing horror that is Peshawar, the following week's skirmish on the Afghan border. Then: Iraq, Yemen, Iran, our own troubles. The original NYT article was disposable enough anyway. Nothing on offer to illuminate the war that has not ever been a war, a war that has not begun yet and is not over.

We wrote to each other several years ago for the duration of a couple months when neither of us were seeing anyone, and she was thinking of coming back to the States. I look at her words now: "...the idea of a/G is still physically repulsive to me. I do not want something in my spinal fluids. I do not want my imagination fueling some dwarf-fantasy, and then I don't want some stranger living that dwarf-fantasy through my spinal fluids. I don't know how you do it, Si. I have no fucking clue. Anti-genius. The name is so *apt*." She described her forever-larval documentary on trauma victims: "I had not guessed there were so many farmers in this world, and that so many people wanted to hurt them." "It is incomplete. Until I can make the viewer feel the insanity of the moment when the victim's world is broken, anything and everything I do will be incomplete. I cannot understand it myself and it is not until I understand it that I will be able to make anyone else understand it, and I will never understand it until I experience it, and I will never experience it because I am a coward, we are all cowards, because who would ever set out to experience such a thing?" We stopped writing to each other, as people who do not see each others' real faces, who cannot touch each other on the shoulder, will do. I do not know if she discovered how I took her words. How much goddamn money I made out of them.

The Motherfucker is on me. I have no idea what he looks like, what her voice sounds like, but it has the appointment book and cuts the checks, and they are not pleased with me. Thirteen individual appointments for WTC '93, all broken, all rescheduled, all broken. The command: *See it, or get back to providing background narrative for The Tattoo of the Ice-Drum.*

Spider-walk.

South Wall. North Tower. Level B-2.

Yousef with the four vials of nitro on his lap; Ismoil parking. Last-minute checks, priming the four boxes, cardboard, urea nitrate and fuel oil, bound with scrap paper. Lining that: tanks of compressed hydrogen. Four twenty-foot long fuses. A single 1,000-pound charge.

12:17:37 p.m. February 26, 1993

Four levels of concrete up, seven stories deep. Shearing through: electrical wires, concrete, glass, asbestos, stone, soil, foliage, flesh, plastic, wood, skin.

"It felt like an airplane hit the building."

A pillar of white smoke going up 93 stories of stairway like an offering diverted.

Brokers and lawyers and maintenance workers bash windows, covered in soot, them and the windows both, they gasp and gasp and gasp and put their hands to their throats and look down 34 29 94 24 floors, they look down at the ground in a way they have never looked down at the ground they look down at the ground in way they have never looked down at the ground before

Those in Emergency Stairwell A know they are trapped. Behind them, the doors have locked automatically; the smoke is building fast, blackening them at their eyes and mouths. Emergency lighting casts no shadow, and the PA system is not working. Climbing twenty floors down. Climbing another fifty floors down. There are 25,000 people in the building. You can feel them around you, you can feel their human flesh, their

fingers in your hair

and her hand goes

sliding down my face

Ican't see it. I can only see one thing. I write the Motherfucker, sit at the terminal and wait. The Motherfucker writes back in sixteen minutes: *Do it, and I will sell the living shit out of it.*

Information is limited, of course, on the ordinance used. History might reveal these things, or it might cover them like a death-shroud. It doesn't matter. No one knows what breed of horse stood calmly in front of Buda's wagon adjacent to the Corner, Wall Street '20, but we can still scream with the downed beast, admire the gray fog rising. MQ-9, Hellfire, Predator, GBU-38 JDAM; we know their names, so they must be antiques. The authorities have not even released the name of the intended target, though they maintain he was "very highly placed in Al-Qaeda", but that to reveal his identity would compromise further efforts directed against him. But give us this much, Fareen, there was a target.

Merriam-Webster: "The male of a bee (as the honeybee) that has no sting and gathers no honey."

Pashtuns call them machays, which means "wasps".

There is only one picture in which she looks like herself.

In it, she sits with her back to the wall of a small hut. She is swathed in white, surrounded by other women, ages varying, similarly garbed. The stock isn't good, but you can make out intricate patterns in some cloth. The women look at the camera; one smiles, cheeks swelling like a girl I knew in the third grade who was unselfconscious and charmless. Fareen looks to the left, unaware, eyes wide and white and black-dolloped in the middle. There is a cut of a smile in her face that is not a smile; it is something I saw on her face once when I came into teacher's lounge when she had just hung up the phone. I did not know what she had been talking about, and I did not know what she was thinking about. There was no way for me to know. The other pictures in her album, no matter how they reproduce recognizable Fareen reliefs (camera operator, junkie, drunken smiler, cut-rate student model), show someone twiggy, feminine, assured, affected. Not her.

The Motherfucker writes: *No one cares about WTC '93 anymore. All they want is Karachi '11.*

"It seems that they really want to kill everyone..."

Spider-walk.

Florida. Out the window: mobile homes, swamp land, endless loops of concrete, mini-malls, the heat of the day smearing the glass. Clouds truck from the sea, ride across the land like a fantasy gif. The road is smooth, and you have your music on. You are eating your breakfast sandwich. There is more coffee in the tall building. You punch up your terminal. There are hellos to say, as everyone settles to their work. In Pakistan, it is now 6:32 PM. Pay attention. Narrow your vision. The screen shows you live: blue, long and narrow, and focused. Camera-eye: you hang suspended, silent (they say they can hear you buzzing when the wind is right; they are lying.) Indulge momentarily in the only poet you give a damn about (Irish, of course; we have culture/history/literature): "A lonely impulse of delight," does not, after all, have to be so lonely. You are not the predator. You sit there and you wait. When it becomes the time to press the button, you press the button.

The heat comes off the sky, comes off the sea, comes off the glass. You shrug into an American wife-beater, the counter-pane twisted around your left foot, all this way into the kitchen. Light a cigarette and stare at the coffee dripping. Jerk open the sliding door. Look down at the vacant beach: used for military exercises and not much else these days. The sky's empty. You step back into your lair. Remember: needles and knock-out and the smell of yourself, when you still smelled like you instead of this shampooed thing. Lift your wrists to your nostril: smell and smile. An animal knows itself. You flip your screen up, slap some Flaming Lips on, you turn to the coffee, stretching your left arm out to the side, hearing the bones crackle. You think about what you have to do today, and nothing comes to mind. You think you hear something like the stirring of insectoid wings. You turn and you look to the empty sky but you don't see the empty sky all you see is your face in the glass and you have a smile that is not a smile and then the smile

is gone with the glass and

you cannot stand where you stood

so you stand

Pigeon-footed and naked, neck twisted, her profile made incomplete by the slope of her right shoulder allowing me just the dull gleam of a single eye. Despite the dormroom halogen, her skin was burnt; everything about her was burnt. Her spine, broad and mountain-range, was accentuated by her aching posture. I could barely breathe, back on the bed, heart triple-tempo, skin raw. The room smelled of rain and sweat. I waited for her to turn around. When she'd come, there was a little shout, like a dog kicked in the side of the head, followed by the glancing blow of elbow to collarbone. She'd relaxed slowly against me, then drew my hand out of her quickly and inched forward so we were not touching. My mouth tasted of her unwashed teeth and her cigarettes and her cunt. I couldn't understand it; I couldn't understand anything. Now her skull was framed by a boxy window looking on three sides of the tan, twenty-five floor dorm, above a blue empty parallelogram, down on the glass roof of the cafeteria I could never see without also seeing a hunk of flame-spewing metal slamming into it, reaving, everything shattered and immolated, suddenly, irrevocably, and with endless screaming.

THERE IS NO COMTE DE ST. GERMAIN FOR I AM HE

Imagine an endless bar, perhaps a shot in a film, a tracking shot, with the camera slowly moving down an uneven, warped surface of different wood grains tacked together, moving past a constant progression of old drinkers, the kind you see in any boozing establishment anywhere in the world. They are wizard-like in their silence, their questing glances around the room, their reserve towards those they meet, their acknowledgment of each other, their amazing thinness of body and of spirit, and the empty shells of their minds devoted to: this place, this drink, this me, this is all there is, this is all I want. They drink stout they drink grappa they drink whiskey they drink rice wine they smoke hookah they smoke cigarettes they drink small dark coffees they scratch at their thin beards they read the paper they pretend to read the paper they treat the bartenders like their grandchildren, sweet and reserved, thin thin thin, their emotion is thin, it is all gone.

Eighty years? Seventy-five? And it is all gone. You look at them and you say it is the drink? You'd be wrong to think that. But the bar, the bar, let us not forget the bar. So your camera-eye, your well-trained cinematographer in his waking-dream, your lens, is moving us slowly down the palimpsest of dead trees, and we are observing the faces of these thin men, and perhaps some of them are mumbling into each other's ears like old lovers, talking of the horses of the dogs of the news of the bartender's tits or rank breath or maybe even of another ancient patron, absent or finally fucking dead, and some of them, they hold the edges of the bar, standing despite the adjacent stool, they are red in the face, their eyes are shut, they croon softly to themselves, perhaps not so softly, you can tell they are next, ready for that final fucking death. The bartender is nowhere to be seen; what are we to do when this old thin one finally has the heart attack stroke kidney failure syphilitic brain burst that we are imagining, just looking at the poor bastard? Let him flop around on the floor like an orgasmic fish? Watch as his legs kick and skitter across the ground? Do we remain silent in observance of his particular problem, his own particular final fucking death? Or do we laugh, knowing that we're next? I, of course, would not laugh. And so, finally, we come to the end of the bar. It curves around to the side, meets the wall. Perhaps there is a little hatch that can be brought up and down for the bartenders to come in and out. And there rests me, slightly hunched over myself, though not so much as I must be careful with my back, it has lasted me this long and I don't wish to enrage it. I drink seltzer or orange juice and I am quiet and not so thin, though I am not stout, I am tall and I fill my tallness well, though am I not so tall, I walk with a slope forward, I am powerful but you wouldn't know it, shaking my hand. I stand and watch the old men drink, and I watch them do the things that old men have always done; old men have always done the same things. I no longer drink alcohol. I no longer smoke hashish or tobacco. I no longer fuck. It is not that these things exert me. I do not think that exerting myself is bad, I have been known to climb, though that has become boring to me in recent years as I am no longer terrified by it for whatever reason. I have lived at every level of society, I have taken up every profession not barred to me by my life-long aversion to the open sea, I have taught and I have learnt everything there is to know, at least what is not hidden by the haar of time. I have felt every kind of pain; that too has ceased to interest me. You're probably wondering why I'm still dancing around the statement of the obvious. Well then, let me be obvious: I have been alive at least since the invention of agriculture. I do not remember hunting and gathering, but then there is quite a bit that I don't remember that took place at times when I am quite certain I was alive. The sixteenth century for example: not even a blur. Just gone. I don't remember what continent I was born on; there is a significant chance that I am Mediterranean, however, perhaps Egyptian, because my skin darkens under harsh sunlight and grows paler in the North. One would expect, I suppose, that like these old men here, I would live in my memories, forever hanging upon each lost moment as if it had been supremely important, my life now nothing but a hollow shell. But I am not that deluded. Life is now as it ever has been. The world is as it ever has been. Humanity, the same. It has not changed; I have changed. There is one other thing that gives me pleasure, though it may be considered something more of a minor self-imposed task. A hobby perhaps. It is, unlike most hobbies, not born of intellectual curiosity (that died in either 1812 or 1845, I can't remember) or of meaningless obsession or of devotion to aesthetic pleasure. And it is here, in New York City, just off the Brooklyn Bridge, Manhattan side, waiting interminably in the aptly named Bridge Bar, that I have come to indulge myself. Whorehouse, grocery store, pub, now restaurant, the Bridge Bar claims to be the oldest bar in New York City. I suppose older types would sneer at the usual clientele here: they would call them yuppies and tourists. I cannot use these terms; they would be disingenuous. Everyone to me is a yuppie, and I am everywhere a tourist. Now, however, is the post-lunch lull; white light bathes the place. A waitress with dark red hair and a terrifying nose marring an otherwise pleasing visage sits in the corner folding pristine whale bone-white napkins. Another, squat and calm, smokes cheap menthols outside, gazing dumbly at glimpses of automobiles through the slats in the great bridge. The bartender's name is Alexandra; she cleans the martini triangles and whiskey scoops slowly and carefully, dancing her fingers along the gleaming bar to the Spanish-gypsy rattle-tune. I'm her only customer, but she leaves me alone. I've been here lunch-times these last three days, waiting for a man named Lazlo. I have spent, in my roundabout way, more than three years following his movements. He's been around for far longer than that, but there was some business that was pressing most exhaustingly on me, and then I had to take time to recover. There are no photographs of this Lazlo; I wonder at that. Not allowing one to take your picture is the opposite of prudent; it draws far too much attention. From description and gossip and a few bloggers' rants, however, I know what this Lazlo looks like. Short stature, long tangled black hair, grey-white beard, open melony smile, large hands rough with work and nicotine, roving ocean-green eyes, creased face. People revert to mediocre prose-poems when they talk about Lazlo. He sold mescaline in New Mexico in the '50s, he started one of the first organic food shops in San Francisco in the '60s. He's played the tin whistle with the Pogues and made millions running one of the first MMA betting parlors in Brasilia. You walk down the street with him in Amsterdam and politicians want to shake his hand; bums embrace him in Oslo; he has a child in Tokyo, the mother dead in her birth throes. What does he do for money? He does everything for money. What does he do for pleasure? He does everything for pleasure. It is claimed that he is the Comte de St. Germain. Do you know the story of the Comte? I will make it brief. For a very brief period of time in the early 1700s, I convinced myself that I was uniquely suited to being a natural philosopher, as I appeared to be immortal and thought myself far wiser than any other living being. So, for the space of approximately eighty years, I paraded about high society, conducting experiments with potions and elixirs, perfecting the art of being very mysterious, and dispensing wealth from a great store I had set up over the millennia. I never told anyone I was immortal or that I could, pheh, levitate. I was not in France, I was in Austria, and I certainly never met Casanova, though I heard he rather enjoyed being on the receiving end of a good bukkake, though it was called something rather less Japanese at the time. Various bullshit artists and basket cases wove the legend of the inventor/magickian/composer/dandy Comte obviously using me as a base. The most ridiculous kind of lies, propagated by the most bathetic simians. However. One day, at my own hand most probably, I will depart this fetid life, and due to my own rather reticent views towards history and power, the title of the Comte de St. Germain remains the only hint towards anything like my true nature that exists in the collected knowledge of this world. It is my only legacy. As a result, I become extremely irritated when others lay claim to it. Now, this Lazlo has never called himself the Comte de St. Germain; that makes him a special kind of pretender. The ones who give themselves the name, who entrance occultist dime-store novelists and rich post-hippies with flowery titles and nonsensical mumblings are shams easily dispatched with. The kind who veil themselves, create an aura that others give name to, these are the truly dangerous ones. For, if there was a true Comte, he would never tell anyone his true name. This Lazlo tells stories that no mortal man, or at least no man of average life-span, could tell. He's talked to NYU freshman in decrepit Irish bars on Canal Street about the way cannon-mist stung your eyes so fiercely it brought tears at Waterloo. To coked-out gonzo journalists in the back of campaign buses, he's mentioned smoking opium with Tom Paine in Paris, hearing the deluded democrat's teen-dreams of going on the account and seizing ships, bullion, and freedom with the same aplomb. I haven't encountered in almost a hundred years a case as well-known, a man as well-loved, a deception so deeply ingrained. I will actually enjoy killing him, I think. Why? you ask. Why don't I believe that there could be another like me? Why can't this Lazlo be the true Comte? Do I think I'm the spawn of angels? A trained dog of demons? Am I Cain, wandering forever East? Oh come the fuck off it. I'm alive because I haven't learned how to die. Why else? Lazlo is a man of passions. Extraordinary passions. His wife Lucinda drowned in the Ganges in the early 1970s; he wept bitterly at her funeral, keened actually. Went into seclusion in a small cabin in the Appalachians for almost a year. He's taken a new wife since then, a Filipino poetess, actually; the Japanese girl was a mistress. He's currently a baptized Roman Catholic, converted in '98; he attends church twice a week, no matter where his business takes him. And businesses. He's on the boards of several flailing internet start-ups, he always maintains a restaurant of some kind (right now: Japanese-inspired nouveau-American noodle shops in Cleveland), and he occasionally DJs in the lower-rent Johannesburg night-clubs. The man described by his associates, by my informants, by the authorities, is a man of outstanding energy, a man who takes a special joy in life. How do I know that he is not the Comte? Take a fucking guess. I know what it is like to live for four centuries. There is no joy left. There is no love left. I'd understand a decade-long heroin addiction. I'd understand a disciplined athlete. I'd understand a serial rapist. That long alive, one descends into the most primal pleasures, pleasures that one's moral code has told one to ignore. One tests oneself against the world, against one's physical nature. It is some time indeed before all that dies out, granted. Thousands of years. But joy, joy has no place in a life even *that* long-lived. I know. I am sure. So I drink my seltzer and bathe in the white light, tending my possibilities, waiting for this Lazlo. This is a well-known haunt of his, and I have patience. I order a salad with cheese and walnuts and balsamic vinaigrette. The after-work crowd arrive. I watch them and lose myself for a small time. Not in their movements or speech. Those hold no interest for me anymore. No, I lose myself in memory. Or rather, in the sheer act of memory. I remember shapes, like colors in dreams. I remember hair, tousled raven black hair. I remember the smell of the sea, which one? Just glimpses. They are enough for me. "Another?" Alexandra asks. I raise my eyebrows. I must have been further away than I realized; it's the first word she's said all day to me. I nod; she brings it, I tip. What a fucking meaningless exchange. I drink half the seltzer up, and she titters. "Thirsty?" she says. "No," I say far too coldly, and one of her eyebrows droops. She waits for my joke, but I have none, and so she backs off, walks down to the far end. A young man with an over-developed black beard and dangling rat-tail is taking off his watch, getting ready for the shift. She nudges him, and I look away. She's telling him to serve me from now on. The quiet guy with a lot to say down there is getting a little much. So this little shit'll do his bravado on me, try and get me pissed off, out of here. I bite my lower lip, turn my face away, brow burning, thinking I must leave, leave and not come back. They know me now; I'm not just the pathetic old man with time to kill who's a bit off. I'm a creep, and they'll remember me. No good when you're about to commit a murder. I finish the seltzer and turn to the door, and standing just a pace away from me is a stubby-small man with wild tangly coal-black hair, a white beard, and glinting green eyes, his mouth slightly open like he's post-orgasm. I squint. He sees me he knows me there's no possible fucking way he knows me I know him there's no possible fucking way I know him. Lazlo, and surely it must be, bird-cocks his head down then draws it up with the strength of his whole body. His smile splits like a brick in the face. "Well," he says, extending his hand with such warmth and assurance and gentlemanly calm, and I am thinking surely I met this man last year surely I met this man five years ago surely ten surely twenty he's aged hasn't he he's aged, this is not not not what he looked like when we last met. "The oldest bar in New York City," he says, giving my hand a light squeeze, which I return in kind. "That's what they call irony, isn't it?" He narrows his eyes, comically. "When was it, exactly?" And just hearing him say that, I remember. A cafe in Catalonia. Early nineteenth century. We talked about the Agraviados, we played dice; he lost. Short of money, he tried to give me his woman for the night, though she didn't seem too pleased about it. When I wouldn't accept, my own copulatory needs having become extremely precise by this point, he proceeded to tell my future, tracing tributaries on my palm. He made up such utter nonsense: I would marry a rich ex-beggar with the keys to the secret gold reserves of Carlos V; I would eat of roots that had been crushed in Babba Yaga's mortar and I would be made so sexually potent that any woman who lay with me would explode. The man was a masterful storyteller; he wove such intricacies around me that I allowed his debt to disappear, not my usual M.O. He was called something excessively Spanish then, Beto or Lencho. But none of these was his true name. He shrugs now, curling out a lower lip. "Doesn't matter, does it?" His voice is tinged with old-world grime but is sharp as a butcher's knife. He turns his eyes back to mine. "I see you're speechless. Me too, well, hell, I mean I should be. This has never happened to me before. I mean, I've assumed there were others out there. But... But hell, sorry, I do this when I'm caught unawares." He spirals his hands around like a pair of wafting doves. "Talk and talk and talk. But you remember. I told stories then. Whenever it was, whatever they were about." His gaze rests on my collar and stays there for a moment, as vacant as his smile. "I've given that up long ago, of course." He gives another small shrug and looks back up to me. "And you? Did you come here to meet me? It's well known that I love this bar." He holds up a finger to Alexandra, who grins large at him, begins making a Manhattan. "This city." He sucks his lower lip. "It makes me forget, it makes me remember. I can't get away from this fucking city." He says it with so much gusto, so much vigor, I almost physically back away from him. Alexandra brings the whiskey and bitters over and he takes a first bracing sip of it, makes a guttural sound of slurping joy. Alexandra is so taken with the small man's spirit that she smiles at me, even after the recent outburst. "No more for me," I say, forcing a weak smile, then look back down to Lazlo, Beto, whatever his name is. "You won't have a drink?" he asks, shock running through his face like it might run through the visage of an infant left abandoned. I shake my head. "Liver," I say, my voice a hasty croak. He nods sagely. "So," he says, "you did not come here to meet me. A coincidence then." He smiles sweetbread. "This city, my friend. It is like the world in miniature. There are always surprises. Certainly not all as pleasant as this one, but..." His hands spiral up again, and I am seized with a moment of heavy nausea. I clutch the bar with one hand, wince forward. His fingers meet my shoulder, support me for the briefest of moments. I recoil, lean heavily against the wooden wall, panting, staring down at my shoes. I must get out. At all costs I must get out. "Are you alright?" says the old man. "Here, let me get a stool." Though I still feel weak and spindly, I hold up a hand, steady myself with the other. "No," I say. "Medication. You understand." He nods. "I must leave," I say through a sick small smile. "Tomorrow though? We will meet here tomorrow and you will tell me stories?" Lazlo nods slowly, joy beaming from his small, broken face. "Yes," he says. "A thousand times yes! But you are still ill. Shall I hail you a cab?" I shake my head no, but he insists on helping me to the door. I can feel the intense thrill of him through my car-coat sleeve. A compatriot. A comrade. A contemporary. He pats me on the shoulder. "Tomorrow," he says, as I slip headlong away from him into the evening shade. "Not such a long time, eh?" He turns and totters back into the bar, sucking up the last of his brown drink. I rush across a street revealed as empty by a defaced dull coin of a moon. There is a small collection of cars underneath the bridge. I duck behind a red Toyota, breathing heavily. Slouch to the ground, clutching my roiling, acidic stomach. My eyes go white; I see the top of my head. My heart is beating with the slam of wheels on the boards above me. My head is moving with the crash of the equinox wind. My fingers dance along my ribs, nuzzling at armpits. I am surely going insane. I slouch down further, shoulder to the ground, staring up above me at the undercarriage of the bridge, split by light, wracked by sound, and for some long time, as the dark deepens and the voices of the whoevers spill as one, I am nothing more than a human being, breathing and clutching myself, my mind poisoned by the terrible unreality of what has occurred. But soon, or perhaps not so soon, I begin to sit up. I close my eyes. I straighten my spine. I breathe normally once more. The very last thing: my hands relax, no longer claws. I open my eyes and stand. I look to the Bridge Bar. Packed now. Feasters. Fuckers. All of them. The world in Manhattan and Manhattan in a bar. I want to go in. Even if he's not there. Even if he's gone. I want to go in and be among them, even if I am not one of them, even if I can never hope to be. How can he still be one of them? How can he still be engaged? How can he still be happy? How can he still feel pain and joy and suffering and take lovers? Could I possibly have been wrong? There are so many questions I need to ask him. I must go in. I must find him. I must. But I do not. I stand rooted to the spot. The cars pass above my head. The drinkers inside carry on. Smokers stand on the edge of the sidewalk, chatting into cell phones. The world is the same as it had been before. As it has always been. I am the same. This is no trick. The man before me hours ago was the same man before me hundreds of years ago. And it is no trick that he is joyful. I have seen enough human-animals to recognize a forced or false emotion. But these things change nothing. I breathe. Time passes. He exits after some time. Weaving a little. A finger in the air, delineating one last point for a pair of friends. Two blonde-haired young things. Woman and man. He embraces the man heartily. Kisses the woman on the cheek. They call, "Lazlo, Lazlo." That is not his true name; I knew his true name once. He turns from them, reeling off down the street. His smile is that a drunken pedophile, of a sainted virgin pierced by scimitars and ungainly verbs, of some chubby child, indolent in the crib, wet and wicked and ready for a lifetime. I cross the street, my hand moving beneath my car coat, seeking the name, seeking the handle of my knife.

THE LOA AND THE GAPING JAW

The ship is just far enough offshore that its occupants cannot be seen. It is a holding of one of those mammoth cruise lines that make their annual winter pilgrimages down from the Northeast, carrying loads of the comfortable, aging middle-class of America. If you believe what people say, there are others just like it littering the entirety of the Haitian coast: oil tankers, cargo ships, UN transport vessels, fishing crafts far adrift from their home ports. Boyer, who swam half-way out, says there is another one past it, just beyond the horizon: a massive, rusted container ship resting there in the Golfe de le Gonave. It is amazing, Simone thinks, that none of them have run aground on an island as large as ours, that a people as populous as ours should be, so far, safe. After all, it has been over a week. What she has gleaned from CNN and the BBC likens the plague to a brushfire, crossing miles quickly and carelessly. The island of Hispaniola has avoided the first wave, and, odder still, it appears to be alone in that distinction. Still, she supposes, it is only a matter of time. The ship is just far enough offshore that its occupants cannot be seen, but in the quiet of the evening, over the gentle lapping of the waves, they can be heard.

"It is not the same thing," says Dupont, playing idly with a small lizard that has run up his leg to his bare knee.

Boyer merely blinks.

"It will not help you." Dupont carefully removes the lizard from his knee and places it on the sand.

Simone leans slightly in. "Monsieur Dupont. Please."

Dupont regards Simone for the breadth of a breeze playing with her hair. "It was time for the midday meal. I found myself listless. Not hungry. Upon setting back to work in the fields, I found it difficult to breathe. I became exhausted. I was a strong man, almost never sick, back then." Dupont gives a little smile, his eyes tracing the ground before him. "Because of my pride I kept working until I collapsed. They took me inside my sister's hut, where I lay, unable to speak. Many thought it was fever, until a man who had been to Port-au-Prince said he was sure it was AIDS. After that, the hut emptied out except for my sister and her husband. I soon found myself completely paralyzed. I was there when they pronounced me dead. I do not remember the funeral. I do not remember receiving this scar." Dupont points to the large, hairless gash running from the edge of his right eye down the side of his skull. "A gift from one of the coffin's nails. When I woke, I was already buried, and I was floating above my grave. The bokor had called my soul. They dug me up, beat and bound me. They marched me to a large plantation near Saint-Claire, which is a tiny village near Hinche, almost to the border. There I worked for nothing every day for almost three years. We tilled the fields; we fixed the grounds. We were fed once a day. Everything was squashed and dream-like. I did not know my name. I could not speak. I could not make choices. I do not know why, but after the first five years, the bokor became more vicious. He beat us more often and more violently. During one of these beatings, one of my fellows snapped and ran the bokor through with a broken tree branch. We were all shocked. With the bokor dead, his power passed from us, and we were free. I wandered, mostly around the North, until I spoke with the American who took my story." He gives Simone a small smile, then looks around for the lizard, which is nowhere to be seen.

"Why didn't you go home?" asks Simone.

Dupont looks slowly up the rise of the sand bank to where the village of his birth lies. "It was my brother who sold me to the bokor. We were having a dispute over my land. I was too afraid to return."

"And now?" asks Boyer in his brusque Yankee's Creole. The words are the first he has spoken in almost an hour. His hands are cupped before him.

Dupont shrugs. "He is dead."

"You were dead too," says Boyer.

Dupont's eyes are murky like the waters of a fetid well. "It is not the same thing," he says. "It will not help you."

Boyer looks to Simone, and she stands, brushing the sand off her black jeans. "Thank you, monsieur, for your help. I regret if we caused you any discomfort."

Dupont nods. "Mademoiselle."

Boyer stands, uncupping his hands, and tosses the small lizard to Dupont, who catches it.

The children watch Simone. She is barely seventeen, dressed in a white t-shirt; she braids her hair into a simple plait as she walks. She could neither be a tourist, nor a villager, nor an authority from Port-au-Prince. She moves regally, and one young boy is reminded by her stride of the houngan. She and Boyer find a bit of shade in the shadow of a hut whose occupant sells them a bottle of rum. Boyer, switching to his Parisian French, asks her what she thinks.

"He was nothing like the ones I saw," Simone says, nestling against the thatch wall. "Physically, of course, they all looked as different as mankind can come. But they staggered, poorly coordinated, their faces palsied and fierce. Monsieur Dupont was all simplicity and slowness, but he was deliberate. Though their limbs were too atrophied to bear their intentions, they were all haste."

Boyer lights a cigarette and allows his eyes to wander around the immense, empty sky, pointless point to pointless point. He is white, the only white for fifty miles in any direction probably. He is dressed in khaki pants and a muddied white t-shirt with a torn and twisted plaid collared shirt thrown over it. With his weathered backpack and eight-day beard, he could be easily mistaken for a visiting professor, perhaps an anthropologist or a ethnobotanist, but for his economical motions and dead, blank eyes.

Simone breaks him out of his reverie by flicking her fingers at him. He extends the pack to her, and she smiles, taking a cigarette.

"Do you believe in voudoun?" Boyer asks, as he lights her cigarette.

"I serve the loa," Simone replies before sucking the smoke down into her lungs.

"But you are a Catholic, no?"

Simone smiles again. It is dangerous how innocent and expensive she appears when smiling, Boyer thinks. It is the smile of a girl who, until very recently, attended one of the most expensive boarding schools in the English-speaking world, who discussed international affairs with ministers of state over tea at LSE, and who would come home to her father's ceremonies to let the loa mount her. There she would frenzy: dance like one seizures, eat glass, and walk on fire. Yet it was still the smile of a young girl enjoying an illicit cigarette.

"There is a saying amongst my father's circles in Port-au-Prince," she says, allowing herself only the slightest flinch when she says the word 'father,' "Haiti might be eighty percent Catholic, but it is one hundred and ten percent voudoun. You have seen me dance. Why would you ask me such a question?"

"I was married for six years," Boyer says, "and twice weekly my wife and I would rise early and make the hour-and-ten minute drive to the church. The ceremony was Russian Orthodox, two-and-a-half hours long at its most succinct. We stood the entire time."

"And you could not understand Russian."

"Oh no," Boyer says. "I speak Russian fine. But I did not believe a word of the Russian I heard. I went through the motions, as we Americans like to say, but I did not believe. Love, especially familial love, can make one do things that might otherwise be considered insane."

Simone holds his gaze for a moment, still smiling, smoke leaking from her nostrils. "I only saw them once, in London," she says. "Briefly, while in the helicopter. Hundreds of them were on one block. Several were eating. There was no method: for walking, for trafficking themselves, for feasting. They had no direction. They could not have been under the power of any bokor."

"So you believe," Boyer says, slowly grinding out his cigarette in the dirt, "that there are no similarities between the zombis of the voudoun and the things that wait," he says with a nod of his forehead, "not half a mile to our west?"

Simone draws her knees up to her chest. "I believe neither are alive."

They sit in silence. Simone's cigarette burns down to the filter, and they watch the ember die.

They move south. Simone insists on driving the ancient jeep, and she speeds over the humps and gouges in the road with a silly grin. They pass from the lush valleys where several lakous rest into the arid man-made desert that is most of the island. "I tried to talk to some of the villagers while you were off getting rum," Simone says, holding out her hand for the bottle.

"Yeah." Boyer answers her without taking his eyes off the sky, his hands still clasped around the rum.

"They wouldn't talk to me," Simone says, yanking the bottle out of Boyer's hands. "They called me a mulatto."

"You're a mulatto?" Boyer says, still not looking at her.

Simone shakes her head. "No. They meant... socially."

Boyer slowly turns to look at her. He is wearing thick, heavy sunglasses, the kind that went out of style in the states about twenty years ago; Port-au-Prince's market had been full of them.

"They wouldn't talk to me," Simone says, throwing the bottle back and slurping a long drab of deep black rum. "But I can almost guarantee you what happened. Dupont said he had a dispute with his brother over land. This was in... 1981, right? Haiti was still governed under the Napoleonic code. When the father dies, the land is split evenly between the brothers. I would wager that the 'dispute' in question was Dupont holding back on his brother." She swerves to avoid a dead dog.

"He admitted as much," Boyer says, keeping his eyes on the dog's corpse as they accelerate away from it.

"No." Simone shakes her head. "He didn't tell you why. All the stories I've heard of zombification, whether from my father, my grandmother or the local gossip, have all had one thing in common. All those changed into zombis have been, if not criminals, then in some way social outcasts. Thieves, bastards, bitches. People the community has wished to rid itself of."

Boyer braces himself between the seats as the jeep takes a jump; he watches Simone ride easy with it, barely moving an inch.

"Sorry," Simone says. "Another dog. Remember the TonTon Macoutes? They were widely believed to be zombis, and they wore their famed dark glasses to accentuate the sense of the inhuman. Duvalier was the biggest bokor of them all. In Port-au-Prince, in Saint-Marc, there might be police, there might be armed guards. But this is the true government of Haiti."

"You're saying this was an attempt at justice," says Boyer, lighting her a cigarette.

"Attempt? No. It was authentic justice."

Boyer furrows his brow and takes the bottle away from her.

Simone, her eyes on the road ahead, tsks. "Reserve your first-world bullshit," she says. "Does any man deserve to have his name taken from him? To be buried alive and turned into a slave? I don't know. Does any man deserve to waste away in prison or be injected with sodium thiopental? I don't know that either. Voudoun is order. For all that it is worth."

"And the plague," says Boyer, playing idly with his lighter, "that's come to the rest of the world. That is anarchy?"

"Yes," says Simone.

"Then why are you here?"

Simone doesn't take her eyes off the road. "My father is dead."

Boyer looks up to the sky. After a long time, he says, "You don't have to come. I understand the situation well enough now. I doubt I'll need much more aid."

"You think all this will really help?" Simone says. She titters slightly. "Some kind of cure?"

Boyer's fingers trace the curve of the bottle's lip. "You don't have to come."

Simone swerves the jeep again. She does not look to the side of the road. "Where else would I go?"

The branches of the trees along the roadside scrape the windshield of the jeep like hands.

Near Saint-Marc, a collection of two dozen villas command a high mountain. Tucked into the bush, Boyer spends almost half an hour with his clothing, toiletries, and hair gel. When he is finished, his beard is gone and his cheeks are flush with a ruddy youth Simone's not expecting. He puts on a well-tailored, though fairly rumpled, suit. He takes a slug of rum, then offers the bottle to Simone, who accepts. They set out towards the villas, just a blanc out for a midnight stroll and to fuck with the local village meat.

It is a tense, quiet walk in the dark towards the flood-lit fifty-foot radius around the villas, a proper killing zone. When they step across into the light, Boyer slips his arm around Simone and pulls her close to him, smiling sickly and pretending to whisper deep fuck-talk into her ear. As they pass the first couple of villas, a few guards snicker.

Boyer keeps his hand underneath Simone's dress; she feels it cold, clenched, and hard. Though Simone imagined this part of the charade would be the easiest for him, there is fierce color in Boyer's cheeks, making him look boyish and shameful.

To distract Boyer from himself, she says, "Baron Samedi is the loa of the graveyard, not to mention fertility. He is usually portrayed as a wizened old man, decked out in a top-hat, tuxedo and dark glasses, clenching a cigar in his gleaming smile. His face is always white; often his head is a skull. He is a fierce and boisterous trickster spirit, constantly amused by man's preoccupation with rutting and dying. I don't know if I can convey how insulting it is that a man has taken his name."

Boyer says nothing, clumsily lighting a cigarette.

"My father had little to do with this human Samedi, other than the occasional exchange of harsh words. My father might well have been considered a bokor by many in Port-au-Prince, but he was not. He was a houngan who had to straddle polite, Westernized society, and the beliefs of his people. If there are those that considered him to be a self-promoter and cheap mystic, I don't mind, they can go fuck themselves. But this phony Samedi is everything my father was not," Simone says, spitting the words. "A bad imitation of a black magician. A bokor with no people and a political agenda. I do not rightly know if he has any true power."

"He has," says Boyer, his voice a child's whisper.

Simone does not ask him how he knows.

The villa before them is slight, compared to the three they passed and the others before them. It is built into the rock of the mountain, and its architecture is clearly patterned after a peasant hut: fine wood cut to look like daub and thatch walls. Boyer stalks around the house, then spends twenty seconds with a lockpick, and the door is open.

The first room is a kitchen, small, tidy and smelling distinctly of bleach. They walk through a small hanging curtain into a larger living room, thickly carpeted.

This Baron is not like his namesake. He is tall, thin, and balding, with a long face. He wears kente cloth loosely around his frame, and he sips a small cup of coffee. He looks to them when they enter and opens his mouth. Boyer draws a stubby silenced pistol from the folds of his rumpled suit and shoots the Baron once in the head and once in the right lung. As the tall man collapses, Boyer strides to him, drawing a ten inch Bowie knife from his belt. He kneels to the twitching body and drives the knife into the Baron's heart. The Baron's head jerks up, the strain showing the outlines of his skull, making him, finally, resemble his patron loa. Boyer jerks the knife out of the Baron and in the same fluid motion, severs the man's head from his body. The head rolls lazily across the carpet, until the heavy shag stops its momentum. Boyer stands up, his young face and nice suit saturated with blood. Boyer looks from the body up to her, as if he'd just remembered she was there. "I apologize," he says, thickly.

Simone has both her hands around her throat. She makes a short, cut-off noise.

Boyer gingerly steps away from the blood, taking off his suit jacket. "Simone. I want you to consider something. Your island is the poorest place in the Western Hemisphere. It has been enslaved, pillaged, and raped by Spain, France, America, England, and Germany since its so-called discovery."

"I am aware," says Simone, her throat crackling and her face slack, "of my history, yes."

Boyer strips off the disposable plastic gloves Simone had not seen him put on. "You are aware, then, that the process of zombification directly resembles what happens to a slave: the loss of identity, being owned, the forced labor. Some anthropologists see a direct psychological link between Haiti's colonial history and the zombi-phenomenon." He kicks off his soaked shoes.

"Horseshit," Simone says in her best English.

"Yes, well, probably." Boyer rips his tie off and tosses it on top of the Baron's chest. "And you are also aware that Hispaniola is the only major landmass in the Western Hemisphere, and perhaps, who knows, the whole world, that is not stricken with this plague of zombis?" Boyer takes off his white collared shirt, rorschached with blood, and tosses it at his feet, leaving an unbesmirched t-shirt underneath.

"You didn't come here for a cure," Simone says.

Boyer shakes his head, taking his pants off carefully, so as to not get blood on his hands. He wears shorts underneath. He steps onto the couch then climbs over it so that he is only a foot away from Simone. She flinches back. "I didn't come here for a cure, no. Nor did I come here to figure out a way to stop these marauding things. What their 'secret weakness' is." He laughs lightly. "Why bother? All of North America is gone. Most of South America as well. Europe, Russia, and China didn't look so great last transmission I saw. What would a cure do? Who would it save?"

"Us."

Boyer shrugs. "Perhaps. But the plague isn't coming here."

"It is not the same thing."

"But it is."

Simone looks into Boyer's eyes, and they are alive and alight for the first time she has ever seen. "This is Haiti's vengeance," he says.

"And you are America's vengeance."

He nods once, slightly. "I will find the houngan, the bokors, anyone powerful enough to have crafted this. And I will kill them."

Simone wraps her arms around her stomach and squeezes.

"I'm sorry you had to see this. But I needed you."

She shakes her head, but Boyer is concentrating on his next cigarette. "Thank you," he says. "You helped me understand everything so much better."

"You understand nothing." Her gaze drifts to the ground. "Absolutely nothing."

Boyer slowly works the spit around his mouth. "I'm sorry you feel that way. Let me at least drive you somewhere. You shouldn't stay here."

She shakes her head again.

"Well," he says, reaching towards her. She jerks away from his touch. "Thank you. And, well, I apologize." He cocks his head like a bird, trying to look into her face, but she hunches away from his gaze. He straightens up and turns to go.

"Blanc," she says, and he stops. "You still have blood all over your face."

While Boyer hunches over the sink, slopping water and soap, she walks silently over to the counter where the Bowie knife lays. She picks it up, hefting its weight. She closes her eyes and says a prayer to her father.

The ship is no closer to the shore than before, but the winds lash harder now, and sound carries better. A low, dumb moan permeates the beach; none of the villagers will go there unless they absolutely have to. Over a languorous week, Simone talks with Dupont about his time in the grave. He tells her of the unmistakable feeling that he was about to disembark on a journey. How his spirit did indeed travel over this land, from the heights of the North to the waters of the Canal de Sud, and he, freed of time, understood his island, his people, his world. They do not speak about the bokor calling him back into his body or the events afterwards. With his eyes closed, the sun cracking his skin, and the smallest smile in the country on his face, Dupont does not resemble a living thing, but a golem built from earth, and it is true that when he opens his eyes, and Simone looks into them, she sees nothing whatsoever.

The local société holds a Rada ceremony later in the week, and the houngan invites Simone. There is much anticipation. In the last fifty years, the great loa—Erzulie, Ogoun, Pappa Guede, Damballah, Simbi, Agwe, Legba, Loco, and Ayizan—have mounted fewer and fewer. There is an expression among the servants of the loa: "Great Gods cannot ride little horses." But over the last week, there have been more mountings of great loa than in the last three years. Ogoun mounted a small boy only yesterday, a terrifying occurrence, as the young one insisted on balancing his body on the point of a machete driven into the ground.

Simone stands in the peristyle with the others, watching the houngan draw Legba's vever, the crossroads, on the ground with flour. She is already moving with the off-beat of the ceaseless drums, her arms and hands whipping slightly. The la-place brings the houngan a pair of live cocks, one white and one dark. The houngan takes them, and while the la-place scatters feed on the vever, the houngan traces an elaborate crossroads in the air about him with the fluttering, squawking cocks. Then he brings them down to the vever, their beaks directly over the feed. It is not until the cocks eat the food that they will become identified with Legba and may be sacrificed to him. The cocks squawk, their eyes drawing on the feed.

All wait.

DONALD ASSHOLE AND LOS ELEMENTOS DE ROCK

"Wheeze aint not lake no dimsort banned."

The lines that make up Buss are clean and clear. Blacks and whites, an oval for a face, the occasional ellipse. Regular readers used to sometimes have trouble telling Jacket, Leeze and Buss apart, though the streets they stumble through and the demi-human saloon keepers, guinea-pig stormtroopers, salivating fans, beleaguered family members, lusty social workers, blind pirates, Finnish porn stars, busking gypsy bands, prolapsed Bulgarian revolutionaries, mobile book store-owners, hobos, hobos, and more hobos they encounter are rendered with precise stereotyping, the 3 figures who make up the band De Sal-Mon Crudities all look exactly the same. Except for their hair.

Jacket has none. Leeze has 5 spikes that wave with the wind when they're not standing up straight. Buss has long flowing hair, God only knows what color. They all speak the same too. To wit:

"Preeeteee peepss donna jig nawn ta funny."

"Bleedy tea-cup aint lak may varhy awn muscus."

"Lickmee creation, smhakee eternita."

To the perpetual frustration of the readers of *Los Elementos de Rock*, a monthly 22-page comic put out by Fantagraphics, written and drawn by Milwaukee artist Donald Asshole (nee Maxmilian), while De Sal-Mon Crudities' original line-up was Jacket on g-e-tar, Leeze on bass and mouth-organ, and Buss on hitting stuff, the girls have begun, caught up in a rabid seizure of Greil Marcus-inspired Debord-fever, to not allow anybody in the band play the same instrument 2 nights in a row.

To make matters worse, the girls are omnisexual, and it's not odd for an issue of *Los Elementos* to begin, end, or entirely consist of the 3 of them having limbic, intense, and impossible intercourse, so that even the most obsessed *Los El* fans (though they often have moments of revelation, leading to lambasted and derided posts on message boards on such web sites as Bald World Blues and Appetizer Apes; "you're thinking with your *guts*, man, you gotta have *evidence* for this shit…") cannot tell apart their favorite characters based on who is having sex with whom, because everybody basically has sex with everybody else in a sort of guiltless, AIDS-less world, this being the reason why most over-30 adult males read the comic in the first place; although, to DA (as he is known in the industry), the comic's stated purpose (beyond the chance to experiment with surreal art, and to get paid enough to live on sitting around all day drawing a comic book whose plot, is invariably [except for the issues that were taken up with just, you know, fucking] Girls Go To Play Show; Odd, Terrifying, Impossible People Show Up For Show; Girls Do An Awful Job; Terrifying People Respond With The Level Of Politeness You Would Expect From Them; Everybody Gets Drunk And Then Fights And Then Fucks And Then Vomits And Then Passes Out) was to attempt to plumb the depths of the absurdity and existential despair caused by a lifestyle lived in the pursuit of pure physical pleasure, this being the reason why he had gotten written up in the *New York Times* Book Review last week by no less a notable than Art Spiegelman, who called his 6th trade paperback, a collection (not really a "graphic novel", words that when placed adjacent to one another made DA go into spastic convulsions and show the whites of his eyes to all) entitled *AAAAAAAAHHHHHHHH! spit?*: "No kidding… a prime piece of the best American novel written in the 21st Century." Anyway, to just nail that sucker in there, in recent issues (#54, #55, #56) DA has drawn the 3 "grils" wearing hats alternating from panel to panel. And sometimes not. This has caused, understandably, a flood of accusatory emails, some of which caused DA to laugh so hard he spat blood.

Donald Asshole wasn't famous, or rather he was famous but not like punch-a-photographer-and-do-a-line-with-some-disheveled-Norwegian-rock-star famous, more like famous in a very small, sick circle, the type of circle where people begin to expect things of you they wouldn't from, say, Lee Marvin or Camille Paglia. Like not being a sell-out. Like constant, unending strangeness. Like tits. Like dinosaurs. Like eviscerations.

But that wasn't the problem. It was a problem, but it wasn't like *the* problem.

The problem was that all the women looked the same.

Not in the comic.

He had thought, at first, that he was losing his sight. But pigs and men and drawers and radio towers and cell-phones and Elvis Costello glasses, they all looked the same as before. If anything, they were sharper in relief to the women. The women, all they had was two dots for eyes, a line for a mouth, a perfectly round head, two lashes of hair going down and out in backwards Ss from their scalps. He immediately assumed a waking dream; he had done enough acid for that. So on and off with the light switch. The lighting, indeed, did change. He tried flying, from a standing position in his living room, of course; he wasn't stupid enough to take a trip off a roof or attempt the clear blue sky with his powers unknown. Didn't work. He tried conjuring up belly-dancers. No bellydancers. *All* his waking dreams had belly-dancers. That was years ago, but some things don't change.

Here's something else that had never changed:

Donald Asshole had never gotten on with men. He'd had a father and uncles and 2 grandfathers and at least seven baseball coaches and a squadron of priests and teachers and co-workers and drinking buddies, but he'd never settled around them, never disgorged himself of whatever hatreds and self-immolations and whiney bits of flotsam were stewing about in his soul. Their responses to questions he deemed important seemed minor without being subtle and as interchangeable as he found the sports teams their conversations centered around. He genuinely didn't know why this was, and he didn't think that learning its origin(s) would do a damn bit of good, so he tried not to think about it. His true friends had always been women. He talked to them one-on-one; he kept them apart and referred to each around the others only tangentially. Some of them had been or were or could have been his lovers; others were not and could not have been. Eva and Ysabel and Tara and Lauren and Persephone and Beatrice and Nancy and Margerita and Eleanor and Alexandra and the other Beatrice and Lorie and Hedda and Irene and Karen and Brita. Now, he could not tell them apart on the street, and when he arranged to meet them, their fleshless black-and-white forms moving in for a hug terrified him far more than any large scale biological attack could. For a while he spoke to them on the phone, deriving his feminine solace in that manner. That is, until all their voices became a single sugary sweet thirty-three-year-old-trying-to-sound-like-a-seventeen-year-old's trill. He stopped calling. He tried to form friendships with males, of course, but it did no good. He sat in sports bars and called up some guys from high school and started going to the gym and started hanging out in gay bars, but it did no good. There was not a single male type he could stand. They all left him empty and deeply bored.

So he was friendless. Which was not what was bothering him.

Donald Asshole had always been a hermit of one kind or the other. As a child under the covers at night with his Thor or X-Men, as an undergraduate burrowed somewhere deep in the library forcing himself to read Hegel, as a grown man working a job he hated so he didn't have to have a roommate. He could do without friends for a while. Long enough for this whole thing to sort itself out.

No, what really bothered him was that the women didn't have faces anymore. After some weeks, they lost even the dots for eyes and the lines for mouths. And then all their breasts started to look the same. Same medium weight, same mass. B cup. No cupcake, no gigundo. No sagging ones, no cupcakes. They all had just a little lift. They were boring breasts. He even went to an art class just to see a nude model. The breasts were almost cosmetic surgery-perfect. He snapped all his pencils in half.

He couldn't draw the next day, and he didn't feel like jerking off or watching teevee, so he went for a walk.

All the women wore the same white skirts. Triangles they were. Coming out sharp at the sides. Their legs were just sticks. No shoes. Feet were just black lines.

He went home and sat down and looked at a blank white sheet of paper.

A single word balloon.

"Everything is repetition."

He had drawn a girl. Just a quick sketch. But real and filled out. Looked a bit like… Jesus, who? Some celebrity? Someone he'd known in college? Beatrice or Lauren?

He drew a second word balloon.

"Everything be repetition."

"Eva-arythin ast reppy."

Like Jacket would say it.

Buss hit something in the background. He closed his eyes. She hit it again. It was his computer monitor. He could hear it squeal and creak and crash onto the floor.

He opened his eyes.

Leeze was sitting on the desk in front of him, a short skirt on, her legs open. He stared at the crux where leg met leg. A perfect triangle of trimmed hair. He couldn't discern lips, but there was the shadow of the skirt. On the inside left thigh: a birthmark that looked like the South-West coast of Ireland.

He stood up and stared down at his rigid hard-on like it was a previously unnoticed prosthetic.

Leeze laid back on his work desk slowly, tucking her head under his shades. Dark out. He couldn't see even an outline of her face. He grabbed her knee. Perfectly warm. Bony.

Buss stomped the printer into the ground, 1-2 1-2.

Jacket spoke in his ear, her voice strangely sweet and rough. He had never before wondered what she sounded like. Sounded a bit like him, actually, when he was drunk. He could smell her hundred-dollar perfume and American Spirits menthol cigarettes and wet Doritos musk.

"Oi Aye, righ' soony. Iz purfec to lak sez upon ye. Howz mattas?"

He undid his trousers, and they descended maybe half an inch, and he slipped his cock through the pee-hole of his boxers.

"I'm fine, Jacket," he said. "How are you?"

Buss put her hand through a wall and howled something lovely.

"Decidela demmy-yumma. Weeza lak a dict, bu' no ye no? Jeez lak weez ar-cut-ulate whatssa nees be lak said. Righ'?"

Donald pushed Leeze's right leg open, and she moved her own left leg a little. He reached for her torso, but his hands went down on either side of it. He pushed his cock into her, the triangle enclosing it, nearly cutting him off from it. She was very dry, very tight. It was extremely painful, but he had no desire to remove himself.

Jacket slid a cold finger into his left ear, and Leeze had a warm, soft hold on his balls and gently began to jiggle them.

"Wass weez wanna tell yeez is tha: thars anly 1 kinda musac an' tha' aint mucus."

A line from one of their songs.

He jerked his hips into Leeze, and she jerked in towards him, and she was slippery now, and he kept going, and he felt himself going past her thighs, up into her stomach, and his cock churned through steak and Caesar salad and shrimp (de grils only ate food that started with the sound, not necessarily the letter, S), his hips were barely contained by her rib cage, their tips shredding his buttocks, till his cock was out of Leeze's mouth, and he felt the triangle of her vagina cold and clear and metallic suck up to his sphincter, and she shuddered around him, and Buss beat a boot-black fascist rhythm on the ceiling, and Jacket hizzed as Leeze slipped behind the shades, and he stood on his workdesk, empty white pages crunched between his toes, and Leeze thrashed wildly behind the shades, and it was night day night day night day night day, the moon and sun jerking through the sky like sped-up stop-motion, and Donald Asshole seized wordlessly in the air, and there was a hard wind inside, his eyes shut themselves, and there was the brutal pressure of thumbs on his eyeballs, and he thought he could see something that wasn't ink and paper, something that wasn't flesh and fingernails, and Jacket said, "Wall ye shouln' wash 'cuze washes be harses and yeez be naw cawbay!" and Donald Asshole came again,

BUT
NOTHING
CAME
OUT.

ABOUT THE AUTHOR

Brendan C. Byrne was born in the District of Columbia but has lived most of his adult life in New York City. He has published three novellas: *The Showing of the Instruments* (2011), *The Training Commission* (2019, with Ingrid Burrington) and *Accelerate* (2021). His short fiction and criticism appear in a variety of organs.

ALSO AVAILABLE

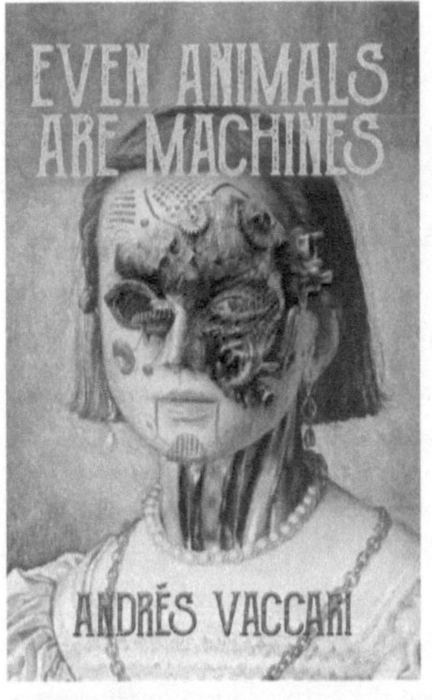

"A rare novel of philosophical ideas that also tells an engaging story—luminous, melancholy and charged with real soul."

—Christopher Brown, author of *Tropic of Kansas*

"A marvellous blend of historiography and provocative allegory."

—Paul McAuley, author of *Four Hundred Billion Stars*

"A work of genuinely original and literary science fiction."

—D. Harlan Wilson, author of *Outré*

1649, North Sea. The great philosopher René Descartes carries a heavy heart and a target on his back. Sick with pneumonia, pursued by powerful enemies, he flees by ship to Sweden and a new life. His companion: a sentient android replica of Francine, his beloved, dead daughter.

But the ship's captain has other plans. Accusing Descartes of sorcery, he tosses the droid overboard, plunging Francine into a bizarre afterlife: a machine graveyard ruled by malignant necromancers. There, she hacks the dying philosopher's mind, glimpsing the birth of A.I. in a timestream parallel to our own.

FILE UNDER BAROQUE-PUNK

Even Animals Are Machines by Andrés Vaccari

www.wantonsun.com/even-animals-are-machines

ISBN 978-0-6456543-0-1

In the near future, Kalsari Jones is hooked on the Vexworld, a global mixed-reality network accessed through neural implants. As his addiction grows, he is plagued by sentient hallucinations, an urge to strip the flesh from his bones, and a latent attraction to artificial intelligence.

Seeking answers, he meets Ingram Ravenscroft, a cult leader who claims a treatment for digisexuality. Kalsari allows his brain to be rewired, only for the operation to leave him with unwanted telepathic powers. Lost in inner space, Kalsari angers a band of rogue AI who've escaped the Vexworld for the time-sinks of the fourth dimension. Battling the shapeshifting bots, he discovers the shocking truth about his virtual obsessions—and Ravenscroft's hidden role in the story of his life.

Code Beast by Simon Sellars
www.wantonsun.com/code-beast
ISBN 978-0-6456543-1-8

HYPERCAPITALISM
AND OTHER TALES OF PLANETARY MADNESS
ANDRÉS VACCARI

Readers, before you go: please remember, user reviews are gold. Your reviews turn the wheels of the small press and help make books.

If *Another World Isn't Possible* moved you in some way, please consider leaving a review or rating on your favourite online channels.

With thanks.